Of Stars and Clay

Of Stars and Clay

Elizabeth M. Herrera

ISBN-13: 978-0-9903492-8-0

Published on January 11, 2018
Revised on August 21, 2019
Revised on March 23, 2023

Mankind's origins are woven with lies, which are exposed when a virus purposely kills the majority of mankind. Those who survive are controlled from behind the scenes by a dark force that has waited millenniums for total domination. Only the mutated Earth Sentinels can free mankind from their unseen shackles.

Dedicated to those who have dared to think the unthinkable.

Acknowledgments

A special thanks to Ian McKenzie-Vincent, whose editing was made with hawk-like precision that without a doubt made this book so much better; and Janet Harvey-Clark, an excellent editor and proofreader, whose support and insights have been invaluable.

In the clay, god and man

Shall be bound,

To a unity brought together;

So that to the end of days

The flesh and the soul

Which in a god have ripened –

That soul in a blood-kinship be bound.

— Ancient Sumerian Tablet

Our creators were alien geneticists,

Claiming to be gods.

We were made to be slaves,

Formed out of stars and clay,

Abused offspring who blindly obeyed,

Generation after generation,

Until the gods fought, and then left,

Leaving us mired with the fallen ones and serpents,

Who took their place.

But their numbers dwindled,

Under the harsh sun and earth's vibration.

So they fled beneath the surface,

Scraping out an existence,

Using humans for subsistence,

Controlling the minds of the masses,

Controlling the ruling classes.

They still exist, but,

Now the battle has begun anew,

As the serpent fights for supremacy,

Manipulating our genes,

Altering the vessel to suit their needs,

Taking the final step,

For total domination.

CHAPTER 1
Amazon Jungle

THE DAY THE world changed forever seemed like an ordinary day in the heart of the Amazon jungle where a handful of tribesmen fished along the shore of the mossy-green river.

Takwa, the tribe's best hunter, brought a gourd to his mouth, taking a long guzzle of the fermented brew. The colorful feathers in his hair hung back. After quenching his thirst, he let out a satisfied sigh, passing the gourd to the man next to him. It was then that Takwa looked to the sky. A passenger plane flew high overhead, leaving behind an iridescent exhaust trail. He pointed at it. "Look!"

All of the tribesmen stared at the strange flying beast. They didn't often see an airliner this far from civilization.

Standing among them was a young man named Zachary, who was notably different from the others—tall and lanky with sandy-blond hair, and fair skin that was perpetually sunburned. He had no painted lines on his body, and instead of a loincloth, he wore cut-off jeans and a ragged t-shirt with a Pittsburgh Steelers logo on it. He put his hand to his forehead to shield his green eyes from the sun as he gazed at the plane. He frowned because he knew the exhaust fumes weren't normal. The pearly sheen of the far-reaching trail made it obvious that something was amiss—at least to him.

Farther from the shore, wandering alone through the scrub

was the tribe's shaman, Pahtia, an older man with gray hair who was searching for the herb *Pau D'arco*, which, when found, would be cut and dried, and then used at a later date as a remedy for warding off infections. He stopped his quest when he noticed his fellow tribesmen staring at the sky. Curious, Pahtia hobbled through the underbrush, making his way to the riverbank where the jungle canopy gave way to the open skies. He stood behind the other men, leaning on his staff while studying the plane's exhaust trail that reflected the colors of the rainbow. He muttered, "Bad omen."

Zachary overheard his father-in-law's comment and felt he was right, but, at that moment, a fish nibbled on his bait. The young man jerked on the line, swiftly sinking the hook into the mouth of an impressive-sized Pacu—one of the best-tasting fish in the Amazon. The fish fought for its life, wriggling out of the water, shimmering in the sunlight before plunging back into the depths.

The other men salivated at the thought of roasting the delicious Pacu, wrapped in banana leaves, over an open fire.

"Careful!" one of the men shouted.

"Not too fast," another advised.

Takwa tried to steal the line from Zachary's hand. "Let me do it." But Zachary resisted. It was his fish. Takwa gave up, but stood nearby, disgruntled.

The Pacu flipped and flopped, desperate to free itself, causing the line to spin off the stick that served as the fishing pole. Zachary rewound the line, trying to exhaust the fish. His amateurish technique frustrated the other men.

The stakes were raised when a fourteen-foot Black Caiman noticed the commotion. The prehistoric creature slid into the river, gliding toward an easy meal. Although caimans, like alligators and crocodiles, were not usually a threat to grown men, preferring smaller game and fish, one could never be too careful, so Zachary kept an eye on the encroaching beast as well as his fish.

No longer a passive bystander, Pahtia warned his son-in-law, "Hurry up! Or you will lose it!"

Sweat ran down Zachary's forehead. *Too fast. Too slow.* He tightened the line.

The caiman swished its tail more vigorously, closing the gap, its primordial eyes and ridged spine cutting through the rippling waters. Then the reptile submerged.

The tribesmen knew the caiman would attack from below.

"Pull!" yelled Pahtia.

Zachary yanked the line, causing it to cut into his fingers. The fish flew into the air, bounding toward the shore. Everyone's eyes followed the glistening Pacu. The line slackened as it soared. And as it did, Zachary envisioned himself being the one to bring in the prize catch of the day. However, his dreams of grandeur died a quick death when the caiman lunged out of the water, opening its tooth-riddled jaws, consuming the entire fish and cutting the line before splashing back into the river.

The men groaned.

"You will never fit in," Takwa said.

Pahtia sighed and shook his head, but then he noticed the blood running down Zachary's fingers. The healer knew the cut could fester in this hot humid rainforest, easily turning into a life-threatening infection. Not wanting his daughter's scorn, he reluctantly offered to help the young man. "Come with me."

Zachary hung his head low with indignation. He hated relying on Pahtia for anything, but it was better than staying here among the other men. Takwa's contempt was obvious even with his back toward him.

Pahtia shuffled along, his staff steadying his gait as he led Zachary down a narrow path that meandered through dense foliage, tangled vines and ancient trees, heading toward his hut on the outskirts of the village. Few tribe members visited the shaman there. Most only came to see him when they were sick or needed guidance. His powers scared them a bit. After all, if he had the power to heal, didn't he also have the power to make them sick? Or worse? But this arrangement suited Pahtia just fine. He was happiest away from the others. He liked being undisturbed while hunting for herbs or journeying to the spirit realm. He knew that one could only clearly hear the spirits' voices when the mind was quiet.

As the two of them neared their destination, a flock of blue-headed parrots scattered. From an overhead branch, a toucan studied them, its observant button eyes peering past its enormous black-tipped orange beak. Squirrel monkeys, hidden in the trees, hooted.

The shaman's thatched-roof hut came into view. Its walls were made out of bamboo slats spaced evenly apart. The gaps let the breezes flow through. They also allowed Pahtia to detect if anyone was approaching, yet still gave him some measure of privacy. Inside, dried wild flowers, roots and herbs were tacked to the walls while others hung from the ceiling. Some fresh gatherings were spread across the worktable.

Pahtia instructed Zachary to sit near the ash-filled fire pit, then walked to the back of the hut where he rummaged through his assorted botanicals, selecting a few leaves and roots, placing them in a stone bowl. He added a splash of *chicha*, then began grinding the ingredients together.

Meanwhile, Zachary sat staring out the doorway, thinking about the ill-boding plane trail. "Pahtia?"

The old man stopped mixing, looking up. Deep creases surrounded his eyes.

"Why don't we visit Bechard and ask him about the plane?" Zachary asked.

"Never again! That spirit tricked us."

"He meant well."

Pahtia shook his head. "He holds a darkness in his heart." He tapped his chest to emphasize his point.

"Pahtia?"

With a touch of irritation, he answered, "Yes?"

"I've got a bad feeling about the plane."

"I know." The shaman walked toward Zachary carrying the stone bowl. He sat down to finish mixing the compound.

"What should we do?"

"I am not sure. I will visit Maka later. She always has good advice." Pahtia was referring to his spirit guide, who helped him with healings, divination and guidance on physical, mental and spiritual matters. The man gathered a clump of the smelly herbal remedy with his gnarled fingers. "This will go on your wound to keep it from getting infected so Conchita will not be mad at me." He added, "You can die from infection, you know."

Zachary sighed. "Yes, I know." He hated being treated like a complete idiot.

5

Pahtia shaped the clump into a ball, casually mentioning, "When I die, I will shapeshift into a great caiman." His eyes gleamed as he imagined reincarnating as this noble beast. "Maybe next time, I will take your fish." He let out a rare chuckle, annoying his son-in-law, and then hummed while applying the fresh salve to the young man's injured fingers.

Zachary winced.

Pahtia smiled.

Too embarrassed to return to the river, Zachary went home to his wife, Conchita, who stood in their hut cradling their infant son. Her long black hair hung over her face as she gazed down at the baby while singing a traditional lullaby. The moment Zachary saw them, he forgot all about the failed fishing incident.

Conchita smiled at her husband, but her joy quickly faded when she noticed his hand was bandaged with leaves and bamboo twine. She asked with concern, "What happened?"

"Oh, it's nothing," he answered, wanting to forget the whole thing.

"Let me see it."

He reluctantly held out his injured hand for inspection by the shaman's daughter.

She balanced the baby on her hip, then used her free hand to examine the patch job, sniffing to detect which herbs had been used, flipping his hand over to study the other side, finally conceding, "Father did a good job."

"Yes, he did." Zachary glanced around the hut. "Where's Eva?"

"Outside. See." Conchita pointed out the doorway at the sunlit center of the village where the young children were having fun with a Capuchin monkey, which jumped from one child's shoulder to the next, playing a game of catch-me-if-you-can. Four-year-old Eva ran toward the scampering rascal with her hands outstretched, only to have the monkey leap over her sun-bleached curls, landing on top of another child's shoulder. The children squealed with delight.

Zachary laughed at their antics until he glanced up at the sky. Remnants of the shimmering plane trail still lingered.

Conchita noticed his troubled expression. "What is wrong?"

Zachary decided to shake off his worries. After all, what could he do about the plane trail? So instead of answering, he smiled, brushing his wife's long hair away from her face, kissing her neck, softly saying, "Nothing's wrong. Sit with me." He sat down on the palm leaves that covered the floor, patting them with his uninjured hand to encourage her to join him. Conchita handed Zachary the baby, then settled beside him, giving her son a quick peck on the forehead to assure him that she was still nearby. The infant gurgled with elation.

It was times like these that caused Zachary to remember why he had come here.

During the night, Pahtia hobbled through the rainforest using his staff to steady his steps. In his other hand, he held a burning torch to light the way. The moon and stars were hidden behind the dark storm clouds forming over the jungle's canopy. Thunder pounded in the distance, causing the old shaman to quicken his pace.

He made his way across the quiet village where everyone was safely tucked inside their huts, sound asleep. He peered inside his daughter's dwelling, past the lattice gate made out of bamboo poles that protected the doorway from night-roaming predators. Pahtia whispered, "Conchita..." She stirred, but did not wake. He held onto the doorframe, poking his staff through the gate, nudging her.

Conchita opened her eyes and saw a silhouetted figure standing outside the hut. She wondered if she was dreaming. It wasn't until a gust of wind threw the torch flames past Pahtia's face that she recognized him. "Father?"

He tersely responded, "Come with me."

She drowsily got up, quietly opening the gate, stepping outside, careful not to disturb her loved ones.

Conchita trailed behind her father, passing the outskirts of the village, continuing down a barely visible path. Branches and vines, flailing in the storm's gusts of wind, hindered their progress. She glanced behind herself, feeling an overwhelming urge to return to her children and husband. The farther she went, the stronger the urge became. She came to a standstill, asserting herself. "Father!"

Pahtia stopped walking and looked back at her.

She said, "I am not going. Not tonight. I will come tomorrow."

He solemnly responded, "I have something to share with you, but it must be tonight." He continued along the path. Lightning crackled, flashing through the trees.

Against her better judgment, Conchita followed him. "Why not morning?" she asked, her voice nearly drowned out by the rolling thunder.

Without turning around, he declared, "Morning is too late!"

They reached Pahtia's hut. The flames in the fire pit burned brightly, welcoming them home. Conchita sat near the fire in her usual spot, combing her windswept hair with her fingers while observing the storm brewing outside, its ardent breath huffing through the slatted walls.

Pahtia went to his workbench, reverently picking up a leather medicine pouch. He returned to sit beside his daughter. With sentimental eyes, he said to her, "You have been a good apprentice. Learned all I had to teach." He set the medicine pouch on his lap so he could use both hands to remove the amulet that hung from a leather cord around his neck. "This was my father's, and now it is yours. Shaman to shaman."

Conchita lowered her head to accept the gift. It was a great honor to be declared a shaman. She looked down at the amulet resting against her chest, picking it up, holding it between her fingers, still not believing the shiny stone her father had worn since she was a child was now hers.

9

He continued, "I will ask my helper spirits to be your helpers. All that I have is now yours." Pahtia opened the medicine pouch's drawstrings, reaching inside to take out an amethyst cluster. He held it up between his bony fingers. "This has magical powers. Hold out your hand." He placed it securely in her palm. "This stone holds the vibrations of Mother Earth. Keep it safe." He pulled out a jaguar's curved claw. "Not Taslia," he clarified, referring to his totem animal, which also happened to be a jaguar. "This was my first kill. I was brave and used only a spear. Very dangerous. Very strong energy." He handed it to Conchita before he once more dug into his bag, removing a dried plant root. "This is a wise root. It knows the secrets of the rainforest." Pahtia placed it in Conchita's hand beside the other sacred articles. Next, he extracted a human tooth, staring at it as if he was remembering how he acquired it so many years ago, then, without an explanation, he returned it to the pouch.

"Father, why are you giving me these things?"

"I had a vision, a prophecy. And in this vision, I saw blood-red skies and a snake slither out of its hole, standing like a man with a gold crown on its head. I heard the moaning of men, women and children in pain, lying on the ground. Too many to count. The snake took joy in their sorrow, eating them."

"Stop it. You are scaring me."

Pahtia became angry. "No daughter of mine is afraid!" His harsh tone made Conchita regret coming here. His demeanor softened. "Forget what I said. I know you are strong. Let us journey together one more time. I need to ask Maka for guidance."

Outside, the storm unleashed its heavy rains.

Conchita believed in her father's prophecies, but that didn't mean this one would happen tonight—maybe not even in their lifetimes. However, he was more riled up about this one than usual. All she wanted to do was return home and sleep with her family, but the downpour made her hesitant to leave. Besides, she knew her father would prod her until she relented, so she reluctantly said, "I will journey with you."

"Good. Let me get the herb." The shaman used his staff to stand up, stiffly hobbling across the floor.

Conchita noticed for the first time how much her father had aged. His frame was frail, and his hair was almost entirely gray. She looked away before he returned.

Pahtia sat beside his daughter once more. He said a prayer while bringing the herb close to his face, honoring it before dropping the sacred leaves into the fire. Smoke burst out of the flames, billowing all around them. The pair closed their eyes, breathing deeply, letting the smoke fill their lungs.

The shaman called for his totem animal, "Taslia, please come!"

From out of the storm, an ethereal black jaguar padded through the doorway, entering the smoke-filled hut. The ghostly feline stood there swishing her tail, her golden eyes reflecting the flames.

Pahtia acknowledged Taslia's presence, "Thank you, old friend, for coming. I need to speak to Maka. Will you please take us to her?"

Taslia nodded.

Pahtia's spirit rose out of his body and climbed onto the jaguar's back. Conchita's spirit joined her father's, sitting behind him. The totem animal carried the pair out of the hut, entering the mystical realm of the jungle. Rain dripped from the shadowy leaves as they moved through the trees. Conchita held tightly onto her father. Even if they weren't in mortal danger, she knew spirits surrounded them—most were benevolent, but some were malicious. Pahtia, on the other hand, was enjoying the ride as if it might be his last, listening to the jungle sounds and taking in the sights. He breathed deeply, smelling the humus aroma the rain brought to the surface. The faint sensation of wet leaves dragging across his face and exposed skin didn't irritate him as it normally would have, instead the cold austere contact made him feel alive.

They moved through a blanket of fog, and the rain stopped.

The totem animal strolled out of the trees. In front of them was a roaring waterfall. The cascading water reflected the moonlight as it fell into an ebony lake. Pahtia dismounted, then ambled

11

through the dense ferns. He stood at the edge of the dark water with his daughter by his side, calling to his spirit guide, "Maka, please come!"

A ball of light appeared from out of the starry sky, hovering above the lake. It expanded into the form of a beautiful woman, who wore white-fringed animal skins decorated with colorful feathers and beads. Her black hair hung down to her knees. She gave the visitors a warm smile. "Greetings! It is good to see you again."

Pahtia bowed his head out of respect. "Greetings to you as well, Maka. Thank you for answering my call. We need your help. I believe the end is near."

"The end of what, dear Pahtia?"

"The end of this life—for me and my tribe."

"Pahtia, you know there is no death. Only change. Why do you falter now?"

The shaman bolstered his chest, touting, "I do not falter! I came for help."

"I understand your concerns, but keep this in mind: That which seems to be the end is always the beginning. Remember, for the caterpillar to become a butterfly is a difficult process—one that requires a tremendous amount of trust before the metamorphosis completes itself. But never does the butterfly mourn the loss of its former self, although, for the caterpillar, the transformation feels like death. To take away the impending change would hinder your spiritual growth. This I cannot do." Maka stopped speaking. Her body glowed brighter and brighter until she was lost in the brilliance, splintering into a thousand sparkling lights, dissipating into the night.

CHAPTER 2
Curator's House

HIGH IN THE misty foothills of the Ōu Mountains in Japan, built on the grounds of an ancient temple, stood a one-room curator's house that had been crafted out of stones excavated from the mountainside. A 200-year-old rose bush clung to its southern wall, dotting the stonework with thorny canes and yellow blossoms.

Inside the dwelling, the morning sunlight peeked through a gap in the faded cotton curtains, the warm rays falling over the futon where a man and woman lay together. The man, a Native American named Billy White Smoke, had made his living by working construction and odd jobs back in the States until he ventured across the ocean to find the woman beside him. Her name was Haruto. She was an Earth Sentinel, like Billy, but also a Miko like her mother, grandmother and great-grandmother before her—a tradition dating back thousands of years to when female shamans mingled with Japan's ruling class, acting as healers, mediums and ritual dancers. Her flowing black hair, tinged with a few grays, was sprawled across the pillow. Billy held her close, kissing her forehead before rubbing her pregnant belly with his calloused hand.

Haruto wistfully said, "I wish this moment could last forever."

His deep voice tenderly responded, "But then the baby would never come."

"True."

"Still think it's a girl?"

She nodded.

"We'll have to think of a name for her. Maybe your mother's?"

"Maybe."

Billy hesitated, then said, "I was thinking, before the baby comes, we could get married." He waited for her response.

Haruto frowned. "We've talked about this before."

He turned away, lying on his back, clasping his hands behind his head, trying to remain calm.

She said, "We are in love and have a baby on the way. I don't understand why that's not enough for you."

Billy answered louder than he intended, "Because I've traveled around the world to be with you!" He immediately regretted raising his voice. "I just thought you'd meet me halfway."

"You know I want to be with you forever, but—"

"But what?"

"I just thought that you, of all people, would appreciate not conforming to society's expectations. To its patriarchal controls—"

"God knows, no man would ever control you."

Haruto shrugged. There was some truth to his words. "We can talk later, but, right now, I have to get ready for an appointment."

Billy wasn't happy at where the conversation ended, but he was old enough to know you have to pick your battles, so he said, "Fine, I'll walk with you." He flung the duvet off himself, getting out of bed to rifle through his clothes piled on top of the dresser, putting on a pair of work jeans and a black t-shirt. He snatched his black-brimmed hat decorated with silver conchos and turquoise from a peg on the wall, placing it on his head, adjusting it to make

14

sure the tilt was just right.

Haruto grabbed her scarlet-colored silk pants off the chair in the corner, pulling them on, wrapping the ties around her protruding stomach. She looked forward to this small act every morning. It helped her to measure the baby's growth as the pant ties seemed to become shorter and shorter with each passing day. She let the white silk blouse fall over her head, sliding her arms through the draping sleeves, leaving the hem untucked so it would fit over her rounded belly.

Ready to face the world, the couple stepped out of the house. They strolled along one of the stone paths that meandered through the meditation garden filled with bonsai, cherry, apple and pear trees; lavender; wisteria; and cultivated roses.

As they walked, Billy admired the view until he noticed several overhead planes leaving iridescent trails in the sky, hatch-marking the atmosphere. He stopped walking, and cursed, "God, damn it! I thought we were done with that shit!"

Startled, Haruto glanced back at him, then followed his gaze, solemnly noting the unusual plane trails. "Was it all for nothing?" she questioned.

"Maybe. Maybe it was a fool's journey to even try."

Discouraged, she let out a deep sigh before offering Billy the only advice she could think of, "Just let it go..."

He gave her a reluctant smile.

Haruto stretched out her hand, opening Billy's clenched fist, slipping her fingers between his, leading him through the garden toward the temple. "Everything looks wonderful," she complimented him, hoping to brighten his mood.

"Thanks. It's coming along." Billy was being modest. He

15

had transformed the neglected garden into a thing of beauty by reinvigorating the trees, resetting the stone paths, and patching the numerous steps that had become hazardous. His favorite improvement was the addition of the medicinal herbs planted throughout the grounds, which introduced an element of untamed wildness and balanced the vibrational qualities of the landscape.

They moved toward the ancient temple at the forefront of the property. The three-story structure sat on top of a foothill overlooking the road below. It had originally been built for Buddhist monks, who had abandoned the place due to a lack of parishioners and dwindling financial support. Its distinct gabled roof was a combination of Chinese and Japanese architectural styles, which, at one time, were used exclusively for those in power.

16

The couple stopped at the rear of the temple. Here, steps led to an expansive landing that supported a wooden pergola holding an enormous bell—seldom rung these days.

Haruto faced Billy. "See you tonight," she said, standing on her tiptoes to give him a quick peck on the lips.

Two Mikos, who happened to be strolling along a nearby path, gave them disapproving glances.

Most of the women here had not adapted to Billy residing on the grounds, despite the passing years. Men traditionally weren't allowed to live with Mikos. But in Billy's case an exception had been made, allowing him to dwell in the curator's house in exchange for his gardening and maintenance services. This exception spoke of Haruto's status—one that had risen considerably after her participation in the Earth Sentinels' group.

Billy ignored the other women's disparaging looks, tipping his hat to Haruto. "See you tonight."

She went inside the temple, passing through the foyer and bypassing the stone staircase that led to the upper floors. Haruto entered the common area where a few Mikos mingled with the city dwellers, who wore workout clothes and held rolled mats while they waited for the yoga class to begin in the Great Hall. A plastic banner with the words "Sign Up for Yoga Classes" hung above the fireplace mantle, but it seemed out of place in this age-old building. On a narrow table, pressed against the wall, were jars of honey for sale.

"Haruto!" a young Miko called out, gracefully moving toward her. "A priest is here. Should I send him to you?"

"Yes, please." Haruto always enjoyed a visit from the local Geki—the male version of their sect.

But her anticipation was squashed when a young Catholic priest strolled around the corner. The Japanese man wore the traditional black robe and white collar, and held a Bible in his hand. The gold crucifix hanging from his neck was centered over his heart. His eyes glanced at Haruto's pregnant belly. If he held any judgments, he concealed them well.

The priest bowed. "It's a pleasure to meet you."

Haruto hid her displeasure at what she considered to be an intrusion, mostly because she assumed he was here to convert her as so many others had tried before. She politely bowed. "The pleasure is mine. How may I help you?" Being polite was the Japanese, and Miko, way.

"I wish to introduce myself. I'm Father Chong from Saint Agatha Lin's church located downtown. I'm reaching out to the community, and would like to personally invite you and the others to attend our mass on Sundays."

17

"Oh…" slipped off Haruto's tongue before she caught herself, and tactfully responded, "I'm flattered you came all this way, but you see, I'm quite content with my path."

"I do see, and your dedication is commendable, however, sometimes people are looking for…something else."

Haruto was offended by his implication that her path was somehow inferior to his, but she chose to overlook it, saying, "I am familiar with Catholicism. I, like the others here, have studied many different religions and beliefs. It helps us to better understand those who come to us for spiritual guidance and healing, so I'm quite sure your religion is not for me."

"Yes, I also am familiar with the Miko tradition," countered Father Chong who, after glancing at her bulging stomach, mentioned, "but I wasn't aware Mikos were allowed to marry." His words were meant to demonstrate his knowledge of their traditions, not insult her.

Because Haruto believed the priest had inquired sincerely, she answered, "We are allowed to marry, but, if we do so, our status changes to that of priestess."

"Oh…so you're a priestess?"

"No, I'm not married."

The priest was not sure how to respond.

To fill the awkward silence, Haruto said, "I have an upcoming appointment I need to prepare for. Is there anything else I can do for you?"

"Well, again, I welcome you, or any of the others here, to attend our mass, or visit, or call me personally if you have any questions regarding our faith." He opened the cover to the Bible he carried. "If you change your mind, here's our church address…"

He pointed to the first interior page, then offered her the book. "Please take this. It's my gift to you. And if you don't mind, I'd like to return again, and perhaps catch you at a better time."

Haruto graciously accepted the Bible. "Thank you." She moved toward the entrance, encouraging him to walk beside her. As they passed by the table displaying the honey, she picked up a jar, handing it to him. "My gift to you." This token offering allowed her to feel she had repaid Father Chong for the Bible, and thereby released herself from all obligations to meet with him again.

However, her action gave the priest a very different perception. He thought perhaps she was having a change of heart, and was pleased by the parting gift. "Thank you. Honey is one of my favorite treats." He had touched on a topic they could both agree on.

She responded, "One of our Mikos loves taking care of the bees. And the taste is quite delicious, mostly because the pollen comes from our garden. There are roses and jasmine, cherry blossoms, lavender and honeysuckle."

Father Chong salivated at the thought of eating the artisan honey later. "Nothing better than fine honey. Thank you, again, um...I don't believe I got your name."

"It's Haruto." She politely bowed.

Later that evening, dark storm clouds gathered in the sky. The wind howled through the trees, forcing the limbs to dance manically.

Haruto and Billy were having dinner inside the curator's house. They sat at the small table next to the window whose handcrafted glass panes had been rippled by time. Candles lit the room.

She quietly chewed her food.

He wondered if she was still upset about their disagreement from earlier that morning. "Is something wrong?"

Haruto wiped her mouth. "I had a visitor today. A Catholic priest."

A forlorn look came over Billy's face. He set down his fork. "Really? What did he want?"

"To save me." She stabbed at her food. "I know he meant well, but it was...umm..."

"Insulting?"

"Yes. Insulting."

Billy solemnly said, "The white man came and killed our people, took our land, then took our children—beating them with one hand while holding a Bible in the other, trying to make them believe in his *loving* God. I have no taste for their medicine."

"But he's Japanese."

Billy shrugged. "Same Bible."

A gust of wind rattled the window. The candles on the table flickered.

Outside, the mounting storm tore leaves and twigs from their branches, hurling them through the air.

An owl crash-landed on the windowsill. Its speckled breast thumped against the glass.

Haruto gasped, startled by the bird's sudden appearance.

Unharmed, the owl righted itself, struggling to maintain its perch as the wind ruffled its plumage. The bird of prey focused its eyes on Haruto, who felt honored. Owls were considered bearers of good luck in Japan.

Billy did not have the same reaction. In his Native American culture, an owl was an omen of an impending death or tragedy. He felt a strong desire to stand between his lover and the night hunter's line of sight, even as he knew he couldn't save her from the harbinger's premonition.

The downpour pelted the bird as it stared at Haruto through the rain-streaked window. Its strange unrelenting gaze caused an unexpected fear to arise within her.

Lightning ripped through the turbulent sky. Thunder exploded.

The owl screeched, then flew away, disappearing into the ominous darkness, leaving the man and woman with a sense of dread they couldn't quite name.

21

CHAPTER 3
Spider Webs

THE SUNSET GLOWED through the virgin forest surrounding the Bear Claw First Nation Reservation in Alberta, Canada. The tribe members lounged around a bonfire while the children entertained themselves by burning sticks. Some of the men stood outside the circle drinking beer and smoking cigarettes.

John, a spirited young man with long hair, carried an armload of logs to the fire. He shooed away the children before placing the wood on top of the burning embers. Sparks shot into the air. He used a stick to prod the logs until the flames grew bolder, dazzling the little ones who drew closer once more.

A boy, Hoki, stepped away from the blaze, going over to Tom Running Deer, a headstrong man in his mid-thirties who sat beside his equally headstrong wife, Cecile Two Feathers. The boy tugged on Tom's t-shirt, which had the words "The Original Founding Fathers" printed above an illustration of four Native American chiefs.

The man set down his beer. "Yes?"

"Uncle, tell us a story," Hoki requested, his big brown eyes hopeful.

Tom shook his head. "No, not me. Grandmother Hausis is the storyteller."

An old woman stopped chatting with the woman beside her,

and called out, "What!? Did I hear my name?"

Tom explained, talking louder than normal, "Grandmother! Hoki wants a story! Would you do it!?"

When the other children heard the request, they aptly followed the conversation. They loved to listen to the stories.

"What does he want to hear?" she asked.

Hoki pointed at the sky. "Tell me about those."

Everyone gazed up at the hazy opalescent plane trails that marred the darkening sky, tinged with orange as the sun left for the day.

"Those things?" The old woman shook her head. She knew the tribe had no ancient stories of this modern-day phenomenon. "Nay, why don't you do it, Tommy?"

Hoki and the other kids refocused their eager energy on to Tom.

Cecile patted her husband on the back, smiling. "Yeah, let's hear it, big guy."

He cleared his throat while racking his brain. "Ah...give me a minute."

The children settled in the dirt in front of him.

Tom tried to remain optimistic for the young ones, but, deep inside, he was somber. He had done his best to ignore the plane trails all day long because their presence meant the Earth Sentinels' agreement with the world's governments had been violated, and that knowledge was too bitter of a pill to swallow after five years of good medicine.

The fire sizzled and snapped. Everyone grew quiet, waiting for the story to begin.

Tom cleared his throat. "There are prophecies from another tribe that speak of the end of days. One says, 'near the Time of

Purification, there will be spider webs spun in the sky.'"

The children's eyes grew big.

A girl pointed at the misty plane trails, asking with a slight lisp because her front baby teeth were missing, "But...how'd they get there?"

Tom was at a loss for words. He didn't want to ruin the mood of the gathering by explaining, in the past, the government had sprayed chemicals into the atmosphere for unverified reasons. Geo-engineering, such as cloud seeding, was one possibility. He had also read the sprays might contain particles that reflect the sun to counteract global warming. However, because of the secrecy, he suspected something more sinister was afoot. Not wanting to disappoint them, he improvised, "Once upon a time, there was a giant spider that spun webs to keep the stars from floating away."

His opening line captivated the children. Some of the adults chuckled because they knew he was crafting the tale from scratch.

"Whenever a strand was weak, the spider would climb up to fix it, keeping every star in place. And, because of her efforts, everything was good and balanced. But one night, the spider slept too long, and one of the strings broke, letting a star hurl through space." Tom pretended to fling a star.

The children envisioned it flying away, lost in the cosmos.

"The hole needed to be filled, so the Giant Spider went after it, hoping to catch the star and bring it back." Tom moved his fingers like a spider scurrying through space. "But while she was gone, another spider snuck in through the hole.

"Now this new spider was not like the other one. It thought only of itself, and weaved a web across the hole to keep the Giant

Spider from returning. And that—" Tom pointed at the plane trails in the sky, "is the Sneaky Spider's web."

Hoki asked, "How will the Giant Spider get back?"

"When she returns with the missing star, its heat will burn up the Sneaky Spider and its sticky web. And after the star is in place, the world will become balanced once more."

"Is the Giant Spider coming back soon?"

"I hope so."

A steady downpour hit the roof of the shack where Tom and Cecile slept. The clock on the nightstand read 7:04 a.m. The dreamcatcher hanging on the wall above the bed served as the headboard. The sound of rain prodded Cecile awake. She immediately noticed the aches in her body and throbbing head. She wondered how a sickness could come on so quickly. She looked over at her husband. His face was flushed. Concerned, she touched his forehead with the back of her hand. Feverish.

Tom opened his bloodshot eyes.

Cecile gasped. "Tom! Your eyes—" She didn't finish her sentence. A sudden urge to vomit came over her.

She tossed the covers off herself, rushing out of the bedroom, past the frayed green chair in the living room sitting under the rain-spattered window. By the time she made it to the bathroom threshold, she was lightheaded and forced to hold onto the doorframe to steady herself. *What is wrong with me?* She reached for the sink counter, making her way to the toilet. She sunk to her knees, placing her head over the bowl, throwing up.

Tom unsteadily entered the bathroom to check on her. "You okay?"

She shook her head.

"Me, neither. Damn, I feel—" He unexpectedly gagged. He motioned for Cecile to move out of the way. She sat back as Tom kneeled over the bowl, every muscle in his body contracting as he retched. Dizzy, he fell to the vinyl floor, lying face down and moaning.

"Tom!" She pulled on his shoulder, attempting to turn him over, but his moans echoed through her mind.

The room spun.

Cecile became disoriented.

Everything went black.

The makeshift infirmary in the tribe's community center was divided in half by a waist-high barrier created out of blankets and sheets draped over chairs spaced evenly apart. The temporary wall offered a slice of privacy for the sick people lying on the floor. Men were on one side and women on the other of the unlit room. Most of them slept. A few moaned because of their aches and pain. All had blotches that resembled bruises covering their bodies.

Adeelah, a junior in the reservation's high school, walked around the room to see who needed her assistance while holding a pitcher of water in one hand and a few empty mugs in the other. The girl looked much healthier than her older "patients". The blotches on her skin were almost indiscernible.

She noticed Cecile was awake for the first time, and sidestepped the others to check on her. She kneeled beside Cecile, setting her pitcher down to check her forehead, saying, "You're better, but you should drink something." Adeelah poured water into a mug, holding it against the woman's dry lips, telling her, "Just so you know, Tom's here and he's doing fine. He's on the other side."

Cecile pulled her mouth away from the mug. "Can I see him?" She tried to get up, but became woozy.

Adeelah helped her to lie back down. "You should rest. Okay? Don't worry, you'll both be fine."

With her bloodshot eyes, Cecile examined Adeelah's face, trying to detect if the temporary nurse was lying, but she found it too hard to focus. She was simply too tired and weak. Her eyelids drooped.

Adeelah set the half-empty mug next to the sick woman's pillow. "Let me know if you need anything else," she said, then walked away. There were others that needed her help.

Left alone, Cecile groggily noticed the teenagers were the only ones taking care of the others. She wondered, *Where's Grandmother Hausis? The elders? The children?* But she didn't have the strength to ask, and maybe didn't want to know.

Cecile fell asleep, dreaming she was walking down a red road. The sides were lined with arching trees dotted with pink blossoms. Crows flew overhead. The fiery ball in the sky was touching the horizon. Each of her footsteps became heavier than the last, and just when she thought she couldn't go any farther, a stag stepped out from behind the trees, standing in the middle of the road. The sunset silhouetted its strong form and magnificent set of antlers.

The totem animal had a message for her. "This will be your most difficult lesson, but you will find the strength, wisdom and courage to do that which must be done."

The stag became waves of light, swirling around Cecile, joining with her spirit before the woman drifted deeper into her dreams.

CHAPTER 4
The Amazon Bruja

THE AFTERNOON STORM had come and gone. Rain dripped off the tropical leaves. Puddles pooled throughout the lifeless village, one trickling inside a hut, making its way under the palm-leaf mats where Zachary, his infant son and four-year-old daughter, Eva, lay with their eyes closed, their bodies covered with black-and-blue blotches.

It had been two days since the virus first struck, and the little girl had fought hard against the disease, but her tender body just wasn't strong enough to win the battle. Eva gasped for air. Her chest rattled. She released her last breath.

Eva's spirit rose out of her body, but before leaving this place, she floated over to her father, reaching down to gently pat his cheek with her small ethereal hand. *Goodbye, Daddy.* At that moment, the hut disappeared from her sight, revealing the vibrant soul of the jungle outside the walls. Strands of light connected everything. Nature spirits hovered above their botanical hosts— joyful to be discovered by the little girl. Eva heard the angelic choir reverberating throughout the universe, its song carried on waves of golden light, pulsing through her, engulfing her in the divine connection that had been hidden from her physical senses only moments before.

The ethereal rainforest converged. Its trees and foliage spun together to create a living tunnel with animals and birds peering out from behind the leaves, all kindly regarding her. A bright light at the end beckoned Eva, but before she took her first step, her grandfather appeared in front of her, blocking her way.

Surrounded by a golden aura, Pahtia told her, "It is not time yet, little one. You have much to do. Lie down and rest."

A celestial butterfly settled on Eva's hand. She admired its transcendental wings sparkling with colors she had never seen before. The world had become a magical place, prompting her to plead like she was trying to avoid bedtime, "I want to go with you, Papa."

"With me?" The old man laughed gleefully. "But I am shapeshifting. Becoming a caiman. Look for me on the shore. Now go back. Go."

The little girl pouted.

"Eva, one day, we will meet again. On this, you must trust me."

Although Eva didn't like her grandfather's message, she obeyed him. Her spirit returned to the hut and entered her limp body. She took a deep breath, filling her vacant lungs. Her heart beat once more. Eva's hazel eyes, the whites tinged with red, opened. She looked around. Gone were the beautiful colors and golden light. The pain that had previously haunted her frail frame returned.

Moments later, Eva's distraught mother appeared in the doorway. The woman's hair was disheveled, and her skin was covered with the telltale signs of the disease. Conchita had come from her dead father's hut and weakly hobbled through the village where so many of her tribe members had also succumbed to the sickness. Cries of despair filled the air.

29

With her heart pounding, dreading what she might discover, Conchita examined the occupants of her own hut, relieved when Eva looked up at her and Zachary turned in his sleep. However, her son lay motionless. She hesitantly stepped across the dirt floor, reaching over her husband's body to touch her baby's blemished skin.

He was cold.

"No!" Conchita scooped up the dead infant, holding him tightly, overcome with grief.

Her sobs roused Zachary, who could barely open his eyes. With a raspy voice, he asked, "What's wrong?"

Overcome with pain, she cried out, "You should have saved him!"

Zachary was confused by the accusation, wondering what she was talking about.

Her words sank into his mind.

The limp baby hung in Conchita's arms.

The words and sight came together.

Their son was dead and had died in his care.

Grief, mixed with shock and guilt, muddled his mind. The last thing he remembered was the entire family falling asleep together. He didn't know how to defend himself. *Was it inexcusable? Wasn't Conchita here? Oh, God, our son is dead.*

Three weeks later, the surviving teenagers played in the middle of the village, chasing each other and laughing.

Eva ran over to join them, but a boy pushed her down, yelling, "Go away."

She fell to the ground, but, instead of crying, she brushed

herself off and found a rock to sit on.

While the others played, an iridescent Blue Morpho butterfly flew up to Eva, resting on her arm. The insect was soon joined by dozens of the same, which fluttered over the little girl, descending onto her small body. The gentle creatures took refuge on the kindred soul, fanning their cerulean wings.

A teenage girl stopped in her tracks. "Look!" She pointed at Eva, who was covered with butterflies from head to toe. "She is a *bruja!*"

Bruja was the Spanish word for witch—a carry-over from the Amazonian tribes' brief, but violent, interactions with the Spaniards during the 16th century. It was then the monks brought with them the concept of good and evil, projecting their own fears onto the shamans' powers, assuming they must be of the devil. These beliefs were added to the tribes' own superstitions, including cannibalism, which they had practiced until just a few generations ago because they believed they could capture their enemies' souls by eating their flesh in grand ceremonies. Afterwards, they shrank the heads to keep them as badges of honor and for use in battles to demoralize the enemy. Regardless of who was to blame, the concept of black magic had taken hold. Even now, some of the shamans used dark powers to manifest the Evil Eye and cast spells onto their unfortunate victims, sometimes resulting in death. It was believed any shaman could be corrupted. It took a strong mind to resist the temptation of using black magic for personal gain.

All the kids stood still as they examined Eva.

The little girl wore the butterflies like a living cloak, their wings reflecting the sunlight, sparkling like sapphire-and-

31

aquamarine gemstones set in black frames.

The teenagers taunted her.

"*Bruja!*"

"Go away!"

"Evil Eva!"

They threw fistfuls of dirt.

The Blue Morphos darted into the air, swirling up and away from the danger, dissipating into the trees. Eva sat motionless on the rock, her eyes peeking through the sandy soil covering her face.

Eva's defenselessness angered the teenagers even more. They wanted her to take on their fears. "You don't belong here!" one sneered.

They walked over to her, scooping up more dirt, piling it on top of her head. The women cooking nearby turned a blind eye to the hostility. Eva covered her face with her hands to protect her eyes as tears rolled down her filthy cheeks.

Zachary glanced out of the hut and saw the teenagers bullying his daughter. He rushed outside. "Stop it!"

One of the oldest boys, trying to act tough, uttered contemptuously at Eva, "You don't belong here! Or you." He pointed defiantly at her father.

Anger welled up in Zachary, reaching a level he didn't know existed within himself. He understood these kids were grieving over the loss of their parents, siblings and tribe members, but to be so cruel to a child was inexcusable. "You should be ashamed of yourselves! Get out of here!"

The teens scattered.

Zachary turned his attention to his daughter, brushing off the clumps of dirt from her hair and face. The air became hazy with dust. Tears welled in his eyes as he did so.

Eva patted him on the arm, saying, "It's okay, Daddy."

"No, it's not. I don't want you playing with them again. They're too old for you." He knew the problem was two-fold. One, she was the youngest child to survive the outbreak, which meant there was a ten-year gap between her and the youngest teenager. And the second problem was many of the parents resented Eva's survival because their own children had died, forgetting that Zachary and Conchita had also lost their infant son. The only explanation the other parents could come up with was Eva was either protected by black magic or the white man's blood. Although the sentiments were unfounded, the tribe was becoming increasingly hostile to both his and Eva's presence in their midst.

Zachary grasped his daughter's small hand, leading her across the clearing, back to their hut where his wife lay on a palm-leaf mat facing away from the doorway. He softly called to her, "Conchita?"

She turned toward him, her eyes red from crying.

He said, "The kids were picking on Eva."

Conchita lifted her head. "What? Why would they..." She stopped talking when she saw her daughter's forlorn expression. "Come here, Eva."

The little girl tottered toward her mother, expecting to be comforted. As Eva approached, Conchita saw her daughter's face morph into that of her son's and became joyful at the sight of him. Her baby had come back to her! But then the hallucination dissolved and Eva's dirt-stained face returned. Once again, Conchita felt as though her son had been wrenched away from her.

A clamp tightened around her heart. She lay back down, sobbing.

With her mother facing away from her, Eva stood there unsure of what to do.

Zachary intervened, taking his daughter into his arms, giving her a quick hug. "Pumpkin, go outside for a moment. Okay?" She nodded, doing as he asked.

He leaned down, touching Conchita's arm, but she pulled away. He said to her, "You can't go on like this—"

"Don't tell me what to do or how to feel!"

"You're right. You can't help how you feel, but you do need to be here for us, especially Eva. We're still here."

"Are you saying I was not here for the baby?"

"No, not at all. What happened wasn't anyone's fault. Whether you were here or there, doesn't matter. There was nothing you could have done."

"But you were here. Maybe if you had held him, or—"

Zachary sighed. He was tired of being blamed for their son's death. He reminded her, "You were with the shaman, yet he couldn't save himself or the tribe. Why would you expect me to—"

"You are blaming my father for our son's death!?"

"What!? No! I didn't say—"

"I need to be alone." Conchita scrambled to her feet, hurrying out of the hut.

Zachary rubbed his face with his hands, unsure of how to deal with the situation.

"Daddy?" Eva peeked around the doorway, remaining outside as she had been told to do.

He looked at her. She was filthy. A few more grains of dirt fell from her hair. Zachary realized he needed to clean her up. With forced cheerfulness, he suggested, "Let's give you a bath, kiddo. Would you like that?"

She nodded.

"Okay, let's go." Zachary escorted Eva through the village, past the women who had done nothing to protect her from the teenagers. He grabbed a bucket off the ground, carrying it as they headed toward the river.

Walking along the well-worn path, he stewed over the betrayal and isolation inflicted by his wife and the other tribe members, although he hid his feelings from his daughter who happily surveyed her surroundings.

When they reached the river, Zachary swept the mucky shoreline with a long willowy branch to scare away any caimans or snakes that might be hiding there. A gold-and-white fish flitted away. After the cloudy water cleared, he filled the bucket, then poured it over Eva's head.

She grimaced as the chilly water flowed over her sun-infused skin. "Ooo, it's cold!" Goosebumps covered her arms.

He said, "One more ought to do it."

Meanwhile, unbeknownst to Zachary, an anaconda had left its den at the river's edge, and swam undetected just below the surface with only its nostrils protruding above the ripples.

Despite the snake being camouflaged by its brownish-green scales, Eva saw its spirit glowing in the water. Excited, she pointed at it. "Look!"

Zachary had barely turned around when the 500-pound snake lunged out of the river, sinking its multiple rows of needle-sharp teeth into his ankle. The young man screamed in pain. The bucket fell to the ground.

With its prey held securely in place, the anaconda calmly slithered out of the river, methodically coiling its tail up around Zachary's legs, reaching his mid-section, moving higher until it fully encompassed the young man's body, then it constricted its massive muscles.

Zachary became light-headed from the suffocating grip. Just before he passed out, he uttered to Eva, "Run..."

But she didn't obey him, instead she approached the great snake whose round eyes carefully observed her, even as it suffocated its victim. She pleaded, "Please let my daddy go!" Eva couldn't understand how these two magnificent spirits could be at odds with one another.

Sensing the love the little girl had for her father, and how desperate she was to save him, the anaconda felt empathy for her and decided to honor her request by loosening its stranglehold on the young man, who was turning blue. The predator's extensive body unraveled, and Zachary fell unconscious onto the shore.

The snake slithered toward Eva, lifting its head, meeting her face to face, its forked tongue tickling her nose.

The little girl said, "Thank you."

The anaconda's thoughts drifted into Eva's mind. *You are most welcome, dear one.* Then something caught its attention. Using the special pits running along its upper lip, the snake sensed the warm bodies of the humans who were hiding in the bushes. *Be careful,* it warned Eva before sliding back into the river.

With the snake gone, Eva focused on her father, squatting beside him, shouting in a high-pitched voice, "Wake up! Wake up!" She shook him until he regained consciousness.

Zachary tried to focus on his daughter, but his vision was

blurry. "Give me a minute," he sputtered, laying there taking deep breaths, oxygenating his body.

While Eva waited, she drew in the sand with her finger, creating an outline of a snake and a stickman.

Finally, Zachary sat up. Still lightheaded, he needed a moment to adjust.

Eva tugged on her father's arm, encouraging him to stand. He obliged her and got to his feet, quickly realizing he was having difficulty putting weight on his injured leg.

Hidden in the dense foliage, the tribe's teenagers watched Zachary hobble beside his daughter. After the pair moved out of sight, the teenagers ran through the underbrush to remain undetected as they sprinted toward the village.

37

CHAPTER 5
The Soldiers Arrive

HARUTO STOOD IN the temple garden surrounded by a bed of purple lavender. The gentle fragrance wafted through the air. She tried to embrace the moment to lessen the pain of losing her baby as well as the elder Mikos who had been her extended family members and mentors, but grief had wrapped itself around her heart with a vise-like grip, causing a constant ache that was so intense she could barely breathe. She needed to find peace—if only for a moment—so she clasped her hands and bowed her head, whispering, "Sweet Devas, I offer my pain to you. Please take it and heal it."

Her prayer was heard, and a part of her anguish lifted like a morning fog. With a lightened heart, Haruto's mind traveled from the past to the present.

With the agility of a cat, she jumped on top of the stone wall that surrounded the grounds. She stood there breathing in the mountain air while viewing the picturesque countryside and the foothills that rolled down to the metropolis at the edge of the sea. There, the highways sat empty. Steam no longer billowed out of the factory smokestacks. The houses and buildings were gray and barren. She had never expected to miss the noise from Fukushima. Then she heard a sound she hadn't heard in weeks—truck engines rumbled on the road at the base of the foothill.

Both concerned and curious, Haruto jumped off the wall, landing on her feet, briskly moving through the garden, bypassing a gnarled cherry tree, following the stone path that rounded the temple, finally coming to the front where she peered down the foothill.

At the bottom, the dust settled around the military trucks parked on the gravel visitor spots. A dozen soldiers climbed out, glancing up at the Mikos' sanctuary, realizing they would have to hike up the terraced staircases built into the hillside.

Haruto's heart pounded. *Were these soldiers bringing supplies?* Even if it was a humanitarian effort, she knew the interaction could quickly escalate into something perilous.

She ran to the rear of the temple, scurrying up the steps and across the landing to where the bell hung from the pergola. She grabbed the horizontal pole that was suspended by rope, swinging it back, letting it rush forward with full force, striking the bell. The low-toned ring echoed over the mountainside.

The soldiers looked up, wary that a warning had been sounded.

Haruto hurried inside the temple to wait for her fellow Mikos, who dashed out of their rooms, their silk white shirts and red wide-legged pants fluttering as they hastily moved down the hallways and staircase.

The women gathered in the common area, wondering why they had been summoned.

Konomi asked, her eyes filled with panic, "What's wrong, Haruto!?"

Hoshino, the oldest Miko after Haruto, demanded to know, "What is going on?"

Haruto tried to appear calm as she informed them, "There are soldiers at our doorstep."

"Soldiers!?" several of the women exclaimed.

"What do they want?" Hoshino asked.

"Let's hope they're here to help us, but let's also be cautious," Haruto said. "Things could easily turn ugly. And no matter how afraid you are, don't show it. Fear always increases fear."

Outside, the soldiers huffed up the hillside stairs, reaching the halfway point.

Haruto asked Hoshino, "Will you take the lead? I'm going to find Billy and let him know what's going on."

The woman bowed her head, agreeing to the responsibility.

Haruto rushed out the rear entrance, bounding through the garden. She was out of breath by the time she reached the curator's house and flung open the door, but the house was empty.

Haruto turned around, scanning the grounds. Billy stood in the cemetery at the rear of the garden, shaded by an old oak tree whose broad limbs spread over the gravesites like a mother hen protecting her chicks. He was paying his respects beside their daughter's final resting place, holding his hat in his hands.

Haruto walked toward him, stepping over the rocky border outlining the burial ground and onto the soft moss thriving in the cool moist soil. "Billy?"

He continued gazing at the small mound covering their angel, who had never taken a breath during her short time on earth.

"Soldiers are here," Haruto informed him.

Billy nodded.

The Miko solemnly regarded the grave. The wooden marker, which Billy had carved himself, simply read "Among the Stars". No name. No date. Grief once again tightened its hold on her heart.

A gentle wind swept past the couple, rustling the leaves. An owl, perched in the branches, awoke from its slumber, hooting a somber warning. Haruto sharply drew in her breath, afraid the bird of prey brought yet another bad omen.

Billy said what was on his mind, "Our people have been through this many times before. At the start, soldiers will claim to restore order, but in the end, they always steal, and rape, and kill."

"Please don't let your past make this worse than it is."

But the past was etched into his genetic memory—hundreds of years of screaming women and children, stolen land, and tragedies like Wounded Knee and the Trail of Tears. Not to mention his ancestors being forced to live on reservations as prisoners until they were granted "citizenship" on the land that was once theirs. Billy knew those in power were all the same—no matter the country.

He stepped around the burial plot to be near his lover, embracing her as if it might be their last time together. Both of them dreaded going back to the temple, yet felt an obligation to stand with the others. Billy released his hold on her, then placed his black hat on his head, tapping it lightly.

The two of them left the cemetery, stepping out into the sunlight, walking hand in hand through the garden. As they passed by a cherry tree, a flash of blue caught Billy's eye. He halted, pulling on Haruto's hand, cautiously whispering, "Someone's here."

Billy warily crept around the trunk, pressing his back against the bark as he stole a glance. His expression changed from concern to disbelief when he saw a fallen angel lounging on a stone bench. This ancient being wore a sapphire-colored robe that draped to the ground, and had enormous white wings with blue tips. His hair was jet-black, and his eyes were the color of the Mediterranean Sea. The lost soul's impressive-sized body was framed by a wooden trellis that supported a tangled wisteria vine whose lavender blooms hung like bunches of grapes ready to be harvested—an iconic scene worthy of being painted by an old master.

"Bechard?" Billy uttered, not even realizing he had said the fallen angel's name out loud.

Haruto exclaimed, "What!?" She bustled around the tree to see for herself.

Bechard got to his feet, standing nearly nine-feet tall. He smiled fondly at the two of them. "Greetings! It's been too long, old friends."

Haruto winced at being called a friend. "Please don't tell me you had something to do with this."

"Not specifically. However, I have come to warn you."

"Warn us!? Why didn't you warn us about the virus!?"

Undeterred by the accusation, Bechard asked, "Did I ever tell you the parable about the old farmer whose horse ran away—"

"I've heard this one before."

"But it's worth repeating," he countered, proceeding anyway, "After an old farmer's horse had run away, his neighbors came to visit him, telling him it was bad luck. The old farmer replied, 'Maybe it is, maybe it isn't.' The next morning, the runaway horse returned with three wild mares. This time, the neighbors exclaimed, 'What good luck!' And yet again, the old farmer said, 'Maybe it is, maybe it isn't.' The day after that, his son broke his leg trying to tame one of the wild mares. And again, the neighbors came, claiming it was bad luck, and again, the old farmer said, 'Maybe.' However, the very next day, the army showed up at the village demanding that all the young men come with them, but when they saw the son's broken leg, they left him—"

"Seriously!?" Haruto scoffed. "It's been five years, and you show up to tell us this old, old story? We don't have time for this! Billy and I need to get back to the temple."

Ignoring her outburst, Bechard explained, "The moral of the story is: That which seems bad, isn't always so. We don't always see the big picture or realize sometimes a misfortune can lead us to our greatness."

"What do you mean by that?"

"You were not chosen to be an Earth Sentinel by accident. All of these events were always spinning through the cosmos as a possibility."

43

Haruto's face became red with rage. "You knew!"

"Before you get upset, keep in mind, I couldn't have stopped this, even if—"

Mad beyond reason, Haruto charged at the fallen angel. Billy grabbed her, holding her back, preventing her kicks and punches from reaching Bechard, despite wanting to do the same thing himself.

Haruto screamed, "My baby died! You're evil! Evil!" She broke down crying, sinking to the ground.

Billy wished he could protect his lover from her agony, but he couldn't, so instead he focused his fierce brown eyes on the fallen angel and, in a restrained voice, declared, "You'd better have a damn good reason, Bechard."

"I do, but it's going to take more time than we have right now.

When the two of you are ready, you know where to find me."

Bechard disappeared just before Konomi came around the cherry tree.

The young woman was startled to see her fellow Miko on the ground with tears running down her face. "Is everything okay?"

Haruto wiped away her tears, embarrassed to be seen crying. "Everything's fine."

Konomi didn't press her for an answer, mostly because the small army occupying the temple was distracting her thoughts. "I came to tell you the soldiers need to speak with the two of you."

"What do they want?" Haruto asked as Billy lent her his hand, helping her to her feet.

"I'm not sure. They said something about a census. Can we go? I don't want to keep them waiting."

Haruto brushed the dirt from her pants, then the three of them walked through the garden not saying a word. When they arrived at the rear entrance, Konomi briskly climbed up the stairs, but Haruto and Billy hesitated.

A warning blared through Haruto's mind, *Run away...run away...* She wanted to do just that—run away and hide with Billy, but a sense of duty propelled her to go inside.

The couple entered the common area where the Japanese soldiers and Mikos stood in separate groups. The military men wore camouflaged fatigues and helmets, and carried automatic weapons strapped over their shoulders. The women appeared outwardly calm, but Haruto perceived their fears.

Billy's presence caused the soldiers to grip their guns a little tighter.

The military leader looked and dressed differently than the

others. He was Caucasian with blond hair and blue eyes, and wore a black dress uniform. The bright-blue patch sewn on his sleeve affirmed his commanding position within the United Nations organization. It had white olive branches stitched on each side of an iconic globe. Arched at the top were the words "New World Order", and the large letters "UN" were embroidered underneath. The UN leader didn't carry a gun, instead he held a sleek silver tablet as he moved forward, saying, "Haruto?" His cold demeanor detracted from his handsome face.

"Yes?"

"I'll need to scan you for our records. Okay?"

He had posed it as a question, but Haruto knew her compliance was mandatory.

The UN leader held the tablet in front of her face. A shutter sound was heard. On the screen, her photo appeared next to her name. Then he used the tablet to scan her body from head to toe. Two beeps rang out. He read the screen with concern. "One more time, please." Haruto's body was scanned once more. And again, the tablet beeped twice, however, this time a black message box appeared in the center of the screen with the words "Detain— Virus Mutation Detected". The UN leader said, "We're picking up some irregularities. You may be carrying the virus. We'll need to quarantine you."

"Quarantine? But I'm not hurting anyone here. Everyone's already been exposed."

"Visitors may not be so lucky. You'll need to come with us."

"I don't think driving me around the countryside is safer for anyone."

"It's an order," he stated, then instructed two of his soldiers

45

to escort her to the military wagon at the bottom of the foothill.

Without thinking, Billy stepped between Haruto and the soldiers. His action caused the tension in the room to skyrocket. The soldiers raised their guns while a lone soldier stealthily snuck up behind Billy, who spun around, but not before a handheld device was jabbed into his back, injecting him with a short-acting sedative. He lost consciousness, falling to the floor. His face hit the stone slab, knocking off his black hat, which rocked back and forth next to his head.

The Mikos gasped. One screamed.

Haruto cried out, "Billy!" She knelt beside him, feeling his pulse to make sure he was alive. She didn't notice the same soldier coming at her until it was too late.

46
⚔

The mobile prison journeyed throughout the night. Haruto lay on a metal bench shivering. The vehicle slowed down, coming to a standstill. The engine idled. She heard the muffled voices of men, then the vehicle inched forward. A metal grate clanked as the tires drove over it.

Both curious and concerned, Haruto got up and went to the back door, pressing her face against the barred window, peering outside. She saw a military base enclosed by a chain-link fence with barbed wire strung across the top. Japanese soldiers patrolled the area. Rows of military trucks were parked in the lot. High in the tower, a spotlight flashed overhead.

The vehicle abruptly stopped. Haruto heard soldiers approaching, so she sat back down.

The door swung open. A handful of Japanese soldiers stood on the pavement. One shouted, "Get out!"

Haruto refused to show her contempt or fear, instead she stood up and made her way to the door, jumping down, landing squarely on her feet.

"This way," said a soldier who motioned with his gun.

Two military men flanked each side of Haruto, escorting her across the parking lot while two more guarded her from the rear. It was an excessive number of soldiers for just one woman. Haruto was led toward a black, prisoner transport vehicle with UN emblems affixed to its sides. Once there, her Japanese guards saluted the fair-haired, blue-eyed UN soldiers dressed in black uniforms, but they did not receive the same courtesy in return.

The UN leader, who looked almost identical to the one at the temple, spoke to the men in stilted Japanese, "We'll take her from here," effectively dismissing the native soldiers.

A UN soldier opened the rear door of the vehicle, motioning for Haruto to get inside.

She hesitated. "Where are you taking me?"

He remained silent.

The UN leader turned toward Haruto, curtly answering, "I'm sure you were told. To be quarantined."

"But *where* are you taking me?"

"Get in."

Realizing it was futile and potentially dangerous to continue questioning him, Haruto climbed inside. Nearly hidden in the shadows, two fear-struck women sat side by side on a metal bench. They avoided Haruto's gaze as she sat on the opposite side. The vehicle's interior became dark when the windowless door slammed shut. The only openings were the vents on the sides that had been constructed to obscure the vision line, letting only a

47

minimal amount of light seep through the slits.

The engine revved and the vehicle moved forward. Haruto thought with bitter amusement that all of her martial arts training—a lifetime of devotion—had proven to be fruitless when a gun was pointed at her head. Now she was a prisoner, and all she could do was sit and wait.

The vehicle drove up a steep winding road just as the sun peeked over the horizon. The deserted two lanes eventually entered a tunnel carved out of a mountainside. Electrical conduits ran along the walls. The overhead lights created a strobe-like effect as the mobile prison sped along. Light. Dark. Light. Dark. The echoes of the turbocharged engine woke up Haruto and the two women, who had fallen asleep during the long journey.

The older woman's voice came out of the darkness, prophesying, "We're never going home." A streak of light flashed briefly through the vents, highlighting the despair on her face.

Hours later, the vehicle ground to a halt. The three women sat up, tired and afraid, staring at the back door as it opened, revealing three UN soldiers and their leader. At first glance, the men appeared to be floating heads because their fair hair and pale skin contrasted sharply against their black uniforms and the dimly lit tunnel. The UN leader motioned for the women to exit the vehicle. One by one, each prisoner apprehensively stepped down.

"This way," the UN leader said, steering the women up the concrete stairs to a set of metal doors, built into the wall. The other soldiers followed from behind. The doors slid apart as they approached.

On the other side was a subway station. Unlike normal stations, there were no people, no benches on which to rest, no vending machines, and no advertisements or graffiti lining the walls.

The women were escorted across the terminal, their footsteps reverberating until they reached the platform's edge near the rails.

Haruto stood under the gloomy lights feeling vulnerable in this barren borderland—like a calf that had been separated from its herd. She could only wait helplessly for the encroaching predator, running through the tunnel, to come and devour her.

The subway train appeared out of the shaft, slowing down at the sight of fresh meat, stopping in front of the women, using magnetic levitation to hover over the rails. Its three cars were painted white and brightly lit. After the doors automatically opened, the UN leader motioned for the women to enter the nearest car.

49

Haruto's heart pounded as she moved inside the train's guts where black plastic benches ran its length. Leather straps hung like nooses from the ceiling, swinging back and forth. Metal poles were its bones. Hypnotizing black-and-white linoleum tiles covered its belly.

A buzzer rang out.

The doors closed.

With its hunger satisfied, the subway train crept away, gaining momentum, carrying Haruto and the other captives back to its lair.

CHAPTER 6
Outcasts

WITH EVA BY his side, Zachary limped along a path through the jungle, wincing with each step. His snakebite was swelling. And even though the anaconda was a nonpoisonous snake, its rows of thin-pointed teeth had cut through his skin and into the underlying tissue, inflicting more germs than he cared to think about. He wished Pahtia was still alive so the shaman could mend his leg, but perhaps Conchita would be able to help him. She had learned well from her father.

Zachary's concern took a different turn when they entered the village.

The tribe members stood outside their huts. Since the men wielded spears, Zachary thought they were planning a hunting expedition without him, again. But then he noticed the women and teenagers held a fierce glare in their eyes, which was disconcerting, especially when it became obvious their aggression was directed at him and Eva.

Zachary was accustomed to feeling like an outsider, but for the first time in five years, he felt like the enemy. His heart beat faster as he scanned the angry horde, searching for his wife. He didn't see her, so he called out, "Conchita!"

There was no answer.

Takwa, the same man who had tried to steal his fish, stepped forward, seeming to enjoy the moment, standing arrogantly as the new self-appointed chief. His brown eyes stared menacingly at Zachary, and his words were deliberate and dangerous, "Conchita cannot help you now."

"What are you talking about?"

Takwa looked with disdain at Eva. "Your child has a bad spirit."

Adrenaline pumped through Zachary's veins as the seriousness of the situation became evident. He defended Eva. "She does not!"

The hunter repeated, "She has a bad spirit!" setting the courtroom for her judgment.

Anyone who might have defended Zachary or his daughter, or offered guidance, such as Pahtia or the elders, had all succumbed to the virus. Takwa was taking advantage of the situation to get rid of the man who had stolen Conchita's heart, and it appeared he would use Eva as the pawn to do it.

Zachary tried to reason with him to calm the situation, "The sickness was hard on all of us. My wife..." he briefly faltered when he noticed Takwa bristled at the word "wife", but then he persevered, "Conchita lost her baby and her heart is broken. She is not thinking right."

"Her mind is good. Conchita knows you are bad. And the child is bad. She is no longer your wife."

"What are you talking about?"

"Conchita is in the hut of her father."

Zachary knew of the tribe's custom that allowed a woman to divorce her husband by simply moving out of their hut. But up until three weeks ago—before the outbreak—they were in love.

This made no sense. He stepped toward his hut to see for himself if Conchita had removed her things, but the others blocked his way. Frustrated and fearful, he declared to his accuser, "There is no way Conchita would send Eva away! This is your doing! Why would you do this to a little girl?"

"Girl?" Takwa said contemptuously. "Your daughter is a *bruja*! The young ones saw her talking to the great snake. The fact you are alive is proof enough. Nobody survives the attack of the great snake."

Zachary racked his brain trying to recall the events that had taken place down by the river. He remembered dipping the bucket, an anaconda biting his leg, and then... The next thing he remembered was waking up on the ground with blood seeping from the snakebite. *What did happen? Why am I alive?* Hoping to clear things up, he asked Eva, "Can you tell us what happened?"

The little girl was all too happy to explain. "Uh-huh. I asked the snake...she is nice...to let Daddy live. So, um...she let him go."

Zachary immediately realized it had been a mistake to let Eva speak. He pleaded with the tribe members, "She sees things with the eyes of a child. She doesn't understand what she's saying."

Takwa was fed up with his competitor's excuses. "You do not know the great snake. It fears nothing. Your child has strange powers. A bad spirit is in her. You brought the sickness to us." The other tribe members nodded in agreement. "You must go! Now!"

Eva frowned. She was confused. Why would her family send her away? She cried out, "Mommy! Mommy!"

It broke Zachary's heart to hear his daughter call for her mother. He tried to reason with Takwa one more time. "I do not understand. Everyone here talks with the animals and nature.

Why do you say it's bad when Eva does it?"

A flame of sensibility flickered in Takwa's eyes, but then it blew out. "Eva has a dark power over the animals. It is not talk. It is control. It is not right."

"She is just a little girl..." Zachary tried to appease Takwa by saying, "Look, I'll leave, just let her stay with her mother. You'll never see me again."

The hunter examined Eva, disliking the aspects that made her different from the other tribe members. The golden streaks in her hair. Her hazel eyes. She looked too much like Zachary. Takwa coldly stated, "She is a bad omen. You both must leave."

"Conchita would never agree to this! She would not send Eva away!"

"But she has!"

"I want to hear this from her. To know it's true."

"You are calling me a liar?" Takwa seethed with anger, wanting to murder his adversary. For too long, the hunter had endured the agony of watching Zachary and Conchita create a life together. That all ended today. "Go before I kill you both."

Zachary knew being cast out of the tribe was a death sentence for him and Eva, especially with his leg injury. The two of them were no match for the rainforest on their own. Plus, he found it hard to believe Conchita had agreed to this—somehow Takwa had twisted her words.

The warriors stomped their feet and brandished their weapons. The women and teenagers chanted threateningly, becoming louder.

Zachary could not comprehend the extreme turnabout in the tribe's sentiments toward him and Eva, but he did realize the two

53

of them needed to flee before the situation escalated into violence. He grabbed his daughter's hand, lamely stepping away, the tribe's threatening cries pushing them out.

As they walked, the outcast man contemplated their future, knowing they would be lucky to survive the night. But if they did make it, and followed the river downstream, Zachary speculated they might stumble upon an outpost or missionary campsite.

Eva asked, "Are we going to see Mommy?"

Under his breath, Zachary answered, "Maybe."

They followed the path that led to the river until the village was no longer in sight. Feeling it was safe, Zachary stopped to rest, leaning against a tree, standing on his good leg.

The little girl, anxious to see her mother, didn't understand why they had stopped. "Come on, Daddy."

"Just give me a minute. My leg hurts." He pointed to the snake bite.

The little girl squatted to look at it more closely. "Oh...that is bad." She noticed the dark energy hovering around the wound, and blew on the shadowy mist, watching it swirl, beginning to dissipate.

"Honey, don't blow on it. You'll give it germs."

Although Eva didn't want to stop, she obeyed.

Zachary pushed off the tree. "Ready?" He started down the path, flinching with each step.

When they reached the river's flowing waters, the young man stood on the bank, glancing up at the mid-day sun. If he obeyed Takwa's orders, he would have followed the current downstream, but his heart made him turn in the opposite direction toward Conchita. He knew it was risky, but he needed to see his wife before they left the tribe's territory, otherwise, he would never get a second chance.

From the treetops, the tribesmen silently observed the father and daughter struggling to pass the thorny underbrush hanging over a seldom-used path. Takwa watched just long enough to confirm the outcasts were headed toward Pahtia's old hut. Infuriated that his orders had been ignored, he motioned with his hand. His signal prompted the other hunters to throw their spears, which sailed through the air, dipping below the tree branches, stabbing the ground, creating a makeshift barrier across the path.

Zachary and Eva jerked to a stop, not knowing if the next spear would strike them. The warriors' hoots and shouts scared the little girl, who clung to her father's legs.

Takwa grabbed a vine, swinging down, expertly dropping onto the path. Only the close-knit row of spears stood between him and the exiled pair. He hissed venomously, "I told you to leave."

Zachary justified his actions. "I have a right to see Conchita."

"You will never see her again." Takwa grabbed one of the standing spears, pulling it out of the ground, stepping through the gap.

He aimed the weapon at his rival's heart.

Before Takwa could strike, a black jaguar leaped down from an overhead branch, knocking him to the ground. Snarling, the big cat opened its jaws to bite down on the hunter's neck.

Eva shouted, "No!"

The jaguar hesitated, turning its blazing-yellow eyes onto the little girl.

Before Zachary could stop Eva, she stepped toward the carnivore.

High in the trees, the hunters, who were reaching for their dart guns, froze in place. They wondered if the jaguar would respond in the same manner as the snake. If it did, it would prove beyond a doubt the child was a *bruja*. And if Eva was a witch, none of them wanted to kill her or her animal friend. She would have the power to haunt them after death.

The motionless jaguar studied the little girl as she approached.

Eva came face to face with the predator. Standing there without fear, she silently implored, *Please let him go.*

Takwa struggled beneath the weight of the big cat, which grumbled a warning at him. The man wisely stopped moving. The jaguar returned its attention to Eva. Its thoughts entered her mind. *Why save this man?*

He is family.

I doubt he would do the same for you, but very well. The creature stepped off Takwa's back, then disappeared into the underbrush.

Seizing the opportunity, Takwa jumped up, almost knocking Eva over as he plowed through the row of spears, running away.

The other hunters took hold of thick hanging vines, using them to soar through the trees before making their descent, nearly free-falling as they put one hand under the other, expertly lowering themselves to the ground, following their leader. No one wanted to mess with the *bruja*.

Zachary understood Takwa would hate him more than ever after this humiliating and bizarre incident, and the tribe would never accept his daughter. So out of fear for Eva's life, and to avoid another confrontation, he aborted the mission of seeing his wife. Besides, he wasn't sure Conchita wanted to see them. And even if she did, he couldn't go near her—not with Takwa running wild. She would have to find them if she wanted to be together. There was no other choice. Zachary decided he and Eva would return to the river, and follow it until they either stumbled upon civilization or died trying.

Moving as fast as he could on his injured leg, Zachary led his daughter along the narrow path, retracing their footsteps. As they walked, he contemplated how Eva and the jaguar had seemed to communicate with each other, but his rational mind cried out, *That's not possible!* His thoughts tumbled back and forth until the episode was pushed to the back of his mind by their current predicament. If they were going to live, he needed to focus on the here and now.

The pair reached the river, then trekked along the sandy bank, which sounded simpler than it was. Zachary had to keep an eye out for the caimans and snakes lurking in the water. And, in some areas, the shoreline was nonexistent, forcing them to tromp through the dense jungle. It was a slow and arduous journey, but they had no choice. Progress was the only way out of this inhospitable place. But, at the same time, every footstep broke off a piece of his heart because each one took him farther away from Conchita and the life they had made together.

The afternoon storm clouds, which had been birthed high in the mountains, were ready to shower their life-giving rain over the jungle. The winds picked up. Lightning crackled across the indigo sky, and thunder rolled over the lush canopy.

57

Zachary sought shelter in the crevice of an old Mahogany tree, but there wasn't quite enough room for both him and Eva, which left his shoulder and wounded leg exposed to the torrential downpour that soon ensued. He examined his leg as the rain hit it. There were insect bites around the swollen and infected puncture marks. How he wished he had learned to make some of Pahtia's herbal concoctions, but Conchita was the shaman's apprentice. *She was supposed to take care of me.* He tried not to cry.

A few hours later, the storm stopped. The sun burned through the lingering mist, causing the temperature to rise rapidly, making the air so humid it was difficult to breathe. The jungle transitioned from hues of gray into full-blown color. And once again, the birds sang, insects crawled, and creatures foraged through the trees.

Zachary wrestled himself out of the tree's crevice, stiffly standing on his good leg, stretching. He reached into the hole to rouse Eva from her slumber. "Pumpkin, it's time to go."

She opened her eyes, whining, "I'm hungry, Daddy."

"We'll find something soon, I promise. Now come on. Let's go."

Eva crawled out of the crevice. Her tummy grumbled. For the first time since they left, she cried, "I want Mommy! I want to go home!"

"I know..." Something in the river caught Zachary's eye. He peered through the underbrush and saw a gigantic eighteen-foot Black Caiman floating on the surface, the water still bubbling from its ascent. The young man warily studied the reptile, which stared back at him. They needed to leave this territory. Zachary motioned for Eva to follow him.

To steer clear of the caiman, they avoided the shoreline and journeyed along the bank that overlooked the river. But, as they traveled, the caiman kept pace with them, using its webbed claws to counteract the current, which threatened to carry it away. Its ridged tail acted as a rudder.

"Eva?"

"Yes?"

Zachary asked the question that had been plaguing him, "Why do you think the jaguar let Takwa go?"

She shrugged her tiny shoulders. "Because I asked nicely." She stepped over a root.

"You know jaguars don't generally let people go just because someone asks nicely. Right?"

She shrugged again, not really interested.

Zachary's snakebite was becoming increasingly painful. He really needed a walking stick, but so far had been unable to find one that wasn't rotten from lying on the moist soil.

They reached a clearing overlooking the river. "Let's stop and rest here," he suggested, standing on his good leg.

The caiman maneuvered its enormous body around to face the current, swishing its tail to anchor itself near the humans.

Eva complained, "I'm hungry!"

"I know. We'll come across something soon."

The spirits must have heard them. Seconds later, a flock of green parrots flew into view, their bright-colored wings flashing like emeralds in the sunlight as they dipped out of sight below the embankment. Zachary expected the birds to soar back into view, but they didn't. It was as if they had disappeared. Curious on where they had gone, he peeked over the edge. There below was a Camu Camu shrub jutting out from the side of the bluff, hanging nearly horizontal over the river. The parrots were perched on the

59

willowy branches abundant with dark-red shiny fruit the size of plump cherries. This food was a gift from the gods. The young man examined the slender limbs. Unfortunately, the fruit grew closer to the shrub's tip than its base—much too far for him to reach them. He would have been willing to climb across the branches, but he couldn't risk falling into the river, not with the caiman lurking below.

There had to be a way to get to the berries without climbing.

Zachary scoured the area, painfully hobbling around until he found a stick hanging tenuously from an overhead vine. He reached up and pulled it down, then peeled away all its offshoots, except for the short one near its tip. He examined the stick, which was now a hook, happy with the results, then limped back toward the Camu Camu shrub.

At the edge of the bluff, Zachary lay on his stomach, reaching out with his handcrafted tool. Startled, the green parrots took to flight, heading for another part of the rainforest. He snagged the closest limb with the hook, bending it backwards. When the berries came close enough, he grabbed a handful and set them on the ground. He repeated this action until he had a pile of berries, which was more than enough to feed them now as well as their next meal.

Zachary and Eva dined on the fruit, savoring the flavor, red juice forming in the creases of their mouths. For a few delectable moments, life was good.

After eating their fill, Zachary tied the front of his t-shirt to create a pocket so he could carry the uneaten berries with them. Struggling with the knot, he didn't notice Eva taking his hook.

The little girl copied her father and lay on her stomach, trying to capture a limb loaded with Camu Camu berries, but she reached too far and lost her balance. She fell into the shrub.

"Eva!"

Her small arms flailed as she tried to latch onto the nearest limbs to save herself from falling. Leaves scattered. Fruit plunked into the water below. She caught a branch with one of her hands, but it bowed dangerously.

Zachary was desperate to go out and save Eva, but he couldn't, not without breaking the limb precariously holding her above the river, and caiman, below. He tried to appear calm, ignoring his racing heart, saying to her, "Eva, you'll be all right, just move toward me."

She looked down at the chartreuse water.

He raised his voice. "Don't go in the river!"

The caiman was methodically swimming toward the dangling child, cutting through the current.

"Eva, look at me." Her hazel eyes shifted toward Zachary. "Come to me. Just move one hand at a time."

She slid her hand along the branch, which creaked, threatening to break at any moment.

"Take it slow."

Hand after hand, Eva finally got within his reach.

Zachary grabbed her, pulling her to safety. After a good hug, he examined her. "You okay?"

Eva nodded. She had a few scrapes, but otherwise appeared to be unharmed.

"Don't do that again. Okay?"

She nodded, trying not to cry, afraid she had disappointed her father.

"Oh, honey, it's okay. I just don't want to lose you." He kissed her forehead, then gathered the berries from off the ground, putting them in his t-shirt's makeshift pocket.

Before setting out again, Zachary stole a glance over the embankment to see if the caiman was still stalking them. The reptile had swum to the water's edge, its unwavering eyes stared back at him. It was time to go.

Journeying through the jungle and swatting at insects became the pair's routine. Zachary used his hook as a walking stick, which helped a great deal to ease his pain, but, less than an hour later, it snapped in half. He threw the broken piece in his hand to the ground, angry that nothing was going right. He would keep an eye out for another stick, but he knew he had been fortunate to find the first one.

The young man shuffled along with difficulty, estimating they would be lucky to walk four miles a day. If it weren't for the snakebite, he would have been more optimistic. However, with the way things were, he couldn't imagine having more than a day or two left in him before he wouldn't be able to walk at all. And on top of all that, because of the caiman, they had to avoid the narrower strips of sand along the river, forcing them to fight their way through the rainforest's thick foliage and underbrush until they came to areas where the shoreline widened—like the one that had just become visible around the bend.

Zachary stood on the outskirts of the broad strip of sand, studying it, weighing the pros and cons. If they took this shortcut, it would allow them to bypass a large swath of the tangled jungle and save a considerable amount of time, but it would also bring them closer to the caiman stalking them. Taking the shoreline was definitely a risk, but he felt it was wide enough to give them a good head start should the beast charge at them.

Meanwhile, the caiman floated in the river, observing them.

Damn vulture. Zachary glanced back at the jungle, wondering, if by some slim chance, Conchita had caught up to them, but she was nowhere in sight. It seemed she really had deserted them.

"Daddy?"

"Yes?"

"Wouldn't it be faster to ride the caiman?"

He took a moment to imagine such a ride through his child's eyes, envisioning them sailing down the river, coasting without a care while lounging on their personal living boat. "That would be something," he agreed.

"Caiman says we can ride him."

"Our last one…" he muttered.

"No, silly."

"That's not a good idea, Eva. You stay away from it. Okay?"

"Okay." She turned toward the river, directing her response to someone behind her father. "He said, 'No.'"

Oh, no! Zachary spun around.

The caiman had crept onto the shore, and was less than a body length away from them. Neither of the humans was a match for the reptile's speed, but Zachary figured if he let the beast attack him, then at least his daughter would be spared. Without taking his eyes off the predator, he said, "Eva, walk away. Follow the river."

The caiman took several steps toward him, its giant claws digging into the sand.

"Find help," Zachary instructed her.

63

The creature took another step while issuing a strange hiss.

"Eva, go!" He didn't want her to see him being mauled. He knew it would be a gruesome sight.

As the caiman drew closer, Zachary shut his eyes, waiting for the horrific end to his life. He winced when the creature's snout touched his leg.

But it didn't strike.

It bumped his leg again.

Zachary opened his eyes.

The caiman moved a few feet past him, pressing its armored midsection against his leg, then bellowed. The primordial sound caused the hairs on Zachary's neck to stand up. *I must be dead or dreaming*, he thought.

64

Eva tottered over to the reptile, sitting on its wide rugged back, exclaiming, "Let's go!"

Or hallucinating.

"Daddy, are you listening? Come on!"

Zachary's body suddenly had a mind of its own. He sat on the caiman behind Eva. The creature lifted up its massive armored frame, taking its passengers with it as it stepped over the sand, sliding into the water. The current gently accepted their presence. The caiman swished its tail, gaining speed with remarkably little effort.

Eva relayed a message to her father, "He says, 'Put your feet up.'" It was a reminder there were pirañas in the river.

Zachary quickly lifted his feet, wrapping his legs around his daughter.

Eva napped against Zachary's side, resting her head on his chest as they rode downstream. The young man's skin was more burnt than usual because of the sun reflecting off the water. Fortunately for the little girl, her complexion offered more protection than her father's. Zachary popped a berry into his mouth as he contemplated the possibility of making it out of the jungle alive by the strangest of all things—riding on a caiman. On the other hand, he thought this had to be a dream, albeit, the most realistic one he had ever had.

Pain shot from Zachary's wound, spiking up his leg. He waited for it to subside. The snakebite was becoming increasingly swollen and infected. He knew he didn't have much time before the infection spread throughout his body. He brooded, *If this is a dream, at least make the pain go away. But maybe it isn't. Maybe it's real. Really? Riding a caiman? But...if this is real, maybe Eva really did talk to the snake and jaguar as well. Maybe she inherited the gift from Pahtia.* Zachary tried to recollect of a time when his father-in-law had talked to animals, but he couldn't think of one, except in the spirit realm, of course.

Eva woke up, groggily watching the rainforest float past. She pointed at the toucans, parrots, storks and Kingfishers, one after the other until she suddenly became enthused, sitting up. "Look!"

The father expected another bird sighting, but instead he saw hunters from another tribe menacingly stalking them along the riverbank, their bodies painted with white indigenous designs. The warriors aggressively shook their spears.

"Daddy, get on your belly." Eva moved from his side to lay on her stomach. "Like this."

By now, Zachary had stopped doubting his daughter's messages, and followed her example. He ignored the threat of

65

pirañas, and wrapped his arms and legs around the beast, using his own body to shield Eva who peeked out from under his arm.

The caiman dove beneath the surface of the river, then vigorously swished its tail and paddled its webbed feet, propelling them through the water, skimming just above the riverbed. The water engulfed Zachary and his daughter, trying to pull them apart as the caiman sped along, but the young man refused to let go. He closed his eyes and hung on tight. Eva's cheeks puffed out as she held her breath, but, unlike her father, she kept her eyes open, observing the underpinnings of this aquatic world, mesmerized by its fish, plants and algae-covered rocks.

The enraged tribesmen, threatened by the intruders, shot arrows that sailed to the center of the river, piercing the surface, whizzing through the undercurrent, narrowly missing their targets. To avoid being hit, the caiman quickened its speed, covering an amazing distance in just a few seconds.

Eva started to turn blue. *Need air!* she pleaded.

Sensing her desperation, the caiman glided to the surface where the sunlight danced on the water. Zachary and Eva took deep breaths, filling their lungs.

The tribesmen were now tiny figures on the distant shore and no longer a threat.

The riders sat up on the rugged shell of the great reptile. Their racing hearts calmed as the river carried them away.

CHAPTER 7
To Hell and Back

THE SUBWAY TRAIN sped through the dark tunnel, slowing as it entered the station. Its forlorn whistle woke up Haruto and the other women as it came to a stop. When the car doors opened, the women saw a troop of UN soldiers waiting for them.

Haruto thought, *They all look the same.*

The women warily stepped onto the platform. The soldiers escorted them to the opposite side of the terminal where the metal doors slid opened, revealing a gray-walled corridor.

They were led to an open vehicle sporting eight tires and four rows of black vinyl seating. "Get in," the leader said, motioning with his hand, indicating the prisoners were to occupy the two middle rows. Haruto sat behind the other women and studied the long corridor. There were no doors. No hallways. No means of escape.

The vehicle hummed past the gray walls for several minutes before coming to a "T" in the corridor, stopping in front of a laboratory with gleaming glass doors.

Inside the laboratory were four hospital-styled gurneys and a row of black-topped tables, which held microscopes, glass beakers and metal trays. Two scientists, wearing white lab coats, stood near the entrance. Neither of them appeared to be quite human. They had almond-shaped eyes that were more violet than blue and spaced a bit too far apart. Their skin texture was rough with a faint olive tone, and their ears and noses were smaller than normal.

The glass doors slid open.

Haruto watched the scientists step into the corridor. Their peculiar faces and off-kilter gaits caused an uncontrollable fear to erupt within her. She jumped from the vehicle, attempting to escape, although she had no idea of where to run to. It didn't matter. Anywhere, but here.

She didn't get far.

A soldier caught Haruto by the arm. She struggled to free herself from his powerful grip, spinning around, punching him in the throat. This move should have disabled him, but it didn't. He seized both of her arms, forcing her to her knees.

One of the scientists smiled insincerely, showing his nub-like teeth, saying in a raspy voice, "Calm down. There's nothing to fear. This won't hurt a bit." He attempted to press a handheld device against her shoulder. Haruto screamed in defiance, and, despite her arms being held firmly in place, managed to kick one of her legs sideways, nearly striking the scientist's ankle.

The soldier angrily grabbed a fistful of Haruto's long hair, jerking her head back while roughly stepping on her leg. She cried out in pain, but continued fighting, scratching at his hands with her nails.

A second soldier, who seemed annoyed by the inconvenience, got out of the vehicle to help his comrade. Together, they secured Haruto's arms and legs, but she kept struggling.

The scientist stepped closer to her, saying, "Tssk, tssk, tssk. It will all be over soon." He pressed the device against her arm, pulling the trigger. Haruto's head slumped and eyes closed. The soldiers held up her limp body.

Both of the scientists wore emotionless smiles as they turned toward the other women whose faces expressed an unfathomable fear.

"No, don't!" the youngest one cried out, but she was knocked out cold and fell over the seat.

The third woman was also drugged.

The soldiers carried the unconscious women into the laboratory, placing each one on top of a gurney. The scientists cuffed the victims' arms and legs to the side rails. Once the women were secured, the soldiers left the room.

The scientists busied themselves with work. One grabbed a metal tray, which held medical instruments, neatly arranged like silverware for a king's dinner. The tray was placed on a cart next to the sedated Haruto. A round overhead light was switched on to illuminate the work area. The second scientist picked up a device with a small spinning roller on its end. He moved the abrasive head methodically along Haruto's arm, leaving behind a pink swathe on her skin. After the procedure was finished, the exfoliated epidermis that had accumulated in the device's bin was emptied into several petri dishes. Next, he used a syringe to draw blood. He labeled the vials, then placed them into a slotted tray.

The first scientist said, "Now for the reproductive samples."

Although her eyes remained closed, Haruto began to stir, moving her feet and groaning.

"This one's waking up."

"Unusual. Make a note of it. Perhaps we should give her another dose."

69

Haruto stopped moving, becoming unconscious once more.

"Never mind, let's finish this."

The second scientist used stainless-steel scissors to cut off Haruto's silk pants and underwear, leaving her lower half exposed. The other one reached above his head to flip a second switch on the overhead light. Sound waves began pulsating over Haruto's abdomen. Her mid-section became semi-transparent as her cells danced to the machine's rhythm—vacillating between being pure energy and tangible particles.

The strange sensation woke up Haruto. She took a deep breath while trying to focus. Slowly things became clear. The gurney. The scientists. One of them was positioned over her lower abdomen, concentrating with his violet eyes as he slid a pair of elongated medical tweezers through her ethereal skin and underlying tissues, reaching inside to pluck an ovary.

The sight made Haruto scream at the top of her lungs.

Startled, both of the scientists jumped back. One of them grabbed the handheld device from the metal tray, attempting to re-administer her dose.

But Haruto had no intention of that happening. From the depths of her soul, she cried out, "NOOOO!" The sound reverberated throughout her being.

Time stood still.

For an instant, a knowing came over the Miko. She understood that she controlled her destiny and that nothing happened to her against her will.

She disappeared from the laboratory.

Haruto materialized in the Mikos' garden. She lay on the ground in the same position she had been on the gurney, except now she was free of the restraints.

Her sudden appearance scared a host of sparrows out of a nearby tree. The birds shrilled as they took to flight, gaining the attention of the youngest Miko, Konomi, who was brushing her hair near a window on the third floor of the temple. She watched the sparrows fly away, wondering what had startled them. She spotted Haruto lying half-naked in the garden. "Oh, my God!" Konomi dropped her brush, rushing out of the room, her long black hair trailing behind her.

Haruto struggled to her feet. An image of the scientist reaching into her abdomen flashed through her mind. Feeling violated, she shuddered, wiping at her bare stomach as if it would remove the horrific memory. All she wanted to do was wrap herself in Billy's arms to feel safe.

71

She stumbled through the garden toward the curator's house. Her weak legs carried her along the path. The front of the house was bathed in sunlight. A daisy grew in the pot beside the red door, which creaked as Haruto opened it.

She paused over the threshold. The futon was neatly made. Billy's black hat rested on a peg, and his clothes were stacked on the dresser. But he was nowhere in sight. She started to go back outside to find him, but then she remembered she needed to cover her nakedness. Haruto went into the house to look for pants, but the effort proved to be too much for her. Exhausted and traumatized, she dropped onto the futon. She couldn't deal with the surreality of being dissected like a frog one minute, and then at home the next. Haruto wanted nothing more than to escape into sleep.

A few minutes later, Konomi, Hoshino and several other Mikos arrived at the curator's house. Out of breath, they tentatively opened the door, not sure what they would find inside.

Haruto lay on the futon with her eyes closed. She didn't respond to their presence.

The women slowly approached her bedside. Konomi, whose long hair still hung loose, leaned down, pulling the duvet over Haruto's lower half to provide her with some decency.

Haruto opened her weary eyes, peering at them.

In a hushed tone, Konomi asked, "Are you okay?"

With the barest of motions, Haruto responded by shaking her head. This broke the other Mikos' hearts.

Konomi knelt beside the futon, stroking the distraught woman's arm, but this caused Haruto to wince in pain because the young woman had unknowingly touched her raw sampled skin. "I'm so sorry," Konomi said, getting up, unsure of how to comfort her friend.

No one knew what to say. Haruto's reappearance after being taken by the soldiers didn't bode well for her, especially since she had come back partially naked.

Konomi implored, "Can you tell us what happened?"

Unable to explain the unexplainable, Haruto hoarsely asked, "Where's Billy?"

The group remained quiet.

Haruto glanced at each woman, but each looked away. "Konomi?"

The young girl burst into tears, admitting, "They took him."

Tears welled in Haruto's eyes. She knew what horrors awaited him.

"But you came back," Konomi said with forced enthusiasm,

"and so will Billy."

Haruto shook her head.

Hoshino, the eldest in the group, said, "If you escaped, they will come looking for you, then we'll all be in danger. It's important we know what's going on."

The other women nervously glanced at each other.

Haruto contemplated the recent events, which was difficult because of the anesthesia haze clouding her brain. "I'm not sure what happened."

"You just woke up here?" Hoshino clarified, "In the garden?"

Haruto thought about the clone-like soldiers, the subway tunnel, and the alien scientists with their bizarre sampling of her genetic materials. *Was it all a dream?*

Hoshino leaned forward, pressing for an answer, "Tell us what you remember."

73

Haruto felt herself shutting down. "I don't feel well."

Although Hoshino was anxious for an answer, she backed off, standing upright. "Of course, we can talk later. Until then, get some rest. Do you want us to bring you some food?"

Haruto shook her head.

"We'll check on you later," Hoshino said graciously, but on the way out, she cast a troubled glance back at Haruto.

The interaction had placed an additional burden on the already overwhelmed and exhausted Haruto. Alone, she fell into a disturbing dream, tossing and turning. An hour later, still in the twilight of sleep, she uttered, "Billy." The sound of her own voice woke her up. For a fleeting moment, everything was fine, but then it all rushed back to her. The torment of being taken prisoner. The inhumane experiments. Her inexplicable return home. And Billy.

Where is Billy? Is he safe? Do the scientists have him? Wanting answers, Haruto prayed, "Sweet Devas, please help me."

A vision appeared of a foggy swamp strewn with dead blackened trees. Vultures were perched on the twisted limbs. A fire-breathing dragon slithered out of the mist, his body covered with iridescent green scales, which appeared lackluster in this dreary realm. On top of his head, horns curved over his furry mane. He had multiple rows of razor-sharp teeth, and fiery eyes that stared at Haruto while his forked tongue flicked in and out. But the Miko was not afraid of the beast. They had traveled together many times before. She bowed to greet him.

The dragon grumbled, "Come with me," as if he had been rudely awakened from a nap, then, without another word, he lumbered across the soggy shoreline swishing his long spiny tail. Haruto walked by his side.

It wasn't long before a familiar iron gate appeared out of the mist. The ornate doors swung open upon their arrival. The two of them strolled through the portal. The fog soon gave way to sunlight streaming through a forest. Birds chirped. A yellow-and-black butterfly danced over white wildflowers.

They came to a clearing where five spirit guides sat on logs around a fire pit.

The dragon announced, "Haruto is here to meet with you, *again.*"

Three samurai soldiers stood to bow, holding their helmets by their sides. Each was fitted with a different color of armor—one green, one red and one black. Sheathed swords were tucked inside their waistbands.

A crone, who had wild gray hair and wore a plain black

dress, remained seated, cackling with amusement at the Miko's presence.

A young priestess, wearing a cream-colored gown, approached Haruto. In a gentle voice, the spirit guide said, "It is good to see you. Please join us."

Haruto hesitated because the last time she was here she had ignored their advice, and now she wondered if she would be judged harshly for her past transgression. Nonetheless, she sat on a log between the priestess and the samurai outfitted in red, who said, "It has been too long, my dear friend. Much too long." His kind words helped Haruto to relax.

She agreed, "Yes, a lot has happened since then."

"Would you care to tell us about your saga?" He rested his armored arm on his thigh, ready to listen.

75

"But you must know already."

"Tell us anyway. It will be cathartic for you."

There was so much to tell them that it was difficult to know where to begin, so Haruto started with the first time they had met, "As you know, I ignored your advice and went to another realm where Bechard the fallen angel resided. He convinced me and others to join his cause to save the planet from mankind's greed and indifference. It seemed like a noble cause until the world retaliated." She lamented, "It nearly cost the lives of many innocent people. Sure, there were some concessions, but none worth the risk. On a positive note, I did meet the love of my life, but now he's been taken by soldiers." She added bitterly, "There's always an endless supply of soldiers. And now, I can only pray he's safe." Finally, Haruto stated her main concern, "I need help saving Billy. Can you please help me?"

The priestess responded, "When you are ready, you will do it yourself. It will be part of your journey—the one that began when the virus afflicted you."

"I don't understand."

"This virus did more than cause billions of deaths around the world—"

"Billions!?" Haruto was shocked by the enormity of the casualties.

"Yes, it was cataclysmic. Its rippling effects are still flowing throughout the universe, impacting timeline after timeline. However, this virus impacted you differently than most. For you, it is in the process of mutating your genes by activating the DNA strands, which have been locked away from mankind for millenniums."

The samurai in red informed her, "There are others like you."

"Like me? What do you mean?"

"You and others are mutating."

"Into what? Monsters?"

The priestess shook her head. "People always assume the worst. No, this change is part of your destiny. You signed up for this, Haruto, before you came into this lifetime."

Haruto mulled over the spirit guide's message, acknowledging she had chosen a difficult spiritual path. *But what about the rest of the world?* "It's hard to believe everyone signed up for this."

"Yes and no. It wasn't a specific part of the plan for most, but it was always a possibility. The engineered virus was cast to the wind without regard for its impact on humanity. The act violated the Law of Oneness. There will be repercussions."

"You should have warned me."

76

"That is not true. The knowledge would have impacted your decisions, which in turn would have interfered with your spiritual advancement. You see, your activated DNA has opened a door that will allow you to step into the full awareness of your true self. The choice to follow where it may lead is yours, of course."

The priestess continued, "This is a pivotal time for mankind—a time when destinies are merging, separating, and sometimes colliding. Our advice to you is this: Work on establishing your powers that are coming into being. It is through these powers that you will be able to help yourself and Billy. But be discreet. The presiding forces in your world do not fully understand the transformation that is taking place within you. The less they know, the better."

The vision abruptly ended.

Haruto opened her eyes. She gazed out the window, past the part in the curtains, watching the clouds in the blue sky morph from one shape to another, recreating themselves over and over again, while she pondered the spirit guides' messages.

There was a rustle at the end of the room. Haruto instinctively turned her head toward the sound.

Bechard sat at the dining table in a chair that seemed child-sized under his exceptionally tall frame. His blue-tipped wings were far too large for the small space and pressed against the free-standing sink. His dark-blue robe draped to the floor, puddling around his feet. The fallen angel stared at Haruto with his ultramarine eyes. "It's time we talked."

She shook her head. "Not now."

"I know this hasn't been easy for you." Bechard paused a moment, then delivered the news he knew she longed to hear.

"Billy is alive."

Overcome with relief, Haruto sat up, modestly holding the blanket over herself. "Is he safe?"

"For now, yes."

"Promise me, please...you'll let me know if he's in danger."

The fallen angel hesitated. He knew the fallibility of making promises and of the variable outcomes the future held, but he also knew he would do his best to keep the promise, so he agreed.

With that out of the way, Haruto became somewhat adversarial. She asked in a quivering voice, thinking of her deceased baby, "You knew. Since the first time you summoned us, you knew this would happen. Yet you never told me or the others. Why?"

"This catastrophe was always a possibility, but it didn't have to be. When I had asked for your help, it was to prevent this from occurring."

Haruto contemplated his words. *Perhaps, we all should have tried harder. But harder at what?* She asked him, "Why did those soldiers take me and the others? And why were they cooperating with those alien scientists? Were they forced? Paid?"

"It's a long story, which I will gladly explain in great detail, but at a later date. Right now, the only thing that matters is getting you somewhere safe—at least until your DNA mutation takes full effect. But you must hurry. Your presence here is putting you and your friends at risk because the soldiers *will* come looking for you."

Haruto mourned the thought of leaving. She had only just returned home—the only one she had ever known. Haruto didn't want to flee, but she also didn't want to jeopardize her extended family. She admitted, "I don't have anywhere else to go."

"I know a place," Bechard said, smiling devilishly.

CHAPTER 8
Leaving the Temple

HARUTO STOOD IN the entrance of the temple. She wore a red-hooded cape that hung below her knees and clutched a travel bag sewn by her mother. Embroidered butterflies fluttered across the black silk. She ran her fingers over the well-placed threads admiring the handiwork, remembering as a young girl watching her mother expertly stitch the design while telling her, "Haruto, these butterflies represent the women here, who went through many difficult changes to become the beautiful creatures they are today. Don't ever be afraid of change." She missed her mother more than ever at this moment.

Haruto turned the brass knob, opening the handcrafted wooden door, which groaned under its own weight. She went outside and stood on the landing, admiring the breathtaking view of the foothills and dormant city below, the hazy blue sea caressing its shores.

It was time to leave. She took a deep breath to brace herself, then stepped down, her red cape fluttering in the gentle wind.

It took the rest of the day for Haruto to reach the outskirts of Fukushima. Dirt covered her shoes as she walked past a suburb, which soon gave way to the empty downtown streets lined by tall office buildings and skyscrapers casting long shadows.

The ground-level retail stores had all been looted. She hurried down the sidewalk, noting the address numbers on the facades. Although tired, she persevered through the desolate city, wanting to reach her destination before nightfall.

The sound of a heavy-duty truck engine growled a few blocks away, alarming Haruto. She couldn't risk being seized by the soldiers again, so she ducked into an alley.

The engine noise grew louder. Haruto pressed her back against the concrete-block wall, sinking into the shadows.

At the end of the street, a roofless Humvee, painted with splashes of tan, brown and olive-green, slowly approached. Japanese soldiers were perched on the raised seats in the back, resting their boots on the side panels and clutching automatic rifles while surveying the city. A UN leader sat in the passenger seat holding a tablet, occasionally glancing at the screen.

A strange and sudden windstorm swept down the avenue, picking up dirt from the street and gutters, blasting over the soldiers who covered their faces to keep out the grit.

The UN leader ignored his own discomfort. He was more concerned about protecting the tablet, which he tried to tuck back into its protective case, but it was too late. The light at the top flashed yellow—an indication the device had become inoperable. "Damn it!" he cursed.

The Humvee drove past the alley and out of sight.

As soon as the engine noise faded away, the windstorm abruptly subsided.

Haruto crept to the front of the narrow passageway, peeking in both directions. All clear.

Anxious over the lost time, especially since the sun was

sinking behind the mountaintops, Haruto resumed her mission, briskly making her way down the sidewalk.

A few blocks later, she arrived at an old church built in a Gothic-revival style, which seemed alien amid the modern buildings of the city. This place of worship had three sets of arched entrance doors. The middle set was the largest. Above it was a stained-glass medallion window. The gabled roof was adorned with a stone cross at its peak and guarded by bell towers, one on each side. A bronze plaque affixed near the main doors read "Dedicated in 1899 by Father Nakaui".

Haruto went to the double door in the center and tugged on a handle. It was locked. Exhausted, she wondered what to do next. It was then she noticed a parsonage on the adjacent grounds that perfectly matched the church architecture, but on a smaller scale. A flickering light in the front window beckoned her.

She returned to the sidewalk, then pushed through the iron gate that guarded the courtyard hidden in the evening shadows. She followed the winding sidewalk to the priest's house, stepping onto the covered stoop, rapping the brass knocker. Crickets chirped. Haruto waited nervously for the sound of approaching footsteps. After too much time had passed, and nothing was heard, she decided to knock again, but just as she raised her hand, the door opened.

Father Chong stood there wearing a red smoking jacket, which, oddly enough, matched Haruto's red cape. They both noticed the similarity. The priest broke the awkward silence. "You're the Miko from the temple, aren't you?"

"Yes, Father Chong, it is I, Haruto."

He glanced out the doorway, looking up and down the street,

then said, "Please, come inside."

Haruto entered the living room illuminated only by the candles on the coffee table. Wax trickled down the silver candlesticks.

The priest seemed perplexed as he shut the door. "Did you walk here?"

"Yes. It was a very, very long walk."

"I can only imagine. You must be exhausted. Please, have a seat and rest your feet. Here, let me take your bag."

"No, thank you. I'll hang onto it." Haruto walked across the dimly lit room, sitting down on the leather sofa.

The priest trailed behind her, coming to his favorite high-back chair where he sat facing his guest. "You're the first person I've seen in weeks. But where are my manners? Let me make you some tea, and we can talk about why you're here and how things are out there."

Before she could say anything, he grabbed one of the candles, heading into the kitchen.

Alone, Haruto took this time to examine the room. The remaining candle burned next to a tin of tobacco and a wooden rack holding several smoking pipes. Built-in bookcases lined a wall. The hand-carved mahogany mantel on the stone fireplace proudly displayed decorative crosses and a statue of the Virgin Mary holding out her hands as if she was welcoming the stranger into her midst. A Persian rug covered the floor. Haruto assumed it was authentic.

Dishes clinked. A teapot whistled in the kitchen.

Haruto stared out the front window. It was strange to see the dark abandoned streets up close. From the Mikos' temple, high in the foothills, she had often observed the city's hustle and bustle at all hours of the day and night, but now, it sat perfectly still.

The priest returned carrying a tray. His candle flickered beside the beautiful cloisonné teapot with a bamboo handle. Steam wafted out of the spout. Beside it were two porcelain cups and matching saucers. He had taken off his red smoking jacket and now wore only a white buttoned shirt and black dress pants.

Father Chong carefully set the tray on the coffee table between them. He seemed a little nervous, as if he didn't quite understand this social interaction. To compensate, he kept the conversation light. "Here we go. I hope you enjoy this blend of green tea. I save it for special occasions. It's one of the finest I've ever tasted—given to me by a devoted member of my flock. It took a little longer to make than usual. I've been using an old camping stove to heat the water. We haven't had electricity here since the outbreak..." A look of sadness passed over his eyes. "This whole situation has been terrible. We lost Father Chin and Father Fugimura."

"I'm so sorry to hear that. We lost many as well." Haruto didn't mention her baby, but her flat stomach spoke of the loss on her behalf.

He said, "I'm sorry. Forgive me, I didn't mean to be insensitive. It's been a very difficult time for everyone." The priest poured tea into her cup, then picked it up by the saucer, handing it to her. "Here you go. I hope you enjoy it as much as I do."

"Thank you." Haruto took a sip, appreciating the flavor, then said, "Oh, I almost forgot. I have something for you as well." She set the cup down to open her travel bag, pulling out two jars of honey and a pint of honey wine, placing the items on the table.

The jars sparkled in the candlelight, delighting Father Chong, who inquired, "Is that mead?"

"It is. Fermented for over ten years from a long-standing recipe."

He picked up the pint, admiring the golden color. "Shall we partake of it now?"

"If you wish, but first, I would like to drink this tea. I'm thirsty, and it's been a long day."

"Of course. Why don't we sweeten it with some of the honey you brought?" Father Chong unscrewed one of the jars. "Would you like some?"

Haruto nodded.

Father Chong drizzled the sticky nectar into her tea, and then his own. After a quick stir, each took a sip, savoring the sweetened brew. For a moment, the priest was far away from all the death and pain caused by the virus. After another sip, he inquired, "So what brings you on such a long and dangerous journey?"

"Dangerous?"

He set his cup down. "Don't you know?"

"Know what?"

"Martial law is in effect. Anyone caught on the streets is arrested. A zealous overreaction—at least in my opinion. Although, the looting was a problem initially."

Haruto hid her anger as she seethed internally, *Damn that Bechard! He had me walking through a minefield.* She smiled tersely. "No, I did not know that."

"Yes, well, that leaves us in a quandary. Doesn't it? You can't go back out there, especially at night."

She was secretly pleased. She had hoped to spend the night here. Many nights, in fact.

"You must be tired," he stated.

"I am. The walk was...um....much longer than I expected."

"You never told me why you came."

Haruto wondered if it was wise to be truthful. *Father Chong won't believe that soldiers abducted me, and then took me to an alien scientists' laboratory. Who would? And what about my unexplainable escape? Or that I'm still fleeing.* She decided a white lie was in order. "I assumed the same outbreak had occurred here in the city, so I came to see if I could be of service, but I had no idea that martial law was in effect or I wouldn't have come." The latter part was true. She took a sip of tea to hide her guilty conscience.

"Understood. Well...you certainly can't go back out there."

Haruto waited for his suggestion.

As a man of God, Father Chong felt it was his duty to house her. "The church has always offered people sanctuary. I insist you stay here until it's safe to travel again." But that wasn't the only reason for his offer. After being holed up in the house alone for weeks, he was grateful for her company.

She responded, "Thank you for the kind invitation. I'd be happy to stay here."

"Yes, well, it's getting late, and I'm sure you're exhausted. Would you care to see your room?"

"Yes, please."

Father Chong stood up, grabbing the candle from the tray. "Please take the other one."

Haruto picked up the candle from the coffee table, along with her travel bag, then followed him across the living room. They moved up the staircase, stepping on the narrow rug that ran down the center. The hand rail and balusters were elaborately detailed.

She commented, "This is a beautiful home."

"Yes, it is. It's as old as the church. They just don't make them like this anymore."

They reached the top, and walked down the hallway. The candles' quivering flames made the paintings of the former popes and bishops, which hung on the wood-paneled walls, come alive. Their pious eyes watched them pass by.

Father Chong stopped at the third door, opening it. "This was Father Chin's. God rest his soul." He stepped back.

Haruto hesitantly entered the bedroom. It was sparsely furnished with a bed, desk and dresser. She was grateful for a place to lay her head that was far away from her fellow Mikos, who would now be safe in her absence. She said, "Thank you, and good night."

"If you need anything, anything at all, I'm in the first bedroom closest to the stairs. Sleep well." He shut the door for her.

She set her bag and candle on the desk, draping her cape over the back of the chair, then took off her blouse and pants. Underneath, she wore a silk camisole and boxers. She blew out the candle. A trail of blue smoke curled from the wick. The moonlight glowed through the sheers.

Haruto got into bed, pulling the covers over herself. *Ahh.* The mattress was such a comfort to her drained body. Sleep came quickly for her, pulling her down a dark spiraling tunnel where all the recent events spun past her. Billy. The laboratory. The endless subway. Soldiers. Fear and confusion. Bechard.

The images faded.

She dreamed of a clear blue sky. A solitary cloud floated into view. It held a blue door, which slowly opened, releasing a

87

blue mist that rolled across the vaporous floor. Haruto hesitated to walk toward the door because she knew where it led and didn't want to go there, but it appeared to be her only option. A familiar snort distracted the Miko. The sound had come from her totem animal, the dragon, as it descended from above, flapping its webbed wings, landing on the cloud. His iridescent green body shimmered in the sunlight. The creature trudged toward Haruto, his heavy steps sinking into the hazy platform, yet never completely falling through. The dragon said to her, "You always have a choice. Trust yourself. You are more powerful than you realize." A puff of smoke billowed out of his snout, encompassing her until everything became solid white.

Haruto lay in bed studying the room in the morning light. Beside her was a tall dresser with stately brass handles and timeworn drawers. Against the far wall, next to the protruding closet, sat a desk. A crucifix hung on the wall above it. Jesus' forlorn face stared down at the old-fashioned writing instruments and the short stack of blank paper on the desktop next to her travel bag. She wondered if the previous occupant had been a writer.

Pans clanked in the kitchen below. Haruto suspected that Father Chong was making breakfast. The thought made her stomach grumble with hunger.

She got out of bed, going over to her travel bag, rummaging through it, taking out a tan cotton blouse and black wide-leg pants. Both were wrinkled, but they would have to do. She got dressed, slipping on black flats.

Haruto headed out of the bedroom, tiptoeing down the stairs. The old wooden steps creaked. At the bottom, she loitered at the edge of the living room, unsure of where to go or what to do. She called out, "Father Chong!"

"In here!" The priest peeked out of the kitchen, pressing the swinging door open with his shoulder. In each hand, he held a bowl of cold rice. "Come join me," he cheerfully requested, waiting for Haruto to pass through the doorway.

She had expected to eat in the kitchen, but instead Father Chong led her to the back door. They stepped out into a large atrium, which spanned the width of the parsonage and possessed exquisite details, such as a stone foundation, beveled glass walls framed with patinated brass, and a glass domed ceiling crowned with a cupola. Flourishing inside the humid warm sanctuary were flowers, orchids and greenery, in addition to well-manicured bonsai trees. Some of the potted plants rested on the white crushed-stone floor while others sat on tables and shelves. The air smelled of fertilizer and peat moss.

In the midst of this botanical paradise was a white-painted, wrought-iron bistro table and chairs where Father Chong set their breakfast. "Please, have a seat," he said. "I'll get the rest." He headed back to the kitchen.

Haruto sat admiring the panoramic view of the courtyard filled with perennials, shrubbery and majestic trees. Curved sidewalks encouraged the church members to wander around the grounds or sit on the stone benches where they could rest and reflect. The grass was overgrown, but that was understandable considering the circumstances. At the rear of the courtyard was an old cemetery overflowing with tombstones marking the graves of the deceased clergy and church members. Ornate ostentatious crypts held the wealthier patrons. A cast-stone statue of an angel,

89

wielding a sword, guarded the entrance. Its fiery glare threatened anyone who dared to enter.

A minute later, Father Chong returned with a bowl of Mandarin orange slices resting in their own juices, and a jar of Miko honey. He carefully placed the items on the table.

Haruto appreciated his efforts. "This looks delicious. Thank you."

"You're welcome. The army only gave us dried beans and rice. Not that I'm complaining, mind you, but luckily, the cupboards were well stocked before all of this happened. And we've had running water all throughout this ordeal, although I've yet to get used to lukewarm baths." He shivered at the thought. "Hopefully, things will return to normal soon. Please have some."

As Haruto spooned the orange slices onto her plate, she thought about the soldiers who had taken her to the alien scientists' laboratory, and wondered if anything would ever return to normal.

Father Chong continued, "This whole outbreak has been beyond what anyone could have imagined. It's been very frustrating not to be able to help my parish during this difficult time. No confessions. No church services. I can't even console them by phone. But what's one to do?" He took a breath, refocusing. "To quote Reinhold Niebuhr, 'God grant me the serenity to accept the things I cannot change, and the courage to change the things I can, and the wisdom to know the difference.' I believe I got that right. Anyway, I'm tired of all this complaining. How about a new topic?"

"What would you like to talk about?"

"God. Religion. The meaning of life. You choose. I always love a great..."

As the priest rambled, Haruto saw a golden light infiltrate the atrium, encompassing everything, including Father Chong. Strings of sparkling light, pulsing with life, were connected to the glass walls and plants. Even the jar of honey shimmered. All were imbued with this glorious energy that filled her with a joy more intense and pure than anything she had ever experienced before.

Father Chong noticed his guest was staring off into space. "Haruto?"

The golden light vanished, but the sense of peace it had brought remained with Haruto. She wondered if the golden light was an indication that her DNA was mutating as her spirit guides had mentioned earlier. Or was it a sign of a spiritual awakening? Either way, she now trusted a grander plan was at work.

"Haruto, are you okay?"

She looked at the priest, but couldn't find the words to explain what had just happened, so she excused her behavior by saying, "I'm sorry...I'm...just a little tired, I guess."

"Maybe you're still recovering from your long journey."

"Possibly. I'm not quite myself."

"Well, no more long journeys for you until you're well rested." He raised his cup of tea in a toast to her health.

Smiling, Haruto clinked her cup with his.

CHAPTER 9
Darkest Before the Dawn

THE BLACK CAIMAN calmly reserved its strength, letting the current carry its massive body, and the passengers it held, down the Amazon River. Zachary drowsily lay on his side using his arm for a pillow to protect his head from the uncomfortable ridges on the reptile's back. Delirium was setting in. His leg throbbed in pain. The young man suppressed his moans, not wanting to scare Eva who happily sat near the beast's head, her small bare feet resting between its eyes. The last thing Zachary remembered before falling asleep was the sound of rippling water.

"He's awake," a woman said.

A handful of Caucasian men and women stood over Zachary, who was sprawled on the shore. He tried to open his eyelids, but they were too heavy.

"He doesn't look well. Does he? See his leg?"

The missionaries examined the young man's swollen and infected wound. Purple streaks flared under his skin.

"That looks septic. Don't you think?"

"Let's take him back. Clean him up."

"Can you hear me?"

Zachary managed a nod.

"We're going to take care of you. Okay?"

He whispered, "Eva..."

"What'd he say?"

"I'm not sure."

The people picked up the young man by his arms and legs, careful to avoid the infected area, carrying him to their campsite, which was comprised of a half-dozen tents and a small bamboo hut. Zachary was placed in the more permanent structure on top of palm-leaf mats where he shivered with fever.

A young prim woman, with brown hair pulled back into a ponytail, leaned down to feel his forehead. She frowned. "Reverend, would you say a prayer for him?"

The thirty-five-year-old man of God, dressed in khaki shorts and a t-shirt, nodded. The humidity had curled his sun-bleached hair. His beard was scruffy. He didn't look like a clergyman, but the jungle had a way of conforming a man to its wild ways. He bowed his head and closed his eyes. "Lord, we ask that you heal this man, if not in body, then in spirit. Please guide us to do what is right for him. In Jesus' name. Amen."

Healing mode. The group did their best to tend to Zachary's wound. They bathed his leg, lightly pressing rags around the edges of the snakebite, coaxing the pus out, and applying antibiotic cream taken from their first-aid kit. If they had possessed oral antibiotics, they would have given him some, but the supply was long gone—used up during the outbreak—not that it had done any good. Now all they could do was wait, and pray some more.

By the next day, Zachary's condition had worsened. His breathing was shallow, and, because of his weakened state, the telltale signs of the virus reemerged, casting blotches over his skin.

Alone in the hut, he reached the final stages of life.

His pain disappeared as his bodily functions shut down.

His beating heart slowed until it finally stopped.

Dead, Zachary's spirit rose out of his body, heading toward the bright light at the end of the tunnel. But, before he could travel to the other side, his mom and dad appeared in front of him, their bodies glowing. Larry wore his favorite plaid shirt and blue jeans, and held his arm around Marilyn who smiled radiantly as she comforted her son, "Zach, it's going to be all right."

"Mom? Dad? It's so good to see you!"

His father said, "Same here. We've missed you, too. But we've been watching you."

"I don't understand. How could you see..." His voice trailed off. "Oh."

"Yeah, we caught the virus just like everyone else, and well... we didn't make it as you can see."

"I'm so sorry. I had hoped to come home one day. Bring the kids. Bring the wife. Except me and Conchita—"

His mother interrupted, "We know. And we're sorry you two have been torn apart."

"I guess you were right. I had a death wish going into the jungle."

"No, you were right. You've been living your life to the fullest, and we're proud of you."

"Really?"

"Yeah, but there's just one catch. You need to go back."

"No, Mom, I can't. I just don't have the strength to do that. Not anymore."

"We know. But a friend of yours showed up. He said he was

enlisting help from shamans around the world, and they'd start working on you." Marilyn looked at her husband. "What did he say? Something about 'healing energy,' right?"

Larry nodded. "Uh-hum. He said they were going to heal you so you could save the world." He chuckled. "Bechard's a bit dramatic. Isn't he?"

Suddenly, rays of golden light streamed from every direction, encompassing Zachary.

His mother exclaimed, "Wow! It looks like they started. Well, we'll get out of the way. Good luck, Zach. We love you, son."

A funeral. The missionaries placed Zachary's lifeless body in a sheet, wrapping it around him. Then, holding each end, they carried him from the campsite to the river where they planned to dump his body. The caimans and pirañas would take care of the rest.

"We don't even know his name."

"Let's call him John."

"John...that's nice."

When they reached the shoreline, the reverend said, "I'd like to say a prayer first." Everyone bowed his or her head. "Our Father, who art in heaven, hallowed be thy Name. Thy Kingdom come. Thy will be done on earth, as it is in heaven..."

While the reverend prayed, Zachary felt his spirit return to his stiff body. His cells woke up. His heart pumped. The blood flowed. Now that he was fully encased within the flesh, he tried to speak, but his muscles had a mild case of rigor mortis. With great effort, he willed his eyes to open.

Solid white.

Zachary panicked until he realized there was a sheet covering his head. But his momentary relief evaporated when he heard the Lord's Prayer being recited. *Oh, my God, they're going to bury me!* He earnestly attempted to move his arms and legs, feeling a spark of mobility.

"Amen."

Zachary struggled to move. Nothing.

The people stepped into the shallows.

The young man heard the rush of the river. Scared, the adrenaline kicked in, and he gave it all he had, managing to wiggle his extremities. The maneuver caused his weight to shift, and the sheet slipped from the missionaries' hands.

Zachary's linen-encased body fell onto the riverbank, his lower half jutting into the water, which careened around his cloth-covered legs. He struggled within the sheet, flinging it off.

The women screamed.

The men jumped back, shocked and confused.

The reverend exclaimed, "It's a miracle!"

All of the pain that had died within Zachary's body came back to life with a vengeance as the people dragged him out of the water and over the rocky shore.

"I can't believe we almost threw this man into the water alive!"

"I'm telling you, he was dead!"

"Are you okay?"

"Give him a minute."

The bright sun stung the young man's eyes.

A half-dozen blurry faces stared down at him.

"What's your name?" one asked.

"Za..." His voice gave out. He cleared his throat, then tried again, "Zachary."

"Nice to meet you, Zachary."

"Where's my daughter?"

"Who?"

"Eva. My daughter."

"Sorry, but you were all alone."

A fear welled up in Zachary greater than anything he had ever felt before. He struggled to sit up, but became dizzy. The reverend knelt beside him, propping him up by the shoulders. Zachary scanned the jungle along the riverbank, weakly calling out, "Eva..."

The others sympathized with his situation.

The prim woman gently told him, "We haven't seen anyone else. I'm sorry."

Tears rolled down Zachary's cheeks as he anguished internally, *Why was I brought back for this?*

It was morning, but the sun had yet to peek over the treetops. Zachary lay awake in the semi-dark hut. Although his body was healing at a rapid pace, his heart hurt as he anguished over Eva's disappearance. *Is she alive? Is she calling for me? Is she scared?* He needed to find her. He thought of all the possible places Eva could be. *Did she wander ashore? Or fall in the river? What if she and the caiman continued on without me? Or circled back to the tribe? Or worse.* He didn't want to think about her possible death. The only thing he knew for certain was a child wandering through the jungle, stumbling into aggressive territories, would not last long.

The prim woman approached the hut, standing in the doorway.

The pale-blue light, which blanketed the campsite behind her, silhouetted her form. She said to him, "Good morning. Are you doing okay?"

Zachary shook his head.

The reverend stepped beside the woman. He peered inside the hut, asking with forced cheerfulness, "How are you feeling this morning, Zachary?"

The woman knew the young man wasn't in the mood to talk, so she answered on his behalf, "Reverend, he's still recovering. Why don't we make some breakfast?"

The reverend became concerned, furrowing his brow, creating creases in his sunburned forehead. "How much food do we have left?"

"Not much. And I don't think the delivery's coming. Not in time, anyway."

"Hmmm...did you try the satellite phone?"

"The line's still dead."

"We need those supplies."

"I know."

"Maybe Zachary can tell us what's going on out there?" The reverend had tossed out the question a little louder than normal, hoping to coax him into the conversation.

The woman tilted her head, indicating she would like to speak to the reverend away from the hut. Standing near the fire pit, she said in a hushed tone, "He's grief-stricken. Let's just give him some time. Get some food in him, then maybe he'll open up."

Stress caused the reverend to respond harsher than he normally would have, "We've all lost someone lately. Grief's a luxury right now."

"But it's a fresh wound for him."

He sighed, conceding, "All right, I'll make the fire."

CHAPTER 10
The Desolate Reservation

THE SURVIVORS AT the Bear Claw's reservation had divvied up the workload and their efforts were paying off. The well-tended garden promised to grow more than enough produce to last them throughout the winter. The men's hunting expeditions were providing an ample meat supply. The women had become adept at frying and roasting over an open fire, and, when the time came, they would use Grandma Hausis's wood-burning stove for canning.

Since survival seemed assured without any help from the outside world, and it was the middle of summer, a beautiful season in Canada, Tom and Cecile had taken a handful of young people on a retreat into the surrounding forest to teach them about the old ways, hoping to prevent the tribe's customs and knowledge from following the elders to their graves. During this time, the couple had taught the kids how to set up a traditional teepee; find herbs, mushrooms and medicinal plants; and shamanic journey—the traditional practice of communicating with spirit guides, totem animals and ancestors who resided in the spirit realm.

The girls who had signed up for the adventure were Adeelah, 17, the terrific nurse during the virus outbreak; the shy Eyota, 15; and the tomboy Taima, 19. The two boys were Rowtag and Manuel, both 18, aimless and angry. Their hair was cut to shoulder-length—a compromise between their tribe's traditions and Western civilization's expectations.

The group had been away for four days and was returning to the village. Two American Paint horses carried the supplies and equipment through the trees while the adults and teens hiked on foot.

"So...what was the favorite thing you learned?" Cecile asked the teenagers.

Adeelah answered, "I liked listening to the stories by the fire."

"But what did you learn?"

"Um...that I could talk with our ancestors and my grandmother. That was cool."

"Rowtag? Manuel? How about you?"

Rowtag shrugged his shoulders. He didn't want to admit he had enjoyed himself.

Manuel replied, "Fishing was fun. And Tom is a good storyteller."

They reached the outskirts of the village. Tom peered through the trees, viewing the rutted dirt road that meandered between the run-down houses and unkempt yards. The whole place was oddly quiet. No one was in sight, except for a pair of listless dogs. Something was wrong. Tom motioned for Cecile and the teenagers to remain where they stood. They obeyed, but glanced at each other wondering what was going on. The horses took advantage of the standstill and nibbled on low-hanging leaves.

Without saying a word, Tom cautiously snuck out of the forest, using an old shed as cover. From here, he surveyed the surroundings, still not seeing anyone. He hustled to an old two-toned Ford truck, one end of its rusted bumper hanging on the ground. His breathing quickened as he studied the vacant reservation. The two dogs ran up to him, wagging their tails and whimpering with excitement. Normally, Tom would have given them a quick pat on the head, but, right now, he was too distracted by his concerns.

He went to the nearest shack, stepping onto the warped boards that acted as the porch, pushing open the wooden door, which was already ajar. The place was empty. On the dining table, flies gathered over a plate of decaying sliced tomatoes and the desiccated remains of a spilled drink. A chair had fallen to the floor. *What's happened? Where is everyone?*

Tom rushed outside, his heart pounding in his chest. The dogs followed him to the middle of the road where the man desperately spun in all directions, shouting, "Hello! Anyone!?" The dogs, scared by his outburst, slunk away. Grief overcame Tom. He fell to his knees in the dirt. It was only then he noticed the heavy-duty tire marks intermixed with the scuffled footprints of thick-tread boots and smooth-bottomed moccasins.

Tom raised his head to the heavens in supplication. The spirits responded immediately in the form of a vision. In his mind's eye, he saw military trucks and a bus entering the reservation just before the sun lit up the sky. The armed Canadian troop, which was commanded by a UN leader, quickly disembarked, then stealthily disseminated throughout the village. His people were pulled from their beds at gunpoint, then made to stand in the middle of the road surrounded by the soldiers.

Lost in the trance, Tom did not hear Cecile approaching. She stopped beside him. The teenagers and horses were close behind her.

102

She gently called his name.

He lifted his head, looking up at his wife through tear-filled eyes.

"Tom, what is it!?"

Stuck between the two realities, he was unable to find the words.

"Tom, tell me!"

He finally uttered, "They're gone."

CHAPTER 11
Haruto's Transformation

THE SUMMER SUN warmed the atrium where Haruto and Father Chong sat at the bistro table having a lively discussion.

Haruto set her teacup on the saucer, saying, "This is hypothetical, of course, but let's say that a fallen angel regrets his decision of rebelling against God, and decides to, well, repent. Would he be forgiven and what would one call this fallen angel? An un-fallen angel?"

Father Chong laughed, nearly choking on his tea. "Oh, Haruto, where do you come up with this stuff?" He wiped his mouth with a napkin.

She asked slyly, "Well...can you answer it?"

The priest was stumped for a moment. "Okay...let's say this fallen angel truly asks for forgiveness, and, keep in mind, there is no scripture for this, but the church's stance is 'the fall from grace is irrevocable, comparable to a man's death.'"

Haruto countered, "But this fallen angel isn't dead, and still has the ability to choose. So I'm asking you for your personal opinion. What do *you* think?"

"Well...I suspect God would forgive him, just as he is willing to forgive us."

"Do you think if the fallen angel were forgiven, he would return to heaven at that moment?"

He sipped his tea, savoring the flavor, then set his cup down. "Maybe not immediately. I'd assume he'd have to go through the same process we do: believing in Christ, asking for forgiveness, redemption, then finally acceptance into heaven when he dies... hmmm...except he wouldn't die. That's a bit tricky."

"So this immortal being would be stuck here until the end of time?"

"Until the Second Coming of Christ, I suppose. But this is silly. Why don't we discuss something more pertinent?"

Haruto smiled, enjoying the conversation. "Of course. Why don't you start the next one?"

Someone pounded on the front door, interrupting the pair's conversation. The sound drifted into the atrium.

Father Chong was perplexed. "Who could that be? Excuse me." He got up, his shoes crunching on the white gravel. He opened the back door, not bothering to close it as he rushed to answer the knock.

A moment later, Haruto heard a muffled voice ask in an authoritarian tone, "Father Chong?"

She couldn't hear the priest's response, so she got up, going to the side of the doorway, pressing her back against the wall where she caught snippets of the conversation taking place in the living room.

The authoritarian voice asked, "Is—residing here?"

The priest answered, "—guest. Why—?"

"Step aside!"

Heavy footsteps tromped through the house, moving toward the rear. An electronic tablet blared out a warning. Beep! Beep!

From the living room, Father Chong called out, "What's she

done!?"

"Stand back!"

The footsteps came closer.

The beeps grew louder.

Haruto panicked. Someone was coming for her.

A UN leader dressed in a black military uniform strode through the back doorway, entering the atrium. His entourage of Japanese soldiers followed him. He scanned the area with his tablet, which beeped. He noticed the two cups on the bistro table, although no one was present.

The atrium did not offer a lot of places to hide. Nonetheless, the UN leader scoured the area, tipping over plants and pots. He glared at the Japanese soldiers. "Why are you standing there!? Find her!"

The soldiers jumped into action, combing through the house, turning it upside down without regard to whether they damaged the antique furniture, artwork or rugs. Closets and cupboards were thrown open, and their contents pulled out, falling to the floor. Bedding was tossed. A carved chest scraped across the wooden floor.

Father Chong was visibly upset.

Outside, the soldiers probed the bushes, parting the sprigs with their rifles, and craned their necks to inspect the tree branches. In the cemetery, they peered behind the tombstones and checked the doors on the crypts to make sure they were locked.

Unsuccessful, the soldiers went to the only place they hadn't yet searched. The church. They pulled on the heavy doors, one set after the other, dismayed to find them all safely secured.

The men returned empty-handed to the UN leader, who was

viewing his tablet. He looked up at them. "Well?"

One of the soldiers said, "Sir, nothing so far, but the church is locked."

The UN leader turned toward the house, calling through the open doorway at Father Chong who stood in the living room anxiously waiting for this dilemma to conclude. "Bring me the church keys."

The priest wanted to say, "It's a holy place. Show it the respect it deserves," but instead, he responded, "Yes, of course." From the wall, he grabbed the old-fashioned skeleton keys fastened together with an iron ring. He went outside. "Here you go."

The UN leader snatched the keys. "Father Chong, you had better not be hiding this woman. If you are, for your sake, you need to tell me now."

For the first time in his life, the priest felt his life was in danger, but he concealed his fear. "I assure you, I'm not. I wasn't aware she was a fugitive until you arrived. I have no idea where she is at this moment."

"If we don't find her, and she returns, you *will* notify us." The UN leader handed the priest his business card.

"But there's no way to phone or send an email," Father Chong pointed out, but then glanced at the tablet in the UN leader's hand. Somewhere, the electricity was working.

"That will change soon enough," the UN leader responded before abruptly turning around, leading the soldiers toward the church.

Father Chong followed the brigade, figuring it was the only way he would be sure to get his keys back.

The UN leader stood in front of the largest set of arched doors,

107

examining the multiple keys in his hand.

"It's the brass one," Father Chong volunteered, trying to appear helpful, although he knew Haruto would not be inside. The church had been locked for more than a month, but, at the same time, he wondered how she had slipped away without being seen.

The oversized wooden door creaked open. The soldiers entered the dim reception area where statues of the Virgin Mary, Jesus on the Cross and saints were displayed in the recessed niches.

They moved into the stately sanctuary. The stained-glass windows cast gemstone colors over the varnished wooden pews. The regal altar stood as the focal point in front of the organ pipes, which were grandly and artistically inserted into gilded, hand-carved lattice panels lining the back wall. Murals depicting scenes from the Bible decorated the vaulted ceiling. Impressed by the ornate craftsmanship, the soldiers stood admiring the handiwork.

"Find her!" the UN leader shouted.

The soldiers dispersed like rats fleeing a cat, diligently searching under the pews, and in the balcony, auxiliary rooms, bathrooms and offices, but Haruto was nowhere to be found.

Father Chong returned home. He closed the front door, leaning against it, overcome with emotion at the recent degradation of his house and the church. This wasn't the Japan he knew. He replaced the keys on the hook, then picked up the items that had fallen to the floor, putting them back on the tabletops and shelves. He straightened the cushions on the sofa, wondering, *Why would they need to mess up cushions? So senseless.* The priest stopped for a moment to pray, "God, please help me to forgive those who have trespassed against me, just as you have forgiven those who have trespassed against you. Amen."

After the house was put back in order, Father Chong felt better. He made rice and opened a can of tuna fish, then poured green tea into a cup. As he drizzled the golden nectar into his brew, he thought of Haruto, *I hope she's okay. I can't believe she's a fugitive. She's so nice. But how, in heaven's name, did she manage to escape?*

A woman's voice entered his mind. *You think I'm nice?*

He spun around, searching for her. "Haruto? Where are you? Show yourself." He could not see the invisible Haruto standing right in front of him.

But then you would have to turn me in. Right, Father?

"Hiding from me won't help the situation." He studied the room from top to bottom. "Where are you?"

Haruto wanted to show herself, but was hesitant. The thought of being vulnerable after her run-in with the soldiers ran through her mind.

"Haruto?"

His call brought her back to the present moment. To appease this man of God, and realizing she didn't want to stay invisible forever, Haruto concentrated, envisioning herself becoming physical. But, because she was still somewhat afraid, she unexpectedly ended up materializing as a vivid ghost standing in the kitchen—a compromise between her other two choices: being invisible or being physical.

Father Chong gasped at the sight of her. "Oh, my God!" He looked like he wanted to run away, but his pride held him in place.

Haruto examined her semi-transparent self.

He asked her, "What's going on?"

She shook her head. "I don't know."

"Have you always been able to do this?"

"Today's the first time—"

"What?"

"I'm...I'm not entirely sure what's going on. There have been other things, but this..." Haruto motioned with her hands over her phantasmal body, "this is a first." She explained, "When the soldiers came, I remember thinking, 'I wish I could disappear.' And then I did. The intense fear of being recaptured must have caused it."

"Did you say *recaptured*? Did you escape once already? You should have told me."

"Father, there was so much I didn't know, and still don't, that I wouldn't have expected you to understand what I couldn't really explain."

He calmed down, sympathizing with her. "I see. Well, why don't you tell me what you do know?"

Haruto looked at the food that Father Chong had prepared. His tea was growing cold on the counter. "Let's sit outside where you can eat, and I'll tell you everything I know."

However, the priest found it impossible to eat while Haruto told him how she had been taken by the soldiers, then transported to an underground laboratory where alien scientists performed experiments on her. And how she had unexpectedly disappeared from that chamber of horrors and reappeared at the Mikos' temple, but then had to leave to protect them. She admitted his church had been chosen because it was a reasonable assumption the soldiers wouldn't search for her there, but after she was rebuffed by the locked doors, she ended up on his parsonage doorstep. The only thing Haruto omitted from her confession was coming here had been Bechard's idea.

Father Chong agreed, "Yes, I can see why you thought it was a good idea to come here, but, since we now know they can detect you with that tablet, your presence puts me at risk."

"I understand, and I'll leave. This is my burden to carry."

Haruto's statement made him feel ashamed. As a man of the cloth, he believed it was his duty to offer her sanctuary, but it was obvious he held little clout with the soldiers and was unable to protect her.

The priest examined her celestial form. "Do you think you're capable of being normal again?"

"I assume so." Haruto looked around to make sure they were alone, then she closed her eyes, concentrating, imagining herself as flesh and blood. She would have liked to describe the sensation of changing forms, but there wasn't one. She simply, and instantly, changed back to her old self.

Her shift back to reality brought with it a sense of peace for Father Chong, who was much more comfortable talking to a physical person rather than a "ghost".

Haruto surmised, "It seems these changes occur by simply setting an intention. Amazing, isn't it?"

"Indeed, it is," Father Chong said, trying to appear supportive while secretly containing his worries. He could only hope these supernatural abilities were part of God's plan and not the lesser power.

Haruto's thoughts wandered back to when she had magically left the alien scientists' laboratory and arrived in the temple

111

garden. With this in mind, she wondered if she could transport herself at will without needing the threat of bodily harm.

She stared through the atrium glass walls at the courtyard, focusing on a stone bench under an old oak tree, imagining herself sitting there.

And just like that, she was. The bench felt cool beneath her silk pants.

Next, Haruto wondered how the outdoor sensations would feel if she were semi-physical so she made her body become insubstantial. With this change, she could no longer feel the coolness of the stone bench, although she could still discern its presence. A summer breeze swept through her barely perceivable form, briefly joining with her essence before carrying on its way. Her nose delighted in the fragrance of the nearby rosebushes, but it was more of a knowing than an actual scent. The surrounding physical forms remained visible, although faint, but the golden light emitting from them was bright.

Haruto looked back at the atrium. The priest was obviously disturbed by her disappearance, but despite this, she saw his soul's rays reaching to the heavens.

With her curiosity satisfied, Haruto willed herself to return to her seat at the bistro table, sitting across from Father Chong.

Her ghostly reappearance caused the priest to lose his breath, but he regained his composure, saying, "I don't know whether to encourage you or perform an exorcism."

She laughed. "Father, you're so funny!"

"Well, I wasn't trying to be."

"I suppose that's why it's funny." Haruto had a hunch. "I wonder when I'm invisible or..." she waved her hand over ghost-like body, "like this, if the soldiers can detect me with their tablet?"

"That would be good to know."

"Yes, it would. I'm going to give it a try."

"Now?"

"Yes."

"So soon? What if something goes wrong?"

"I need to know, otherwise, nowhere is safe."

"I suppose you're right. No time like the present." His words belied his concern for her safety.

Haruto concentrated, thinking about the UN leader who had just trashed the place looking for her. A scene appeared in her mind. She saw a Japanese soldier driving a roofless Humvee while the UN leader rode in the passenger seat holding his tablet, scanning the air for rogue DNA as they drove down a desolate street. Soldiers sat in the back of the vehicle keeping an eye out for anyone who dared to step outside.

Since she knew where to find the UN leader who held the tablet, it was time to test her theory.

Haruto made herself invisible, and then transported herself to the Humvee, hunching between the front seats above the flat metal console, ready to take flight if necessary. She stared at the UN leader, waiting to see if his tablet would react to her presence, but its light remained green and no beeping sound ensued.

Pleased, she decided to test the second part of her theory. For an instant, Haruto became semi-transparent. The UN leader glanced over, thinking he had seen something out of the corner of his eye, but his tablet gave him no indication of the mutant intruder. The lack of detection made him disregard his gut instinct.

With the first two tests completed, Haruto had one more to

113

perform. Despite being scared, she allowed her body to become physical for a split second before becoming invisible again.

The UN leader jerked his head around, but the space between the seats was empty.

Unseen, Haruto anxiously waited for the tablet to respond. The small green light at the top changed to blinking red. A warning sound blared. Beep! Beep!

The driver stomped on the brake pedal.

The UN leader read the screen's message, scowling. "It's that woman. She's here, somewhere." He narrowed his eyes and scrutinized the interior of the vehicle, sensing she might be among them.

Haruto came face to face with his ominous glare, but she was no longer afraid. *What can he do to me?* she speculated. *He can't even see me. Being invisible has made me invincible.*

Now that she knew the device's limitations, she had more important things to do—like saving Billy. *Where are you!?* she silently called to her lover.

A vision of a dingy prison cell presented itself. A heavy-metal door and solid-rock walls sealed the chamber. Billy sat cross-legged on the damp floor. His eyes were closed as if in prayer. His braid hung loose, and his body was filthy. He had lost a considerable amount of weight. Seeing her lover like this broke Haruto's heart.

Wanting to go to him, the Miko left behind the UN leader and his band of soldiers, emerging into Billy's cell, careful to remain invisible. She knelt beside him, touching his shoulder with her transparent unfelt hand. Haruto yearned to transform herself into a physical body so she could embrace him, but she knew it

114

would be unwise to risk being detected by the surveillance camera bolted high on the wall and protected by a rusty cage.

Billy sensed her metaphysical presence, lifting his head, his dark brown eyes staring through her, whispering, "Haruto?"

She cast her thoughts into his mind. *Shhh...my love. They'll hear you.* Billy had already paid a steep price for trying to protect her. Who knew what else these alien-led soldiers might do to him if they knew she was here?

Unsure if Haruto was still among the living or speaking to him as a spirit, Billy silently asked her, *Did you survive the soldiers?*

I'm alive and well.

He let out a sigh of relief.

Don't worry, I'll figure a way to get you out of here. Trust me. I always do.

115

Inside the parsonage, an antique grandfather clock ticked at the edge of the living room where Father Chong sat across from the spectral Haruto. He asked, "So...how did it go?"

"Good news. They can only pick up my physical 'scent'. But when I'm invisible, or like this, their scanners are useless."

"Well, if that's true, you're more than welcome to stay here. At least until you find somewhere more suitable."

Just then, the lamp on the end table unexpectedly lit up.

Father Chong exclaimed, "Thank God, the power's back on! Excuse me." He got up, going over to the television on top of the antique chest. He grabbed the remote control. The television screen flickered on, displaying a static message that warned the viewers "Martial Law in Effect, Remain in Your Domicile". He switched the channel, but the message remained the same. He shut it off. "I was hoping to see what was going on out there. God willing, this means everything will be up and running soon."

The spell between them had broken.

The priest remained standing, seeming preoccupied as if he was already thinking about the topic for his next homily.

At the same time, it occurred to Haruto that she could return to the temple and her beloved Mikos as long as she remained in a semi-transparent or invisible state. There, she could practice her newfound powers in the beautiful meditation garden until she figured out a way to save Billy. "Father, you have been a gracious host, but I must be going." She stood up.

He seemed genuinely disappointed. "I will miss our conversations. Please come to visit me from time to time. We'll have tea."

His warm words made Haruto feel as if she had made a true friend. She replied, "I will. And thank you for your hospitality."

Gentle rays of the morning light filtered through the temple window, falling over Haruto's face as she lay sleeping on a padded mat, her head resting on a silk pillow. A simple cotton blanket covered her body. She woke up slowly, listening to the birds greet the sun. It felt good to be home. She had decided to sleep in her own bedroom, which served as her healing room during the day, because, with Billy away, the curator's house painfully reminded her of his absence.

Konomi, who was walking down the hallway, approached Haruto's doorway, peeking inside to say a quick hello, but her cheerful expression turned into panic. "Haruto! You're physical!"

Haruto touched her own cheek. *Oh, no!* Somewhere in the

night, perhaps prompted by a dream, she had changed into a flesh-and-blood body—detectable DNA. Guilt stabbed at her heart as she anguished, *I've endangered them!*

"You promised you wouldn't do this!" Konomi said accusingly.

Haruto felt ashamed. She had believed she knew how to control her abilities, but she obviously still had much to learn. She sat up, apologizing, "I'm so sorry. I didn't mean to." She morphed herself into a phantasmal figure, although, at this moment, she really wanted to be invisible so she could hide from Konomi's glare.

A sad realization swept over Haruto. She knew she needed to leave her beloved home once more.

CHAPTER 12
Zachary's Transformation

ZACHARY HELPED THE missionaries pack their supplies into a pair of aluminum canoes resting on the shore. It had only been two days since Bechard had requested the shamanic healing on his behalf, but almost all of his strength had returned.

The reverend walked up to him, saying, "God willing, we'll make it to the next village before sundown. Sure you won't come with us?"

It was a caring and possibly life-saving invitation, but, for Zachary, it only drove the knife deeper into his heart. He answered with a question, "Would you leave your daughter?"

The reverend nodded, indicating he understood.

The prim woman came over. She held out a tin of oatmeal and several water bottles, saying to Zachary, "Here, take these."

He accepted them. "Thanks."

The woman nudged the reverend, giving him a knowing look.

"What? Oh, one more thing," he mentioned to Zachary, "the neighboring tribe blames us for the outbreak, so I wouldn't go near them if I were you. We had a good, but delicate, relationship until this happened. So...just stay away from that area." With his hand, he indicated the general direction. "It's safest here. In the camp. They think it's cursed."

The woman whispered, "They're cannibals."

"Now...no need to scare him. They're not cannibals—not anymore. Times have changed. I think. Well, we're ready to head out. Good luck, Zachary." The reverend held out his hand.

The young man juggled his newly given supplies so he could shake it. "Thank you. Thanks for everything."

"You're more than welcome. We always try to follow Christ's example." The reverend gave him one last look, knowing it would be the last time he saw him. "I'll pray for you."

"We all will," added the woman.

With the goodbyes out of the way, the missionaries carefully boarded the canoes that teetered back and forth as their weight shifted. Once they were seated, Zachary dug his heels into the wet sand, shoving the first canoe into the river. The water nudged it along. The second canoe was wedged in the sand a bit more tightly, but, with a little extra muscle, he freed it from the shoreline.

The canoes flowed with the current. The prim woman waved at him while the others focused on navigating their way back to civilization. The gleaming silver streaks rounded the bend, flashing in the sunlight, then they were gone.

Zachary returned to the campsite. Bare patches marked where the tents had stood. He went into the hut, sitting cross-legged. He planned to ask Bechard for guidance on finding Eva. At the very least, the fallen angel would be able to point him in the right direction. Zachary closed his eyes and began to shamanic journey in the same manner his mentor (and Haruto's lover), Billy White Smoke, had taught him to do years earlier when he was kind enough to share some of his indigenous customs and spiritual practices.

A vision came to Zachary. Everything was completely white,

except for a blue door, which slowly opened, releasing a blue mist that drifted across the ground, beckoning him to come closer. The young man's spirit followed the vaporous trail through the doorway.

On the other side was a hill overlooking the valley below. Built on top of the grassy mound was a circular cobblestone courtyard laid in a spiral pattern, and at its very center was an enormous crystal ball perched on a marble pedestal.

From out of the sky, Bechard flew down, flapping his blue-tipped wings, landing softly. He tucked his feathers and smiled broadly, displaying his perfect teeth. "Welcome, Zachary. It's been too long."

"Yes, well..." Not wanting to be rude, Zachary did not mention why he had not returned since their last escapade, instead he said, "Bechard, it's good to see you again. And thanks for the healing."

"You're most welcome. It was my pleasure."

Zachary cleared his throat. "The real reason I've come here is I need your help finding my daughter. Eva's only four years old, and lost in the jungle. Can you help me find her? Please."

"Of course." Bechard moved closer to the crystal ball. He stood over it motioning with his hands. The blue mist swirling inside parted to reveal the lush Amazon rainforest. The fallen angel spread his hands farther apart and the image zoomed in, dipping below the treetops. There, the underbrush was protected from the harsh sun. The focal point was a large Bacuri tree abundant with golden fruit, which resembled small grapefruits.

Leaning in to get a better look, Zachary saw Eva sitting on a sturdy branch beside a tiny Emperor Tamarin monkey, easily noted by its brown fur, white underbelly and distinguished white mustache that curved down to its chest. Both the little girl and primate were contentedly eating one of the tree's fruits whose interior looked like a scoop of vanilla ice cream surrounded by a thick lemony shell. The monkey dipped his fingers into the fleshy pulp, bringing it to his mouth, relishing the flavor.

Oh, thank, God! Zachary was so relieved to see his daughter alive and well. He shouted, "Eva!" to get her attention.

She looked around for the source of his voice.

"Eva! It's me! Daddy!"

A broad smile crossed her round face, even though she couldn't see him. She gushed, "Daddy!"

His heart was warmed by her joyful expression. "Hi, honey! Oh, it's so good to see you! Can you tell me where you are?"

"Right here."

Zachary grimaced inside, but kept a smile on his face. "Are you near Mommy?"

"I don't know."

"Are you near where Daddy was left on the shore all by himself?"

"I don't know."

"Do you remember leaving Daddy?"

She shook her head. "I woke up and you were gone."

"Where did you wake up at?"

"On the caiman, silly."

Trying to get information out of a small child was exasperating, so he tried another tactic. "Okay, I see you, but where is the caiman?"

"He went home."

"What!? He left you all alone!?" *What am I saying?*

"No, I'm with Jabbar." She pointed at the monkey next to her. He hooted softly in response. Then she pointed at the ground. "And Ferta."

An unseen jaguar let out a deep rumble, not quite a snarl, but rather an announcement of her presence.

The primitive sound sent a shiver down Zachary's spine. "Eva, watch out! There's a cat!"

The spotted jaguar strolled into view, stopping at the base of the tree.

Zachary nearly had a heart attack when the predator expertly jumped onto the limb beside Eva, then nimbly turned around to lick the little girl's hair as if cleaning her own young. The monkey did not seem the least bit concerned. He kept happily eating the fruit, bits of which stuck to his mustache.

Frustrated, Zachary said to Bechard, "I don't understand what's going on."

The fallen angel chuckled. "She's fine. That's all that matters. Right?"

Visibly upset, he answered, "I don't know!"

"Daddy?"

Zachary looked into the crystal ball. "Yes?"

"I want to play with my friends now."

Oh, God, she thinks they're friends! "No, Eva! Don't go! Please! Daddy needs to find you."

"But I'm right here."

The image faded.

Zachary put his hands to his eyes to hide his tears. Wrought with guilt, he lamented, *How could she be so close, yet so far away? What if the cat eats her?*

Bechard studied the young man, sensing his fears as well as his love for his daughter. Because of this, the fallen angel chose his words carefully, "Don't worry. She has found her own version of a tribe. She'll be safe until you find her, which I expect to be soon."

"Can't you protect her?" pleaded Zachary. "At least until I get there?"

"I'll keep an eye on her, but Eva doesn't need my help. She's fine. I'm more concerned about you. You have a great journey ahead of you, and like all great journeys, the beginning is always the most difficult. It's what I call, 'the dark night of the soul.' A time when you purge all that stands in your way of discovering who you really are and what you are capable of."

The young man's head hung low. His fear of not being able to immediately save Eva weighed heavily on his heart.

"Zachary?"

Lifting his head in response, Zachary forlornly looked up at the magnificent being who towered over him.

"This is your time."

The vision unexpectedly ended.

Zachary opened his eyes, sitting as a solitary man inside the hut, surrounded by the vast rainforest. Furious that he had not received the guidance or direction he needed to find Eva, he clutched his fists and shouted in rage, "Bechard!" his voice echoing throughout the jungle.

Without warning, the young man's legs cramped. The muscle contractions spread throughout his whole body. He cried out in pain as he convulsed. Shaking, twisting and jerking. The suffering was unbearable. *I'm going to die alone!* he anguished just before his muscles tightened even more, forcing him to curl into a fetal position.

He lay contorted and in agony for hours.

The rainforest grew dark as the sun set behind the misty mountains.

Zachary lost nearly all hope of surviving until a ball of light floated down from the stars. The tropical landscape lit up as it descended, alarming the wide-eyed jungle creatures that had already settled in for the night. The campsite was lost in the light's brilliance, which encompassed the young man's body, streaming through his cells, transforming every molecule. He felt his body crack like a brittle clay vessel, turning into dust. And in its place, the light awakened his immortal being.

His new body radiated a light that reached to the heavens, which in return, reached back to him, pulsating from eternity. With this connection, he felt the loving energy of every soul in existence.

Zachary was no longer alone. Instead of being housed within a limited body, he was part of the light that dwelled in all things. The plants. The creatures. The elements. The spirits of the living and the dead, Eva, Conchita, Pahtia, his parents, Marilyn and Larry, Bechard, and those who had no name, joined him from every corner of the universe, and their joy became his own. He lay there cherishing the connection to the infinite oneness, feeling the expansiveness of not being contained within the physical.

Perhaps that should have been enough, but soon his mind shifted toward more practical matters. He wanted to be with his daughter. To hold her while she slept. To protect her. This yearning prompted Zachary to wish with all his heart, *I want to be with Eva.*

He felt his essence rise above the hut, and then above the trees. He soared over the rainforest. From this higher perspective, he could see the shrouded mountains melding into the night sky, and, beneath him, the darkened river slithering through the dense jungle, reflecting slivers of the luminous moon.

After briefly traveling through the air, which no doubt would have taken a thousand times longer by foot, he glided down, dipping below the canopy, slowly descending until his ghostly body floated above the moist sloped ground.

Here, huddled at the base of a tree, nearly hidden in the night, Eva slept beside the jaguar. The monkey was snuggled between them. A confusing mixture of thoughts ran through the young man's mind as he observed Eva and her friends. He wondered how he had gotten here. Or if he really was here. Or if it was just a dream. But after riding the caiman, he was starting to believe anything was possible.

Zachary drifted closer to Eva, kneeling to touch her head with his transparent hand. He was disappointed at not being able to hold her physically. Not knowing what else to do, he sat beside his daughter, his spectral body poised above the ground. He listened to the night jungle sounds, wondering if he had died earlier when his body had experienced those severe muscle contractions. Was he now a spirit between worlds? He also wondered if he would ever sleep again. Those questions were answered in the morning.

Rain pounded down on the monochrome rainforest, waking up Zachary whose wet clothes clung to him like a second skin. At first, he sighed, wondering if things could get any worse, then it occurred to him that he could feel the rain. He had a body! He was alive! Never had he been so glad to be miserably soaked to the bone. Dying had only been a bad dream. He was here. Here with Eva and—

It was a bitter-sweet moment when Zachary realized the deadly jaguar might wake up at any moment and snap his neck like a twig, then eat him for breakfast—long before Eva, who was snuggled next to the predator, opened one of her sleepy eyes to stop her carnivorous friend.

Zachary wondered if he could sneak away without the jaguar noticing, but the big cat's tail was draped over his lap. Feeling Eva held his best chance at survival, he whispered her name.

The big cat's ears flickered.

Ever so carefully, the young man inched his hand toward his daughter, poking her with his finger. Eva stirred, but didn't wake. He poked her again. The little girl wiggled.

The commotion roused the jaguar, which, when she saw Zachary, flattened her ears and growled viciously, her breath forming a mist around her snarling mouth. The jaguar's booming voice caused the young man to shrivel beneath her glare and become invisible. Fear was a strong motivator.

Eva bolted awake, looking around in a daze. But unlike Jabbar and Ferta, she could see her father's energetic body. In a shrill voice, she called out, "Ferta! Be nice! Don't hurt my daddy. Okay?"

The jaguar, which was looking around for the man who had disappeared right before her eyes, resentfully obeyed, closing her mouth, her tail still twitching.

Zachary was amazed at the power his daughter held over this fierce predator, who acted as her loyal guardian. He silently asked Eva, *Why does the cat obey you?*

She heard his thoughts, and answered, "Ferta loves me." Eva petted the jaguar.

Zachary wanted to ask how they had formed such a close bond, but who could explain love? *Well, he seems very fond of you.*

Eva corrected her father, "She."

What?

"Ferta's a girl."

Oh, yes, of course.

Staring through the raindrops, Zachary studied the jaguar. Her paws, which were pressed into the muddy soil, were the size of a man's head. It was easy to understand why this dangerous creature had provoked him into becoming invisible.

Zachary gave his recent transformations more thought, speculating, *If I can disappear by sheer will, perhaps I can do the opposite and become physical.*

There was only one way to find out.

The young man floated a reasonable distance away from the jaguar, then set an intention to become "normal" once more.

It worked.

His unseen body instantly became physical. Amazed by the conversion, Zachary held out his arms to examine them. They seemed none the worse after the magical metamorphosis. But he wasn't the only one who was curious. The jaguar also studied the young man, curling her lip and issuing a low growl, resisting her urge to charge at him.

Eva smiled when she saw her father in his familiar form.

Zachary returned the smile. "Come here, Pumpkin."

She went to her father. He bent down, hugging her tightly.

127

He sighed with contentment. Eva was real and in his grasp. Not wanting to be left out, Jabbar scaled up the little girl's body, sitting on her rain-splattered shoulder, gripping her drenched tangled hair to secure his perch.

Zachary released his hold on Eva and stood up, asking her, "What have you been doing out here?"

"We played. And Jabbar showed me where the food was. He's good."

The monkey tilted his head and lowered his eyelids halfway, looking like a sleepy old man basking in the glory of the compliment.

"That was nice of him." Zachary tried to pet Jabbar, but the monkey nipped at him. "Feisty little fella, isn't he?"

Eva shrugged.

Zachary scanned the jungle. The rain-soaked ground was slippery. They would have to wait for the sun to come out before beginning their travels. The young man took a moment to examine his leg and was pleasantly surprised to see it had completely healed. There was not even a mark where the snake's teeth had ripped into his flesh. He assumed going back and forth from being invisible to physical had regenerated his body. The miraculous healing would definitely make walking easier.

A small pool of rainwater, which had accumulated in a broad leaf above Zachary's head, spilled into his eyes. As he wiped it away, he had a flash of insight. *Wait a minute! Why walk? I didn't walk here.* He remembered how he had simply envisioned being with Eva, and then, a moment later, he was. Being able to "float" from here to there defied the laws of physics, but so did becoming invisible. Another thought occurred to him. *How did my clothes go with me? If I can transport things, can I transport people?*

To test his theory, he touched Eva's arm, saying, "Honey, I'm going to try to take you to the tree over there. Don't be afraid, okay?" Eva nodded. Jabbar, still on her shoulder, copied her, his mustache bobbing. Zachary envisioned the three of them next to the Kapok tree at the bottom of the slope. And just like that, they arrived beneath the massive branches, standing among the roots that slithered over the soil.

The jaguar stood alone in the distance, disgruntled at being left behind.

Eva glanced around, realizing she had been relocated in the blink of an eye. She gazed at her father with awe and admiration.

Laughing with delight, Zachary exclaimed, "It works! This changes everything!" Now that he knew how to transport this motley crew, they could go anywhere. "Eva, I'd like to go some place else. Back to where I came from."

"Why?"

Zachary thought to himself, *Why? Because everyone here wants to kill me. And I'm miserable and homeless. My wife left me—and every part of the jungle reminds me of her. God, I'm so tired of it all.* But he wasn't going to say that out loud to his four-year-old child, instead, he replied, "It'd be nice to see some friendly faces and sleep in a dry bed. Don't you agree?"

She frowned slightly. "I guess."

Zachary considered their options. He could take everyone back to his parents' home in Pennsylvania, but, with them gone, everything would be in disarray. *Maybe I should check on things.* He hesitated, figuring a jaguar wouldn't be welcomed in the farmlands, and Eva wouldn't want to leave her friends behind.

129

Think. Where can I take them that's remote enough for a wild predator, yet still civilized?

Only one place came to his mind.

CHAPTER 13
Together Again

ROWS OF CORN, bearing heavy-hanging ears, fluttered in the Canadian breeze blowing over the garden. The teenagers were picking the ripe beets, green beans, squash, and sweet peppers. Cecile gently placed heirloom tomatoes inside her bushel basket. Tom tediously browsed through the bean pods. He noticed a stray weed and yanked it out.

The newcomer, Haruto, was also in the garden. She had arrived at the reservation a few days earlier, seeking refuge from the Japanese soldiers. Her connection to Tom and Cecile as a fellow Earth Sentinel made her more than welcome here, even if she had to explain her sudden appearance and strange powers to them. Haruto stood over the carrots whose bushy green tops reached for the sun. She was determined to find an easier way to do the laborious work, so she focused on the vegetables, imagining them lifting out of the ground. A detectable wiggle occurred, but the bright-orange roots remained firmly within the soil's grasp, frustrating her.

Tom stood up, sighing and putting his hand on his sore back. He looked over at Haruto, watching her attempt to magically harvest the carrots. He called out to her, "Once you get that figured out, we'll leave all this work to you."

She smiled. "But what would you do with your free time?"

"Ah...let me see...fish, hunt, chop wood, read, and make love to my beautiful wife."

Cecile laughed as she stood up, holding a large tomato in her hand. "Maybe later, big guy. Personally, I like to garden, but if you want to, Tom, you can take the boys and go do something else."

"I think I will—"

A big cat's roar reverberated over the garden, causing everyone to freeze in place. The magnificent Ferta stood at the edge of the plot snarling with her muscles flexed, ready to pounce. The black-and-gold feline felt vulnerable in this wide-open and strange environment, making her especially dangerous—any quick movements could cause her to strike.

Tom, Cecile and the teenagers wanted to flee, but their bodies instinctively had become rigid. Unable to move, and fixated on the fierce creature, the tribe members did not notice Zachary and Eva standing there—even the monkey went unseen. Those in the garden only saw the jaguar glaring at them with her canines bared.

To calm the situation, Eva put her arms around her friend's furry neck, telling her, "It's okay. They won't hurt you."

Ferta came out of her primal trance, and, despite remaining tense, was no longer ready to attack. The little girl continued stroking the big cat's fur, whispering comforting words in her ear until the beast sat down on her haunches, purring to soothe herself.

Zachary watched the predator to ensure his friends' safety. If need be, he would take Ferta back to the jungle.

Haruto, who knew she could transform herself in an instant, wasn't worried, and skirted around the jaguar to greet her old cohort. "Hello." She gave Zachary a quick hug. "It's so good to see you again."

He was overjoyed to see a friendly face. "Wow! This is a surprise. I didn't expect to find you here. Where's Billy?"

She didn't answer his question because she had something more pressing on her mind. "I see you brought the girl and animals with you."

"Yes—"

"How did you do that?"

Zachary hesitated. "I'm not sure you'd believe me."

Haruto slyly grinned. "I might surprise you." She saw the potential for getting Billy out of the hellhole he was trapped in, so she pressed her fellow Earth Sentinel for an answer, "You must tell me how you did it."

"Sure, just let me greet..." Zachary stopped talking when he noticed Tom and Cecile had become invisible. Their intense fear had led to intense focus, which allowed them to do what they really wanted to do—hide from danger. The young man silently waited for them to experience their amazing transformations for the very first time.

Indeed, Tom and Cecile were mesmerized by their own supernatural abilities. Since they had already seen Haruto change from physical to semi-transparent and invisible states, they weren't concerned something had gone wrong. No, not at all. In fact, they felt this was a blessing.

Cecile spun around admiring the golden light, which was infused in everything and everyone. All the illusionary forms had fallen away. The essence of every person, plant and animal pulsed with love. She delighted in the moment, considering it a sacred

133

gift from the Great Spirit.

Tom held his hands in front of his face, amazed he could see through his body, yet still know it was there. Then he willed himself to become semi-transparent. With a ghostly hand, he touched a corn tassel, watching it flutter between his fingers.

Cecile called to Tom, *Neechi?*

He saw her shining spirit, and answered, "Yes?"

Life will be good again.

He smiled.

The Divine energy reminded them that they were eternal beings created out of love. No matter what happened here on earth, a part of them would always remain untouchable.

The couple willed themselves to become physical once more. The teens stared wide-mouthed at their elders.

Adeelah exclaimed, "You, too!? Just like Haruto!"

Tom grinned, tilting his face toward the sky. "Thank you, Great Spirit!" He embraced the communion until he noticed Zachary standing there with his usual goofy grin—a welcomed sight. Tom announced to the others, "Kids, there's someone I want you to meet. It's our old friend, Zachary." He motioned with his hand to indicate who he was talking about, even though it was obvious.

The teenagers studied the lanky Caucasian man with sunburned skin, wondering how he had become such an important part of their elders' lives.

Tom explained, "Zachary was only seventeen when he fought nobly with us as an Earth Sentinel. We are honored to have him here today."

Zachary walked into the garden to formally greet his old

friend. They gave each other a bear hug.

After letting go, Tom said, "It's been too long." It was only then the man noticed Eva standing beside the jaguar with a monkey on her shoulder, the tiny creature nervously grasping her hair. Quite an unusual sight. "And who are you?" he called out to her.

"Eva!" she cheerfully answered. "I'm four." She held up all the fingers on one hand as if to confirm her answer.

"Four? Well, it's nice to meet you, Eva. I'm much older than you. And who are your friends?"

Beaming with pride, she introduced them, "She's Ferta," pointing at the jaguar who sat quietly by her side, "and he's Jabbar," pointing at the monkey.

"Well, those are fine friends, indeed."

Zachary said, "Eva is my and Conchita's girl."

"Really? How is Conchita?"

The smile left Zachary's face.

Tom understood it was a taboo subject and dropped it.

Cecile came forward. "Hello, stranger!" She held Zachary firmly in her arms for a moment. "How have you been?"

"Really good 'til lately. Man, it's all been so..." He stopped talking as the recent deaths and tragic events passed through his mind. "I'm just grateful to be here."

Cecile's mouth turned downward and eyes grew sad, knowing Zachary's loss and hers were probably similar. She said, "The world is a crazy place. We've had our own share of..." Her voice trailed off. She wasn't quite ready to say it out loud. "Why don't we build a fire? We can talk and eat."

The Earth Sentinels sat around the flames, catching up on lost

135

time while the teenagers roasted Snowshoe hares, ears of corn and squash served with sliced tomatoes.

Because the village stocks of beer had run out, Cecile passed around several jars of wine she had made out of sugar beets and vegetable pulp, combined with packets of yeast she had found in the back of a cupboard. While it had an unusual taste, and the color was blood red, its alcohol content was just high enough to loosen their tongues, enabling them to share their bizarre and tragic stories throughout the evening and into the night—in a way only warriors who have learned to trust each other with their lives can do.

CHAPTER 14
Our Origins

AT THE CRACK of dawn, before Zachary, Haruto, Cecile and Tom had a chance to get out of bed and begin practicing their superpowers, they heard Bechard calling to them from the heavens, his voice infiltrating their minds.

Unable to sleep, they flung off their covers, stepped out of their shacks and gathered in the center of the village, standing in the pale morning light. Here, they discussed whether or not to answer the fallen angel's call. The dew dissolved as they debated. The vote was three to one in favor.

So, the four of them walked to the cold fire pit where they sat on the logs. The morning air was brisk. A Purple Finch perched in a Silver Birch tree sang its warbly melody. The smell of pine needles filled the air. The Earth Sentinels closed their eyes and let their spirits roam free. Each of them, in his or her own way, found the mystical blue door, stepping through the passageway to enter the spirit realm.

They came upon Bechard, who was standing next to a crystal ball in the center of the cobblestone courtyard. The fallen angel looked his usual regal self as he raised his arms, dramatically calling out to them, "Welcome, Earth Sentinels! Thank you for coming."

Tom rolled his eyes, annoyed by the theatrics.

"Hello," Zachary said.

Haruto and Cecile also greeted him.

Bechard spoke to the group, "It's been too long since we were last together, even though I understand you had your reasons—"

"I'm so sick of your half truths," Tom said. "It was never going to work, was it? We risked everything. And gained nothing."

The man was referencing the less-than-favorable events that occurred five years earlier when the Earth Sentinels tried to save the planet from people's greed, ignorance and indifference. Their demands that the world's governments make changes to improve earth's water, land and air quality had been partially heeded, but now what little they had gained had obviously been lost.

The fallen angel calmly responded, "When I asked for your help before, there were many possible outcomes, and no one knew for sure which one it would be, but we had to try. It was mankind's last chance before something like this recent virus pandemic occurred."

Tom wasn't happy with the answer, but he knew sometimes there wasn't a good one.

Bechard continued, "I know the recent tragedies have been devastating for you, and you're eager to practice your abilities so you can save your tribe and Billy, but, before you do, I need to explain what led up to the outbreak, and the events that have transpired since then. I believe this information will ensure your rescues are successful—"

Tom interrupted, "Look, we don't have time for your history lessons. The soldiers have taken my people. If you have some advice, that's great, but otherwise, we need to practice and save them. Now."

"I disagree. It is important to know your history. Only then will you understand the dynamics affecting you today, and how best to solve them."

"I think we should hear what Bechard has to say," Zachary commented.

Tom crossed his arms, miffed, believing they were wasting time.

"Thank you," Bechard said. "It all began approximately 400,000 years ago when my planet, Nibiru, crossed your solar system—something that happens every 3,600 years. It was then that my people, the Anunnaki, visited earth. We came looking for gold, which we planned to refine into small particles that would be used to replenish our dissipating atmosphere. But our original plan of filtering ocean water to extract gold through a technological process failed to yield an adequate amount. This meant we had to resort to mining, which went on for thirty thousand years before King Anu came to inspect our progress—"

139

"Thirty thousand years?" Zachary asked in disbelief. "Who waits that long?"

"Keep in mind that on my home planet, 3,600 earth years is only one year for us. As you might have noticed from my own appearance, my people age very, very slowly. For example, Enki, one of the king's sons, oversaw the gold-mining project the entire time, and was still considered a young man. But the king wasn't satisfied with the results—we needed a lot more gold to save our planet—so he put his other son, Enlil, in charge.

"Enlil was determined to outshine Enki by increasing production, so he made the six hundred Anunnaki workers toil in the mines for forty Nibiru orbits, or 144,000 earth years, before they finally revolted, burned their tools and stormed Enlil's abode, imprisoning the prince within his own home.

"Once again, King Anu had to come to earth to help settle the dispute. The workers faced the death penalty for their mutiny. However, after listening to their side of the story, King Anu agreed the work was too hard and had gone on for too long. But we still needed the gold.

"The solution was to take an existing species on earth—the Neanderthals, the dark-haired ones—and alter their genetics by splicing it with our DNA, using in-vitro fertilization and surrogate pregnancies to create suitable workers. It took numerous attempts, and we made a lot of mistakes, but, eventually, we got it right and created the predecessors to what you now call Modern Man—Adams and Eves made in the image of the gods.

"There were some differences, of course. For instance, the crossbreeds were infertile—similar to what happens when you breed a horse with a donkey. The offspring mule can't reproduce. However, you did inherit a portion of our longevity and were living to be nearly a thousand years old—so not being able to reproduce was beneficial for keeping your numbers in check. And, as an added bonus to us, you were docile and obedient, unlike the Neanderthals who couldn't be tamed.

"We justified the manipulation by telling ourselves that we were advancing your intellectual capabilities. We taught you how to farm and dig wells. But, on the other hand, the manipulation unintentionally suppressed your spiritual connection to the earth and all its creatures. In this regard, it was a major step backward for you, but we needed the workers so we defended our actions. And for the next forty thousand years, things went as planned

140

until the Dracos snuck onto the scene."

"Dracos?" asked Haruto.

"They look like lizard people. They wanted to manipulate your genes for their own reasons. Convincing the Adams and Eves to cooperate wasn't difficult. All the Dracos had to do was tell the women the modification gave them the ability to procreate. To have children. To become like the gods. Of course, this appealed to them, and the women quickly convinced the men to participate. But the modification came at a great cost. The Dracos' DNA, which was inserted during the process, linked your consciousness to their hive mind. Fortunately, it wasn't a full connection—you retained your free will—but the alteration did lay the groundwork for future modifications.

Bechard continued, "The Anunnaki considered the Dracos' contamination to be the 'Fall of Man' because the modified ones were procreating like rabbits and outnumbering us. Plus, you became disobedient and uncooperative. You were done working for the gods. To maintain control, we devised all sorts of schemes, including religion, which threatened you with hell if you didn't serve the gods." He chuckled. "It's hard to believe how easily it worked back then, and still does."

141

The others hostilely glared at the fallen angel, prompting him to wipe the smile off his face and clear his throat before moving on with the discussion. "Eventually, your numbers became too great, and most of the humans were asked to leave our land, E.DIN, referred to as the Garden of Eden in the Bible. Only the necessary workers and our favorites were allowed to remain."

Tom clarified, "By favorites, you mean pets. And by workers, you mean slaves. Right?"

Bechard's jaw tensed. "I'm not justifying our actions. I'm simply telling you what happened so you can make better decisions today." He moved forward with the story. "The outcast humans migrated across every continent. Your evolution continued for the next 200,000 years, although it was further complicated by other alien species tinkering with your DNA, and thereby creating several new races."

"Looks like you solved the case of the Missing Link," Zachary joked.

The fallen angel gave him a half-hearted smile. "Yes, 400,000 years is a 'blink of an eye' in terms of evolution. These changes would normally have taken millions of years. But let's move ahead to just before the Great Flood, which all the legends and ancient writings speak of. My people knew of the impending disaster, but my uncle, Enlil, forbade us from warning the humans. He saw it as a chance to wipe out the contaminated ones and start fresh. However, many of us had our favorites and couldn't bear to see them die so...well...we went behind his back and warned them."

Zachary asked, "Did you save any?"

"A few."

"Was the flood a natural disaster?"

"Yes. The Anunnaki scientists stationed in Africa noticed the Antarctica ice cap was slipping off its slushy foundation because of the gravitational pull of our approaching home planet. We knew once the ice cap fell into the ocean, it would cause catastrophic tidal waves around the entire globe, which it did. But, before the watery abyss covered this planet, my people got into our spaceships and hovered above earth. Despite my people's callousness, many wept when they saw you drown."

"I'm touched," Tom said sarcastically.

Bechard ignored the man's comment. "After the flood waters receded enough for the Anunnaki to return, my uncle discovered some of the humans had been spared." The fallen angel shook his head remembering. "Enlil was furious, but he calmed down after we convinced him the survivors would be useful for rebuilding.

"However, another problem sprung up during the aftermath. A fraction of the Anunnaki citizens, including myself, rebelled because we wanted to build our own kingdom instead of rebuilding for the seldom-seen king. The rebellion seemed like a rational decision at the time, but, for our transgressions, we were deemed traitors." He added without bitterness, "We were also demonized. From that point forward, we were referred to as *fallen* angels. And, to make matters worse, after a while I didn't fit in with the rebels. I was on my own on a strange planet. But that's karma for you."

143

The others could tell Bechard was rehashing the events in his mind, perhaps considering what he should have done differently.

Tom tapped his wrist, indicating it was time to conclude the story.

To placate the impatient man, Bechard began talking again, "After the flood waters receded, our geneticists decided to disable ten of the twelve DNA strands in the human survivors. Our intention was to reduce your life span to fewer than 120 years so you wouldn't overpopulate the earth and overrun us."

Cecile scoffed, "There's no way you could have found every one."

"We didn't, and there's tales of people living to be very old, but eventually, through interbreeding, everyone's life span shortened.

If it were possible, we would have also removed the reptilian influence."

"Why couldn't you?"

"The Dracos' modification had become an integral part of your brain that neuroscientists now refer to as the R-complex or Reptilian Brain, which controls your heart rate, breathing and body temperature—the basics for sustaining life. It also holds your more animalistic qualities, such as the desire to fight for dominance and territory, and sexual and survival instincts. Their modification couldn't be removed without killing you. Of course, this is what the Dracos intended. And they are still busy modifying your DNA as well as doing something far more sinister. Here, let me show you."

Bechard waved his hands over the crystal ball. The blue mist parted to reveal a laboratory where alien scientists were working among a half-dozen, unconscious naked men and women, who lay on gurneys with white sheets covering their midsections.

One of the scientists walked across the floor pushing a tall machine topped with a glass dome. A wheel squeaked. He stopped at the nearest gurney, which held a male subject. The scientist flipped a switch on the machine, causing a white light in the glass dome to flicker on. A humming sound arose. From the side panel, the scientist unlatched a black hose, then pressed a red button. A holographic funnel appeared at the end of the tubing, which was positioned over the man's chest. The scientist waited for his assistant to press a handheld device against the man's neck, killing him. A moment later, the man's spirit spiraled out of his chest, and was vacuumed into the black hose where it headed toward the white light in the glass dome. Once there, his spirit was unable to proceed any farther. It was then, the man realized the treachery. This was not the natural progression of a soul passing from this life to the next. He panicked. His spirit took the shape of a ghostly face screaming for help, but the glass dome silenced his pleas.

Without the slightest concern for the victim, the scientist inserted a clear hexagon-shaped crystal, the length of a finger, into a slot in the machine. This prompted the man's spirit to flow out of the glass dome and into the crystal, which became cloudy as it filled. After this operation was completed, a small mechanical arm swung over the quartz cell, etching a number on its flat topmost surface with a red laser. The scientist retracted the crystal, putting it in a rack along with the others. Finished with this human, he rolled the machine toward the next victim.

"What you just saw is our biggest concern," Bechard stated as he waved his hands over the crystal ball, stirring up the blue mist inside to hide the continuing actions of the scientists.

"What the hell was that!?" Cecile demanded to know.

"The Dracos were, and still are, capturing people's consciousnesses—what some might call souls—"

"But that's not possible. Is it?"

"It is. Let me show you." Bechard waved his hands, and the blue mist inside the crystal ball dissolved once more.

This time, the scene showed a white-walled laboratory that housed four-foot-tall glass capsules. Inside them were fetuses, all in various stages of development, floating in green synthetic embryonic fluid. Bubbles gently rose to the surface. Piped throughout the room were sounds of dogs barking, kids playing and people conversing. A lullaby softly played in the background.

A scientist pushed a cart between the capsules searching for a specific subject. When he found the one he was looking for, he stopped, reaching inside his cart, pulling out one of the hexagon-shaped crystals from a rack. He checked its number, then inserted it into a slot on top of the capsule lid.

Immediately, the spirit within the crystal rushed out, swirling inside the capsule, floating above the amniotic fluid until it sensed a viable body, prompting the life force to race through the liquid and enter the strange-looking fetus with an oversized head, unformed nose and rounded bulge between its closed eyes.

Zachary asked, "Is that an alien hybrid?"

Bechard chuckled. "It looks like an alien, doesn't it? But there's no difference in appearance between a human and hybrid fetus."

"Oh." The young man took a closer look, somewhat repulsed.

Cecile stated, "That soul wasn't given a choice. Not a real one, anyway."

"You're right," Bechard agreed with her. "It wasn't, and that's the problem. And, to make matters worse, if the Dracos figure out a way to incorporate your DNA into their hybrids, they'll have unlimited power. So let's hope it's not possible. Meanwhile, the stolen souls that have been forced into these hybrid fetuses are effectively trapped within the hive mind—a matrix within a matrix. Their freewill and access to the universal energy are so hidden from their consciousness that they'll never be able to escape the hive mind on their own. It will take an outside intervention to free them. The Dracos' actions go against the universal Law of Oneness, and they will pay dearly for it in terms of their own karma, just as my people have."

Tom said, "I don't see how your people have been punished at all."

146

Bechard solemnly explained, "The Dracos were concerned the Anunnaki would step in and help mankind because our planet Nibiru was approaching earth once more. They knew the Anunnaki felt responsible for you since they were your original creators. To prevent any sort of intervention, the Dracos gave the United States government advanced laser beam technology, which they used to punch a hole in our atmosphere, quickly destroying all life on my planet." The fallen angel's eyes watered with tears, but he refused to let them fall. He took a deep breath to clear his thoughts. "Every living thing on Nibiru was annihilated shortly before I met you. Any hope I had of returning home was gone forever—so I set my sights on saving this one."

"I'm sorry," Zachary said.

Instead of giving the expected response, Bechard turned his head, studying something inside the crystal ball. After a moment, he commented, "Well, this is new."

147

Curious, everyone focused on the glass sphere. They watched a scientist, who was standing in front of a microscope, hold an industrial silver-hooded light near the slide beneath the lens. A blue beam of light flashed, then the scientist peered into the microscope to examine its effects. After a moment, he lifted his head to type on a laptop.

Wanting to know what was going on, Bechard repositioned the crystal ball's perspective directly over the microscope. The Earth Sentinels stared down the lens. A magnification of 400x revealed a micro-sized clear crystal nestled among red blood cells. This unique crystal had a fiber, which resembled a plant root, growing out of it. The fiber wiggled as it grew in length until two new offshoots spontaneously sprouted from its tip. Each of these runners began forming their own crystal buds.

"What the hell is that!?" Cecile exclaimed.

Bechard gave his opinion, "It appears to be some sort of biological crystal. Very strange. I haven't seen—"

"Shouldn't you know?" Tom asked.

"Contrary to popular belief, I am not God. However, I will keep an eye on this to find out."

Anguish flooded over Zachary. "This just keeps getting worse."

A rare flash of irritation crossed Bechard's face. "If mankind wasn't so weak minded, this virus outbreak would never have occurred."

The young man was perplexed by the fallen angel's comment. "What do you mean? Are you saying it's our fault?"

"In a round-about way, yes." Bechard became sympathetic. "Let me explain. The Interstellar Senate, which is a collective of leaders from throughout the galaxy, has been watching mankind's development ever since the Dracos first modified you, and you began procreating. As a self-perpetuating species, mankind had become part of the universal journey. This status entitled you to protection under the Law of Oneness, which meant no other species could interfere with your progress. It also meant no one outside the human race could rule you directly—"

"Wait a minute, didn't the Anunnaki rule over us?"

"Yes, we did. But, after your 'fall', we were forced to use demigods to rule you. They were half human and half Anunnaki— the Sumerian kings of old. Demigod priests were also useful for maintaining control. Later, to circumvent this same restriction, the Dracos ruled you using their human hybrids, also known as the elite, Illuminati, world leaders, priests and royalty, who were all offered protection, wealth and privileges as incentives to betray mankind."

"Sure, you call it a betrayal when the Dracos do it," Tom scoffed.

"If it will make you happy, both parties were guilty. Shall I move on?"

Tom maintained the scowl on his face, but nodded.

"After millenniums of war and the use of nuclear weapons during World War II, the Interstellar Senate declared that if humans didn't change their ways, interim representatives would be put in place to govern you before you ruined this precious planet.

"Assuming you wouldn't change, the senate put out a call for volunteer representatives, but the only ones to respond were the fallen angels and Dracos. Each claimed a right to oversee the human race, not on a temporary basis, but permanently. Their claims were taken seriously for several reasons. First and foremost, both the fallen angels and Dracos share a common ancestry with you, and second, both live on this planet. It is their home as well. And last, but not least, because of their role in your development, the senate couldn't ignore their right to self-correct their past wrongs. So, despite neither the fallen angels or Dracos having your best interests at heart, the lesser of the two evils was chosen, and the fallen angels were given permission to come out from the shadows and rule mankind. But only if you did not change your ways.

"This decree changed very little for the fallen angels, who were content to wait for your inevitable failure. However, the Dracos saw it as a once-in-a-lifetime opportunity they weren't going to let

149

slip through their fingers. So they stepped up their plan by more aggressively continuing their genetic manipulations, and placing hybrids into every top-level leadership position around the world. These mind-controlled humans were appointed as the presidents, dictators and generals who instigated continual wars; the CEOs and bankers who profited from the wars; the educational trustees who dumbed down your textbooks; the religious leaders who told the believers they were God's favorites; and the scientists who assured you the poisons were safe while never mentioning that GMOs, pesticides and herbicides, and vaccines were designed to alter and weaken your DNA to make your bodies more receptive to the Dracos' genetic blueprint."

"Why didn't the fallen angels stop the Dracos?" Zachary asked.

"It would have been a bloody war. Plus the fallen angels would have risked losing favor with the senate. But mostly, I suspect they were letting the lizards do the dirty work for them, thinking they would bypass the karmic retributions against their own race, not realizing the Dracos were capable of implementing a master plan to take over the world. However, that's just my guess. I'm not sure what the fallen angels were thinking. As master mind readers, they cloak their thoughts very well."

"Couldn't they read the Dracos' minds?"

"No. When the Dracos communicate, they use their hive mind, which has proven to be impenetrable from the outside. However, once their thoughts reach the hybrids, they are easily picked up. To counteract this, the Dracos have been very careful not to divulge their plans to the hybrids, who have been, and still are, compartmentalized very effectively.

"But let's get back to the story. Decades went by before the Interstellar Senate finally gave the fallen angels permission to take over."

"This was recently, correct?" asked Cecile.

"Yes. But the Dracos struck first by spreading the deadly virus, using military, passenger and commercial planes to kill over seventy percent of the human population and nearly all of your leaders—essentially thrusting the world back into the dark ages, leaving you cold and hungry, and paralyzed by fear."

Tom was skeptical. "Didn't the Dracos kill the leaders they put in place?"

"Yes, they did. But even this was part of the plan. Because right after the virus outbreak, the Dracos utilized the existing United Nations' infrastructure, which they created, so they could assign their new and improved hybrids to the UN positions in military bases around the world. These blond-haired, blue-eyed mind-controlled hybrids took charge of every single country's armies without firing a single shot. Ingenious really. The human foot soldiers blindly obeyed, thinking they were restoring order instead of helping to enslave themselves and mankind."

"But why do they want to control us?" Tom asked. "Why not just kill us, and keep the earth's resources for themselves?"

Bechard looked the man straight in the eyes. "*You* are the resource."

Tom's face paled.

"The easiest way to explain it would be to show you." The fallen angel stepped up to the crystal ball. "But be prepared, these are graphic scenes."

A gray-walled room came into view. A dozen reptilian officers sat at a long stone table. They wore black military dress uniforms. Their skin was scaly with an olive tone. They had red-hued eyes with slitted pupils, and pointed teeth. Their forked tongues occasionally flicked in and out of their bony mouths. A ridge formed at the top of their foreheads and ran over their scalps and down their necks, disappearing beneath their collars. Their ears were small, almost nonexistent. And, instead of fingernails, they had sharp claws.

Tom offered his two cents, "They look like gargoyles that bred with humans."

"Shhh," Cecile whispered. She wanted to hear what was said next.

The Supreme Leader, Zycar, who sat at the head of the table, had a distinct appearance from the others. His face resembled a skull because of his ashen skin, sunken eyes and exposed pointed teeth. Ridged horns curved out of the sides of his head. A patch of long white hair grew from the center of his scalp and hung down to his shoulders. He turned toward the silvery door, gruffly shouting, "It's time!"

His command prompted a blue beam to flash over a door that was the color and consistency of mercury slowly swirling. The door became pure energy instead of physical particles, leaving the entryway wide open. A gray alien entered, presumably male because he wore what could only be described as a butler's jacket with no shirt underneath. His hairless body stood about four feet tall. He wasn't wearing pants, although it didn't matter since he had no visible genitalia. His large almond eyes were completely black and spanned the width of his face. His long skinny neck supported his oversized head. And his tiny nose, if you could call it that, was little more than a fold with two slits above where his mouth should have been. The gray alien, who was assisted by a second one, carried the front end of a metal stretcher on which a semi-conscious, prepubescent girl lay whimpering. Her legs and arms were tied down. Cuts had been inflicted all over her small body. Blood oozed from her wounds, congealing at the bottom of the deep-dish metal tray that was set in the middle of the table with the victim's head closest to the commander.

Those sitting around the table hungrily eyed the human entrée, hissing with anticipation.

A third gray alien entered the room carrying a gleaming butcher knife and copper pitcher. With his four-digit hands, he held the pitcher under the girl's neck as he slit her throat. Her eyes flared wide with terror as her blood spurted into the container. She only had time to utter, "Mommy..." before the rapid blood loss caused her to mercifully lose consciousness, then her heart stopped beating.

153

The butler began filling the goblets on the table, starting with those highest in command.

After everyone was served, Zycar picked up his goblet, toasting to the others in the room, communicating through the hive mind, *To our nourishment!*

The Draco officers raised their goblets to return the toast, then greedily gulped the blood until it was gone, flicking their forked tongues to capture the last remaining drops. Refreshed, they uttered sounds of contentment mixed with euphoria.

Leaning over to take the first bite, Zycar sunk his teeth into the girl's shoulder, tearing off a piece of her muscle and skin, exposing the bone beneath. As he chewed, blood trickled down his rough chin.

The sight started a feeding frenzy.

The others ravaged the body.

Teeth clashed.

Flesh tore.

Grunting ensued as they feasted.

The Earth Sentinels turned away from the scene in disgust and horror.

Bechard waved his hands over the crystal ball and the blue mist inside rose to hide the gory buffet. He told the others, "The Dracos have been eating humans for millenniums. It's where your legends of vampires, werewolves and demons come from. The hormones and adrenaline coursing through your veins make the Dracos feel alive. Often, they torture their victims to increase the adrenaline content, but, and here's the most interesting part..." He motioned with his hands and the blue mist dissolved, showing the girl's corpse had been picked clean—just her skeleton, head and lower intestines remained. While a gruesome sight, Bechard wanted the group to see what took place after the Dracos finished eating.

Some of the reptilians transformed into blue-eyed humans with either fair or brown hair. One of them belched. Several others picked their teeth with their newly formed fingernails. Those with a higher percentage of reptilian genetics also transformed, but retained their reddish eyes with slitted pupils, and scaly skin. Their noses grew longer, but were still smaller than normal; and, although spaced a bit too far apart, their teeth were no longer pointed. The Supreme Leader did not change at all, perhaps out of intention, or perhaps because he was too archaic, but either way, Zycar seemed pleased with his lunch, resting his claws on his engorged belly.

Tom uttered, "Shapeshifters."

"You are correct." Bechard explained, "Once the ratio of human to reptilian blood changes, those 'on the fence', so to speak, shift and appear to become human for a little while."

Fearing the worst, Haruto asked, "Will they eat Billy?"

"For now, he and the other tribe members are safe." Bechard moved his hand over the crystal ball. A new scene appeared, showing a nuclear plant that had melted down. "But there is another major concern. Because of the power outages, nuclear plants around the world experienced melt downs, and are spewing radiation as we speak."

Overcome by the devastating news, Haruto sorrowfully declared, "Life will never be the same. Ever." She was all too familiar with the after-effects in her hometown of Fukushima.

"It's true. Life as you knew it is over. The Dracos were strategic on where the nuclear plants were built. This ensured the radiation would be evenly dispersed. You need to remember these reptiles thrive on radiation. Soon, the levels will be closer to what they prefer—going as high as the newest hybrids can tolerate, but definitely much higher than humans can bear long term. This means the Dracos and hybrids' primary meat source will be loaded with radiation and live a shorter life span. For them, it's a win-win."

Haruto asked through her tears, "But what about the animals? The plants? The oceans?"

Bechard was sympathetic. "It's a travesty, but they don't care about diversity unless they can use it or eat it."

155

Tom went up to Bechard, demanding to know, "Why didn't you stop it!? Everything is ruined!"

Bechard looked around the group, seeing the fear and anger in their eyes. "To you, I'm all powerful, but to them, I'm just a solo dissident who has fallen away from the Anunnaki rebels' agenda. You're asking me to fight an entire army. I can't do it alone."

The tall pedestal, on which everyone had placed Bechard, shrank.

The fallen angel continued, "However, a lot of things have changed since then. Mostly you. I believe your powers are the only thing that can save mankind. Don't take them lightly. But back to the radiation. The remote areas are still safe from it, and once you've mastered your superpowers, you could transport the nuclear plants to a distant star, preferably one with no planets, to get rid of the problem." He seemed pleased with his own idea. "We'll add it to the list."

Haruto asked, "What about the damage already done?"

"There are natural solutions, such as microbes, bacteria and mushrooms that could effectively neutralize it. This isn't the first time in history there's been nuclear disasters, so there is hope for restoring the planet."

Zachary's shoulders slumped. "Who knows what else they're doing. It's hard to win when you don't know the rules."

"True enough. We're late to the playing field, but the game is still on, so don't give up, not yet, because, if you do, mankind's evolution in terms of spiritual advancement will be set back by hundreds of thousands of years. But the first step is recognizing your own powers. The rest will follow. To that end, it's time to practice your newfound abilities. Get to know them inside and out, and then you can save your loved ones and the others from this tyrannical regime."

Cecile said, "I agree we need to practice. We don't want to endanger our tribe, but I wish we knew they were all right."

"That's easy enough." Bechard waved his hands over the crystal ball. "Let's start here—right after the tribe was taken off the reservation."

The glass sphere showed a military bus driving down a road escorted by army trucks. The convoy slowed to a stop in front of a fenced compound with barbed wire strung along the top. A reflective metal sign read "Canadian Armed Forces Official Facility, No Trespassing". Inside were rows of khaki-colored canvas tents, which housed brown-eyed people who sat inside their temporary dwellings, listlessly staring out the opened flaps. A military base was stationed on the other side of the fence.

157

The convoy moved past the gate and entered a holding pen that acted as a barrier between the tents and checkpoint to prevent the prisoners from escaping. Behind them, the gate slammed shut. The armed soldiers jumped out of the military trucks, positioning themselves near the bus before the bi-fold door opened.

"Everyone out!" a soldier ordered.

John was the first prisoner to exit. He stepped down, defiantly clenching his jaw. His straight black hair hung loose over his black t-shirt, which was imprinted with the artwork of a powwow festival he attended last year. The other tribe members followed him, one after the other, huddling outside the bus, confused and afraid. John protectively put his arm around his younger sister, Mari, who tried to act brave like her brother.

The UN leader told the group, "You'll be assigned tents. If

you cooperate, this will be a temporary situation until you receive your work orders. Follow me."

Back in the spirit realm, Tom ruefully stared at the scene in the crystal ball, stating the obvious, "They're living in concentration camps."

"It's not great," agreed Bechard, "but the tribe should be fine until you rescue them, so practice well."

CHAPTER 15
Practicing

THE JAGUAR, HIDDEN in the branches of a maple tree, silently observed the people's activities below.

Standing near the fire pit, Tom spoke to the teenagers, Adeelah, Manuel and Rowtag, who were gathered around him, "I'm going to practice moving you together."

"Where to?" Manuel asked, apprehension tainted his voice.

"Over there by the trees," Tom answered. "Now, everyone put your hands on me." He waited for them to do so, and then he concentrated, imagining all of them at the new spot.

In a blink of an eye, everyone in the group, except for Manuel, relocated, appearing on the forest's doorstep, standing in the sparse weeds. The teenagers were amazed.

"This is so cool!" Rowtag exclaimed.

"Wow!" Adeelah gushed.

Tom noticed Manuel was missing. He looked over his shoulder and saw the boy standing in the old spot. He shouted across the way, "Why didn't you come?"

Manuel loudly answered, "I didn't do it on purpose!"

Tom magically transported himself to where Manuel stood. "That's okay. It's good to know this stuff. Can you tell me what you were thinking? It might help."

"I don't know..." The boy seemed embarrassed. "I guess I was freaked out about..you know...doing it."

"Let's see what happens if you don't resist," Tom suggested. He held onto Manuel's arm, saying, "Just relax. Okay?"

He nodded.

"Are you ready to go?"

He nodded again.

Tom took the boy to where the others stood. Adeelah and Rowtag cheered when Manuel arrived.

On the other side of the fire pit, Eva walked on a log like a tightrope walker, placing one foot in front of the other, her tiny toes gripping the bark as she balanced herself with outstretched arms. The miniature mustached monkey stepped behind her, imitating her movements, holding out his hairy arms.

Nearby, Zachary was trying to move objects with his mind. He aimed his hands at the cord of wood located at the edge of the clearing, focusing on one of the uppermost split logs, which he managed to lift a few inches before it fell back onto the pile. He tried again. This time, the log floated up a little higher before falling once more. Zachary decided to focus more intensely. He straightened his fingers, pointing them at the log, which rose unsteadily, but stayed afloat. Pleased, he beckoned it with his hands, and the log followed his motion, wobbling through the air toward him. When it reached the fire pit, he lowered his hands, and the log abruptly dropped into the cold ashes. A cloud of soot billowed.

Eva clapped enthusiastically for her father. The monkey clapped and hooted.

Zachary pretended to bow to a crowd. "Thank you, thank you, one and all."

"Do it again, Daddy!"

Prodded by her admiration, he caused another log to float off the pile, sail above the ground, then land beside the first one. He did this several more times, each one more easily handled, before Eva got bored and resumed her balancing act.

Having lost his audience, Zachary decided to try something new—something that was sure to impress his daughter. He dramatically cast his hands, making hundreds of pine needles rise up from the forest floor, swarming like bees as they flew a circle around Eva and Jabbar, then headed toward the fire pit, settling into a mound beneath the logs. Zachary focused on the pine needles, causing them to smolder. Smoke trickled. The kindling caught fire. He moved his hands higher and the flames grew, lapping over the logs.

Eva and the monkey clapped.

Meanwhile, Haruto was working with Eyota, a shy, but willing participant, who she asked, "Do you have any questions?"

The girl shook her head.

"Okay, good. The first thing I'm going to try to do is move you over there." She pointed at an old oak tree. "Okay?"

The girl nodded.

Haruto touched Eyota's arm, praying this would work. The pair disappeared from where they stood and reappeared near the massive trunk. The Miko smiled. The process had turned out to be much simpler than she expected. And after a little more practice, she would be able to save Billy and anyone else who might need her help.

At the same time, Cecile was practicing her skills with Taima, who she asked, "Are you ready?"

161

Although the young woman usually acted tough, her voice was soft as she answered, "Yes...but there's somewhere I want to visit."

"Oh?"

Taima hesitated before saying, "I never gave them a proper burial."

Cecile knew who the young woman was talking about. "It might be better if we all went together."

"I know, but I'd like to go alone. With you, I mean."

Cecile took ahold of Taima's hand. They disappeared from where they stood and arrived in a field at the edge of the burial grounds where ashes and bones were piled in a heap. The gray cremated remains were a stark contrast to the lush green surroundings.

162

"Don't feel guilty," Cecile comforted her. "You kids did what you had to do. You were still recovering. Something had to be done."

Despite the macabre bones and skulls, Taima stared at the funeral pyre. She rarely cried, but, at this moment, tears ran down her cheeks. With great difficulty, she uttered, "Mom, Dad, if you can hear me, I love you. Please forgive me." She turned toward Cecile, sadly suggesting, "We should bury them."

"We will. But right now, we need to take care of the living."

After several hours of practicing, the Earth Sentinels felt comfortable enough with their newfound powers to discuss rescuing the tribe members. They gathered around the smoldering fire that Zachary had built. The teenagers quietly listened. Eva and the monkey sat down, trying to act like grownups.

Tom took the lead. "Okay, everybody, we need a plan so we can save the tribe." Haruto gave him a look that prompted him to add, "And Billy."

Cecile interjected, "I don't see a problem with that. We can easily transport them, but where will we take 'em? Once they go missing, this will be the first place the army looks."

Tom sighed, frustrated this process was still having complications.

"We could take them to the jungle," Zachary suggested. Eva and Jabbar eagerly nodded. He added, "Although, personally, it wouldn't be my first choice." Eva frowned.

"I was hoping for a location similar to here," Cecile said, glancing at the forest. "You know, not so hot. Maybe there's some place in Canada? Or Alaska?"

"Hmmm." Tom speculated, "Alaska would be tough, even without the aliens looking for us."

"I'd prefer something a little warmer," Zachary commented.

Cecile said, "Yeah, but we could always move again. As long as it keeps them safe for the time being, we shouldn't rule it out."

Haruto asked, "Then where to?"

Tom admitted, "I don't know."

"Do you really think the Dracos care about such a small group of people?" Cecile questioned. "I mean, how much effort would they put into finding the tribe?"

"They cared enough to take them in the first place," he reminded her.

"Yeah...but was it really about them? Or were they looking for us? Are we the reason they were taken?"

"I don't think so. We hadn't mutated yet."

163

"Just because we didn't know about the mutation, doesn't mean they didn't."

Tom growled, "There's so much we don't know."

"Then let's find out for ourselves," Haruto suggested. "Zach and I can visit the Dracos' bases and laboratories, and you two can scout for locations. It shouldn't take us more than a couple of hours."

CHAPTER 16
Scouting

THE CHICAGO PUBLIC Library, built in 1991, replicated the more notable architecture throughout the Windy City. The brick building had high-arched windows and a roofline adorned with gigantic, bronze owl sculptures ready to take flight. Inside on the main floor, every inch of the ceiling was adorned with ornate carvings and reliefs, and topped by a dome crafted out of Tiffany glass panes. It was here that Cecile and Tom arrived, using their supernatural abilities to remain invisible as a safety precaution. They took a moment to admire the magnificent library, which had three levels of bookcases on this floor alone. The escalator was motionless. Dust had accumulated on the lengthy empty tables where the patrons normally sat perusing books.

This place is huge! Cecile exclaimed.

Tom asked, *Where should we start?*

I don't know. The travel section?

Sounds good.

They transported themselves to a row that was over fifty-feet long.

Now that's a lot of books, he commented.

Their ethereal bodies floated down the aisle until they found the section labeled "Remote Destinations". Cecile scanned the shelves. *Oooh, here's one.* She read the title to him, *The Twenty-*

five Most Remote Places in the World. That sounds interesting. She became semi-transparent so she could pull the book off the shelf, opening it. "Okay, this one is in Motuo, China. It says you need a suspension cable to get to it."

I'm not sure about that one.

"Tetepare Island? It's part of the Solomon Islands and used to be inhabited two hundred years ago. There must be fresh water there."

Tom shrugged his invisible shoulders.

"Okay, here's a place in the Australian outback."

Sounds remote.

"Yeah...I'll make that a maybe." She flipped through the pages. "Nope. Nope. Okay, this one's interesting. Deception Island, Antarctica."

166

Brrrr. You know I love Canadian winters, but that's too cold, even for me.

"But it's got volcano-heated waters," she joked, then read the next one, "Okay, this one sounds good: the Palenque Mayan ruins. Warm, sunny and near a waterfall."

Bookmark that one.

"Man, you never realize how small the planet is until you're trying to hide out." Cecile put the book back on the shelf. "Maybe we should just visit some places. It might be faster than thumbing through these books."

Okay, where to?

"You choose!" Cecile made herself invisible and held onto her husband's hand.

Meanwhile, cloaked by invisibility, Haruto and Zachary emerged inside the hub of a military operations control center where hybrid soldiers sat monitoring grids of holographic screens that spanned the circular walls. One bank showcased street scenes from different cities. The images continually switched. On the opposite side of the room, the holographic screens offered a bird's eye view of remote jungles, snowy tundras, deserts and mountains. In the top-right corners of the screens, the text "Satellite Transmission Enabled" displayed. Three reptilian commanders sat in high-back chairs overseeing the activities.

A warning sound ensued from a control panel, prompting the soldier sitting there to take a closer look at one of the screens. The body heat from four people displayed as orange figures.

The reptilian commanders swiveled in their chairs. The soldier glanced back at them, seeming to read their minds before flipping a switch on his control panel.

The holographic screen in question zoomed away from the wall, moving to the center of the room, becoming life-size. The projection showed the band of travelers, two women and two men, wearing heavy coats and scarves that flapped in the strong winds as they trekked up the hazardous mountainside. The three-dimensional image was so life-like that Haruto and Zachary could almost feel the bitter cold nipping at their faces.

The commanders viewed the scene, then simultaneously nodded at the soldier, who pushed a button.

On the monitor, everyone saw a laser beam shoot down from a satellite, striking the travelers. The mountainside exploded. Flames shot up, and a cloud of smoke mushroomed over the site.

Haruto and Zachary instinctively ducked, unaccustomed to such realistic holographic technology.

167

When the smoke cleared, it was obvious the travelers had been vaporized—only their ashes remained within the blackened crater.

The commanders nodded in unison, indicating the task had been satisfactorily completed. The soldier pushed another button, and the holographic image shrank, returning to its original spot on the wall. Everyone resumed their normal duties.

Distressed, Haruto and Zachary slowly stood up from their crouched positions. He expressed his dismay, *Man, that was terrible. They were just trying to survive.* Haruto solemnly nodded. *Let's get out of here,* Zachary suggested. *I've seen enough.*

Agreed. But where?

I'm not sure, but I was thinking these Dracos must have something, somewhere, relaying these camera transmissions. We could check that out.

Okay. Let's go.

Barren ice. Brutally cold winds. Although it was summer in the Northern Hemisphere, here, in Antarctica, it was winter and perpetually dark until springtime. The temperature was currently -80 degrees Fahrenheit or -62 degrees Celsius depending on which scale one used. A man's skin would be frostbitten in less than a minute if he was foolish enough to lose a glove or expose his face to these harsh elements.

High above this forlorn continent, the shimmering Aurora Australis light show danced—spinning shades of green, yellow, orange and purple nearly 150 miles high. The Solar Wind collided with the magnetosphere to create a luminous tango between the upper and lower energies.

When Zachary and Haruto arrived, they were so captivated by the light show, it took them a while to notice the manned outpost right in front of them. Interior lights glowed through the thick-paned round windows in the futuristic, heavily insulated pods supported by sturdy steel legs. Stationed behind the pods were twenty-foot-diameter, white faceted balls, which emitted a strange hum. Generators, the size of train cars, churned nearby. Several heavy-duty snowmobiles were parked out front.

In order to take a closer look, the pair instantly transported themselves inside one of the pods where military engineers, dressed to stay warm, sat at computers with holographic screens that resembled the ones at the Dracos' military base. On the screens were similar images of cities and remote areas under surveillance.

Looks like a sophisticated operation, whispered Haruto.

Why are you whispering?

She talked louder, *I keep forgetting they can't hear us. This place obviously sends and receives transmissions. And being so remote makes it even more suspect. It's literally the end of the world.*

Well, now that we know about this place, what are we going to do about it?

Right now, nothing. We need to rescue the others before doing anything that attracts attention, but it's good to know they use satellites for surveillance. It's something to keep in mind when we choose a place. Are you ready to scout for locations?

Yeah, but before we go, could we peek at the South Pole? Those Aurora lights are so cool. I'd like to see them closer. It'll just take a minute.

169

Haruto hated to waste the time. *We should start scouting.*

Just for a minute, Zachary pleaded. *Please...*

All right, just for a minute.

Thanks!

The pair left behind the military engineers, who were none the wiser they had been spied upon.

When Haruto and Zachary arrived at the South Pole, traveling hundreds of miles in a blink of an eye, they immediately noticed something even more captivating than the southern light show. They were standing on the outskirts of an enormous hole, which was so vast, the other side could not be seen over the curvature of the earth. The snow-covered edge sloped downward, like a funnel, until it reached the mammoth opening. Awestruck, the pair stared at the natural phenomenon.

Zachary said, *Come on, Haruto, let's move closer! See what's inside.* She nodded. Even she couldn't contain her curiosity.

Bypassing the mile-long slope, the pair instantly went to the edge of the icy rim. The two of them looked like ants peering into a bottomless pit.

Zachary thought to himself, *This was definitely omitted from the geography books. How could Google Earth have missed this?*

The two of them barely had time to take in the view when a ball of light emerged from deep within the mysterious tunnel, growing bolder and bigger as it rushed into the colorful night sky, hovering above them. The radiant sphere split into five orbs—zipping, soaring and intersecting with each other until they formed a perfectly spaced row over the crusty snow, which glistened like diamonds. The orbs pulsed as their audible voices simultaneously spoke in a monotone, synthetically generated voice, "Greetings! We are the Guardians. We welcome you." It was obvious the orbs had detected Haruto and Zachary's presence despite them being invisible.

Haruto stood in awe. She had seen a lot of things in her life, but this was the first time she had seen orbs. She responded, *Who are you, again?*

"We are the Guardians. We have come from another galaxy. We are here to help mankind."

Against the Dracos?

"Yes."

Why would you help us?

"We are pleased with the question. We come from a solar system where the planets were taken over, much like yours. The invaders plundered our natural resources and kept the indigenous people as slaves and a food source. It is a barbaric system used by heartless races. We wish to prevent the same fate from happening here on earth, although it may already be too late."

How can you help us?

"We can advise you, and offer a safe haven," replied the orbs as they pulsed in the night sky, maintaining their formation. Their monotone voices continued, "We know you are searching for a residence where the Dracos cannot find you. To help with this, we have set aside a territory for you and your people in inner earth."

Your offer is most generous, but living underground sounds dark and depressing to me.

The orbs bounced around as if chuckling, then realigned themselves in a row, speaking once more, "As above, so below. We believe you will find inner earth to be quite beautiful. Would you

171

like to see it for yourselves?"

Zachary was as giddy as a kid on Christmas morning. The explorer in him burst forth, *Of course!*

Haruto rationalized the orbs couldn't hurt them unless she or Zachary became physical, so she agreed as well.

The orbs responded, "This is good. Please let your minds join with ours."

A mist filled Zachary and Haruto's minds, swirling and gathering, turning into cumulus clouds floating over an amethyst ocean. The red-hot lava sun, held in place by centrifugal force, spun in the center of the lavender sky. The vision zoomed closer, showcasing a Mediterranean city hugging the sea. A Parthenon-styled capital, the crown jewel, was built into the cliffs. Its white columns complimented the lush green backdrop. Closer to the expansive bay, Greek-styled homes with tiled roofs, ornate facades and domed cupolas occupied the shoreline.

The orbs explained, "This is one of a thousand cities here in inner earth. You are welcome to take a closer look."

Deciding to see it for themselves, the Earth Sentinels left the snowy tundra and transported themselves to the market square where the Grecian storefronts displayed merchandise, such as baked goods, shoes and bolts of cloth. A centaur trotted down the cobblestone street carrying a basket of apples. A short distance behind him was a human mother wearing a toga, escorting her two children past the shops.

In the center of the square was a water fountain with marble statues of the Greek Gods: Alpheus, the river god; Delphin, the leader of the dolphins; Poseidon, the Olympian god of the oceans, seas, rivers and storms; and Pan, the patron god of fishing. The

172

mythological figures stood back to back holding vessels that poured life-giving water.

The ball of light, having traveled from the Antarctic surface, flew into view, then, once again, broke into five smaller orbs that hovered over Zachary and Haruto, speaking in unison, "We would like to invite you and your people to live here in inner earth. If you agree, you will receive your own region where you can prosper."

Haruto felt she needed more information in order to properly inform Cecile and Tom about the possibility of bringing their tribe here. *Your offer is very generous, but is it safe from the Dracos?*

"We are pleased with the question. We understand safety is your main concern, and without it, you cannot fully focus on the agenda at hand. To answer your question, inner earth is the safest place in, and on, this planet."

173

Haruto was still wary of relocating the others here, wondering if it was a trap. These orbs might be working with the aliens. She couldn't be sure.

The orbs read her mind, responding, "We understand your concerns, but you do not have the luxury of time you once had to discern friend from foe. Perhaps an old friend of yours can persuade you."

Bechard appeared, standing on the cobblestone street, looking as handsome as ever. Giggling fairies fluttered around him before flying away.

It seemed rude to remain invisible in Bechard's presence, so Zachary let himself become semi-transparent, saying, "It's good to see you."

Bechard smiled. "Good to see you as well."

Haruto reluctantly followed the young man's lead and became

semi-transparent, then she scoffed, "Really? Bechard? You're the one who's supposed to instill trust?"

He chuckled. "Ironic, isn't it?"

The orbs patiently waited to see how the interaction would play out.

Zachary asked Bechard, "Why didn't you tell us about this place?"

"You had to find it on your own."

"Like the Holy Grail?" he joked.

"That's actually a good analogy."

Zachary badgered him, "But what about the tribe? Do they have to find it for themselves as well?"

"As their ambassador, you'll do."

The orbs interjected, "We realize you do not completely trust Bechard, but he has helped us for millenniums—forging alliances and creating a sanctuary that has benefited all of us here. He is not perfect. None of us are. But he has been true to his word. Again, we invite you to bring your people here to live for as long as they like—forever if need be. This will allow you to work with us, without impediment, to overthrow the Dracos."

Zachary whispered in Haruto's ear, "Where else would the tribe, and Billy, and Eva be safe?"

She whispered back, "What if they're lying?"

The orbs grew antsy waiting for an answer, flickering.

Haruto's question made Zachary hesitate. After all, the decision was a matter of life and death. He couldn't afford to be naive, so he quizzed the orbs, "How do we know we'll be safe here?"

"We are pleased with the question. We have protected the

southern region of inner earth, Alteria, for over 200,000 years. We have numerous armies for defense."

"But how do you keep the fallen angels out? Can't they come here like Bechard does?"

"Again, we are pleased with the question. The fallen angels' power to 'come and go' as Bechard does was lost eons ago. The fallen angels' affinity for dark energy has drained their powers. They have become reliant on human flesh to restore themselves, rather like the Dracos, who are also slowly dying. Without you, they would have perished long before now. It's a strange and illogical concept that both the Dracos and fallen angels reject the divine energy, yet rely on humans to furnish it through their bodies."

"Can the Dracos be stopped?"

"We believe with your powers and the wisdom of the Galactic Council, we have a chance at overcoming the dark force that has been thrust upon this planet. However, should you decide to become citizens of Alteria, you must meet with the Galactic Council before taking any further actions or interacting with the Dracos. There is no negotiation on this matter. This includes the rescue of your tribe members. The reason for this is your actions could impact all of us here in Alteria. We think you can understand that."

Haruto requested, "Could you show us where the tribe would live if we agreed to come here?"

"It is our pleasure. Please connect with our minds."

A vision burst forth, displaying an ancient forest, its lush canopy filtering the unending sunlight. Spotted deer grazed on the grassy knolls that gently fell into a plum-colored lake framed by willowy grass. Mountains stood in the distance.

The orbs narrated, "Clean water. Plenty of game. We believe you will find this region more than suitable. We will ask the gnomes and fairies to explain the customs of Alteria to help you acclimate yourselves. One day, you will do the same for others. Are there any other questions?"

Haruto and Zachary shook their heads.

"Please let us know your answer soon. Time is of the essence."

Cecile and Tom nervously waited around the fire pit for Haruto and Zachary to return. The logs had long since burnt out. Tom's legs nervously shook. He wanted to save the tribe. Now. There was no doubt in his mind that it needed to be done as quickly as possible. To pass the time, he took a pinch of tobacco out of a plastic pouch, packing it into his elk-antler pipe. He flicked a lighter, holding the flame over the bowl. He took a few gentle puffs. The tobacco swelled, glowing in the center. He took a deep puff, embracing the sacred plant spirit, then released a cloud of smoke.

"Feel better?" Cecile inquired.

"A little. I hate waiting."

"I know, but it must be important, whatever they're doing. Just be patient."

A blue jay landed on a nearby branch, shrieking as if warning the other creatures in the forest of these people's presence.

Tom asked the bird, "What's wrong, little fella? What are you afraid of? Have I invaded your home? Or you mine?"

The blue jay cocked its head, then shrieked once more before flying away through the trees.

Cecile reminded Tom, "It's home for all of us."

"Not for long."

Fortunately, at that moment, Haruto and Zachary appeared, both wearing smiles. A good sign.

"How'd it go?" Cecile asked.

Haruto answered, "I believe we found a place."

Tom set his pipe down. "Good. We found a few as well, but tell us about yours."

"Sure. But let me start at the beginning. Initially, we went to a Draco military control center. It was a horror show. Terrible. We watched them kill travelers with a laser beam from a satellite. They had detected the people using heat sensors. With this type of technology, there's no doubt in my mind, they will eventually find us—no matter how remote our hiding place is on earth."

Cecile's heart sunk. "If that's true, is any place safe?"

"I believe ours is," Haruto replied. "After we left the control center, we went to a Draco outpost in the Antarctic, which led us to the South Pole where we stumbled upon a gigantic opening."

"How big?"

"Oh, it's hard to say. We couldn't see the other side, but five orbs flew out of this hole—"

"Orbs?"

"I know it's strange, but stay with me. These balls of light knew all about the Dracos and the fallen angels, and offered us, *all* of us, sanctuary inside inner earth—"

Tom interrupted, "Inner earth? I've never heard of such—"

"It's true!" Zachary backed up Haruto's claims, "The hole was a tunnel that led to the earth's core, except there is no core. Instead, there's a whole world inside our planet. It was unbelievable! Oceans...and mountains...and forests..."

"That is hard to believe," Cecile commented.

"I agree, but we saw it for ourselves," said Haruto, who continued, "The orbs claimed they have successfully kept the Dracos out for hundreds of thousands of years."

"How?"

"They mentioned having their own armies. If true, inner earth would be the safest place for us. The only drawback, if you can call it that, is the Galactic Council wants to oversee our actions."

"Who?" Tom was annoyed because each answer only brought up another question.

"The orbs mentioned a council that oversees inner earth. I didn't meet them, so I really can't tell you more than that, except they want the 'final say' on how we save the tribe, and how we interact with the Dracos. But, since they know more about them than we do, that might not be such a bad thing. However, my main concern is, 'Can we trust the orbs and the Galactic Council?' Bechard vouched for them—for what that's worth."

Cecile grimaced. "Bechard? I can't say he breeds trust."

Haruto suggested, "Perhaps we should meet the council before making a decision."

"Perhaps."

Tom said, "I say let's go ahead and meet them. It might be..."

A flapping sound was heard, as if a great bird was approaching. Everyone looked up and saw Bechard descending from the sky, his indigo robe fluttering as his great wings flapped. The fallen angel landed on the other side of the fire pit, stirring up the cold ashes. He tucked his wings, greeting them, "Hello, Earth Sentinels."

With disdain, Tom uttered, "Bechard."

"Tom."

The man stood up from where he sat, taking an adversarial pose and crossing his arms, saying, "I suppose you've got something to say about this."

"I do. It's time for you to meet the Galactic Council."

CHAPTER 17
The Galactic Council

BECHARD, TOM, CECILE, Haruto and Zachary appeared in an expansive sanctuary created entirely out of irregularly shaped crystal walls. At the forefront of the great hall, twelve Galactic Council members stood atop a crescent-shaped platform—a collective of leaders from planets throughout the universe.

The first to greet the visitors was a female Arcturian dressed in a white robe. She stood no more than four feet tall. Her bald head made her pretty face, which looked human except for her exceptionally large green eyes, stand out all the more. "Greetings, Earth Sentinels. I am Synege from the star Arcturus. Welcome to the Crystal City—my home away from home."

"Thank you for meeting with us," Haruto responded.

"It is you who honors us. We know who you are so let us introduce ourselves." She motioned for the council member on her right to speak first.

The thin man had long white hair pulled back in a ponytail, and wore only a loincloth. He smiled warmly. "Hello, Earth Sentinels. My friends call me 'Guru' because I spend my days pondering the meaning of life. We are delighted to have you here."

Next to speak was a giant head created out of points of light that constantly shifted like a flock of swallows spreading and regrouping perfectly in sync. "My name is Phosulent. My planet resides in another galaxy. Its name would mean nothing to you. But we are well aware of the unjust actions taking place on earth's surface, and intend to help. Your desire to bring your tribe and family members here is most welcome, but understand, we must—"

"Contain our numbers. Greetings, I am called Geet," said the creature who had an elephant head and a rotund human body with a protruding belly. He wore a bright saffron-colored cloth tied around his mid-section. Beautifully braided cords draped over his head and large flapping ears, forming a casual free-flowing crown. The mouse perched on his shoulder curiously observed the proceedings. Geet continued, "Believe me when I say we'd love to bring everyone here, but unlike some—"

A small voice squealed, "We honor the Law of Oneness. Even the best of intentions can cause sorrow when imposed on others." The voice belonged to a fairy, who from a distance resembled a glowing pink dot floating among the other council members. The fairy flew closer to the visitors, hovering in front of them so they could better see and hear her. She wore a pink gauzy dress with pink stockings, and her red hair was elaborately styled. "Very good day. I am Faylinn. I live in Alteria with others like myself, who have dwelled in this land for thousands of years. It is a wonderful place to live, but I digress, back to the Law of Oneness. Many people have pre-planned their destinies, so however we proceed must honor that, even if it seems cruel, even to them. We don't want to—"

"Interfere, you might say," said a nine-foot-tall and very thin being whose body, comprised of shades of beige, seemed to flicker in and out of existence. His or her face was there one moment, and then not the next. It was as if its presence was blocked from the

181

Earth Sentinels' perception. They weren't even sure if the being was talking audibly or telepathically. "My name is Telphane. I come from a moon that orbits the planet Saturn. My people are ethereal beings who survive on energy from the sun. I am pleased to meet you. I have been waiting to do so since you first met Bechard. This council and my people care deeply about mankind's fate as well as your right to live without interference and manipulation. But the main effort must come from—"

"You," a giant butterfly interrupted. Her wingspan was nearly six feet wide with a double set of wings. One set was orange and black, and the other was green, blue and iridescent white. "I am Gladise. Pleased to meet you. But you've come for guidance on rescuing your tribe, so I will defer to Synege on that matter."

Zachary noticed that not every council member had introduced themselves, and he wondered why.

Synege answered his unspoken question, "Not everyone here participates in the discussion. Some are here to raise the vibration of this sanctuary so the others can work at their highest level of wisdom and inspiration. Even the crystal structures within our city are sentient beings."

She changed the topic. "You, Earth Sentinels, have been bestowed a great gift that is awakening you to your true selves—a path we all will take at some point in time, but you are among the first. As you progress, you will recognize that everyone and everything is an extension of yourselves, even the Dracos and fallen angels. Each has a lesson to teach us. This council is privileged to watch you travel forth on this journey of self-discovery, even if it's likely to be plagued with heart-wrenching decisions and sacrifices."

Synege finally spoke of the Earth Sentinels' main concern, "The council agrees your loved ones should be rescued and brought here to Alteria. Bechard mentioned you would be transporting them yourselves. Is that correct?"

Cecile and Tom nodded.

"Please tell us your plan."

Tom cleared his throat. "Cecile and I will rescue our tribe members from a UN detainment camp. Haruto will rescue Billy from the Dracos' underground prison, and the Mikos in Japan. Zachary will bring the teenagers and his daughter from the reservation."

Synege nodded. "That is an acceptable plan. However, when explaining the details to your people, please don't mention inner earth or Alteria beforehand. The fallen angels are very adept at reading minds, and the Dracos could torture your loved ones to get the information, so not mentioning your destination is a fairly simple precaution. Agreed?"

The Earth Sentinels nodded their heads. The council members' grace and words had invoked their trust.

"Are there any others you would like to bring here to Alteria? If yes, please say so now." Synege's eyes lingered on Zachary, who, although he thought of Conchita, remained silent. "Very well, once you have completed your mission, please reconvene here to discuss future actions."

Tom said, "I have a question. Can you show me where we would be living? I'd like to see it for myself before taking the others there."

"Of course. Bechard can show you around. Godspeed to all of you, and be safe."

CHAPTER 18
The Tribe's Rescue

A BLACK-UNIFORMED UN leader, trailed by a troop of Canadian soldiers, approached a tent inside the detainment camp. He shouted, "Everyone out, now!"

The command struck fear into the Bear Claw tribe members who looked at John for guidance because he was the strongest in both body and spirit. The young man got up, ducking beneath the low canvas ceiling, his long black hair hanging down. His people followed him outside.

The UN leader motioned for John to step forward, then scanned his body with a tablet. The young man stared past the officer as if he wasn't there, trying to maintain a shred of dignity in this degrading situation. On the screen, at the top of John's profile, a black message box popped up that read "Level 4". The UN leader told him, "You've got work orders. Stand to the side."

Next, the UN leader scanned John's sister, Mari. He stood a little too close to her as he ran the tablet over her body, only stepping back to read the screen. Mari's profile information appeared. She was a "Level 3". He ordered her to stand to the side as well, then motioned for the next tribe member to step forward.

Mari felt like crying, but refused to do so in front of these monsters, instead she stoically stood beside her brother as each tribe member was scanned and told to return to the tent.

Soon, Mari and John were the only ones left standing outside.

The UN leader looked at the pair, then told the soldiers to escort John to the bus.

John surveyed the soldiers and the rifles they carried. He knew he had no choice but to leave. He hugged Mari, who, in return, held onto him tightly, praying it wouldn't be the last time.

The two soldiers marched John past the rows of tents until they reached the edge of the detainment camp. A soldier stationed there pushed open the gate. John felt like a dead man walking as he moved through the opening.

At the bus, John stepped up the grooved-rubber stairs, moving past the driver who refused to make eye contact. He found an unoccupied seat, and sat next to the window where he stared at the chain-link fence and barbed wire, dreading what the future held for him.

185

A short while later, the invisible Tom and Cecile stood in front of the three tents that held their people. There were no soldiers in sight. It was time for the rescue to begin.

Tom glided through one of the tents. Inside, all of the occupants were visibly upset. The would-be rescuer let himself become semi-physical so he could talk to his people. His ghostly appearance startled them. A few gasped. One frantic woman started to speak, but Tom put his finger to his lips, and she fell silent. In a hushed tone, he said to them, "I know this is strange," referring to his phantasmal body, "but I don't have time to explain."

The frantic woman couldn't contain herself any longer, and spoke out, her voice quivering, "John's gone! Sent to a work camp. And Mari..." she fought back her tears, "the soldiers took her."

Tom clenched his jaw with frustration. This rescue was supposed to be quick and easy. Now two were already missing. He told her and the others, "I'll find them. Wait here." As if they had a choice.

To search for Mari, Tom let his mind wander. He saw an image of a military truck parked between two tents.

Tom became invisible once more, then transported himself to where the missing woman was. He arrived, floating beside the vehicle, just as the cab door creaked open. Mari was pushed out, falling to the ground. Her clothes were ripped, and her face and arms were bruised. Numb. Traumatized. She struggled to get up, stumbling forward, dazed and unsure of which direction she was headed.

The UN leader stepped out of the truck, grinning as he zipped up his black pants. The other soldiers turned a blind eye.

Enraged, Tom stormed toward the rapist intending to kill him with his bare hands, but then Mari staggered past him.

Tom stopped.

She needed his help.

The tribe needed his help.

To kill the UN leader now would jeopardize everyone's lives. Revenge and justice would have to wait.

Still invisible, Tom followed Mari as she tried to return to the safety of the tent, but she tripped, falling into the mud. Prodded by her own determined spirit, she attempted to stand again, but lost her balance, landing on her hands and knees.

The UN leader jeered, "Looks like she wants some more."

The other soldiers snickered. Only one looked away, ashamed.

Sensing the situation might escalate, Tom returned to the

tent. He became semi-physical once more, blurting out, "Mari's hurt!" He pointed at two of the women. "Go get her. Now!"

The women hesitated to leave the tent because they knew it was against the rules, but they followed his orders and went outside.

When the women saw Mari crawling on the ground, they forgot their fears, ignored the soldiers and rushed to help her, lifting her up by her arms, dragging her back inside the tent.

Mari collapsed on the canvas floor, curling into a ball, too traumatized to cry. One of the women pulled her into her arms, cradling her like a baby.

Tom kneeled, gently touching the woman who held Mari, then said to the others, "Put your hands on me. I'm taking you out of here."

187

Cecile had an easier time than Tom. She transported two groups of tribe members to inner earth within a few minutes. Her people were overcome with relief and gratitude. Some stared incredulously at the red sun held high in the lavender sky. A rainbow-feathered loon fished along the shoreline of the purple lake. The moment was too surreal for the tribe members to fully comprehend—one minute they were prisoners, the next they were free.

After too much time had passed, Cecile began to worry about Tom's rescue attempt. She was about to check on him when he and his group arrived, appearing on the grassy knoll. The visibly distraught women formed a protective barrier around Mari, who remained in the arms of her friend. The men stepped away to give them privacy.

Cecile rushed over to Tom. "What's happened?"

"Mari was..." he hesitatingly whispered, "raped." Cecile's knees weakened. Tom grabbed her arm to steady her, saying, "We waited too long. If we had acted sooner, like I said, none of this would have happened." He breathed heavily as his anger intensified. "I'm gonna kill that son-of-a-bitch!"

Cecile glanced at her beloved Mari, who lay in anguish. "I'm going to see if she needs..." Overcome by emotion, her voice faltered. Unable to say more, she simply walked away, heading toward her friend.

Tom barely noticed Cecile's departure. His only thoughts were of killing the rapist, until suddenly, a greater concern crossed his mind, causing his rage to turn into fear. He disappeared.

CHAPTER 19
Rescue on the Reservation

WHEN ZACHARY ARRIVED at the Bear Claw First Nation Reservation to save the teenagers and Eva, he found his daughter asleep on a porch, partially protected from the sun by the metal overhang. Ferta and Jabbar were snuggled beside her.

Adeelah, Eyota and Taima were ambling through the village reminiscing, knowing they most likely would never see this place again. But, on the positive side, they knew they would be reunited with their rescued tribe members soon. The two village dogs paced beside them, hoping for a head scratch or treat, or both.

Rowtag and Manuel were riding bareback on the American Paint horses, stepping through the green field, enjoying one last pass over the tribe's ancestral land.

Zachary leaned down, gently nudging Eva. Her hazel eyes opened. She drowsily gazed at her father. He told her, "It's time to go."

The little girl sat up, resting her hand on the sun-bleached boards. Her movement woke up the jaguar, which stretched her enormous front paws while yawning. The monkey struggled to lift his eyelids still heavy with sleep, wiggling his mustache as he smacked his lips. Eva asked, "Where are we going?"

"Somewhere safe." Zachary stood up, shouting at the girls who were still down the road, "Time to go!"

The girls waved to acknowledge they had heard his call, then dawdled toward him, moving as slowly as possible to delay their departure.

Zachary turned in the other direction, hollering at the boys, his voice rolling across the pasture, "Time to go!"

Rowtag and Manuel leaned to the side, prompting their horses to turn toward the village. The horses followed the boys' cues, swishing their tails to drive away the flies.

Understanding how difficult it was to leave a place you loved, Zachary patiently waited for them.

Eva stood up, putting her hand on the jaguar's head, stroking the soft fur between her ears. The monkey climbed onto the little girl's shoulder.

190

It was a perfect moment—one that embraced all that was right about the "dog days" of summer. The air was golden and the sky was clear. A cool breeze blew over the land.

But the perfection vanished when Zachary spied jets on the horizon, heading their way. Something was amiss. There hadn't been a single plane overhead since the virus outbreak. These had to be military planes. Fear tore through him. He knew he needed to get everyone out of here, and he needed to do it fast.

Zachary placed his hand on his daughter, then transported her to where the girls stood studying the sky. Ferta and Jabbar, who were touching Eva, had come by default. Zachary shouted at the girls, "Hurry! Touch me! We need to leave!" They rushed to him, clinging to his arms, but Adeelah and Taima also took the time to reach down, each grabbing a dog by its scruff.

The jets closed in on them. The pilots fired the missiles mounted beneath their wings.

Rowtag and Manuel saw the projectiles whizz through the air, thin trails of smoke following. Without hesitation, the boys yanked on the horses' manes and kicked them into a gallop, hunkering down and holding on tightly as they raced toward the forest.

Zachary transformed the girls, jaguar, monkey and dogs into an ethereal state, which would keep them safe. Then he transported them to the field, directly in front of the boys and stampeding horses. The moment the horses burst through the energetic edges of the semi-transparent group, creating a connection, Zachary took every single person and animal out of there.

A split second later, the missiles hit.

Fireballs exploded.

Black smoke billowed.

Amid the haze of settling debris, flames licked the charred remains of the houses and community hall. The outskirts of the forest were scorched. The reservation was no more.

191

CHAPTER 20
Saving John

THE AIR BRAKES hissed as the bus came to a stop outside a brick-facade factory. A red maple-leaf flag fluttered in the breeze on the pole out front. On the side, big rigs and eighteen-wheelers idled near the loading docks while their attached trailers were being loaded.

The passengers studied the building wondering what job positions they might be given. Relief flooded over John as he gazed out the window. He had been skeptical about the work assignment, assuming the worst. Decades of lies by the Canadian government had led to his mistrust—not to mention his recent imprisonment at the detainment camp, which was eerily similar to the reservations his people were forced to reside on until they were officially granted their citizenship in 1956, retroactive to 1947. (Only in the eyes of the government did that make any sense.) However, this time it seemed the soldiers had told him the truth.

A blond woman waited on the sidewalk. As soon as the bus door folded open, she boarded, standing beside the driver. She held a clipboard snug against her chest, and wore a black pantsuit accented with a light-blue scarf. She smiled, then spoke loudly to make sure those at the back could hear her. "Welcome, everyone! My name's Sara, and I'm the HR representative in charge of taking you through the steps of your work assignments, which will include a physical exam to make sure you're healthy enough for the job. After that, you'll get your ID badges."

Someone asked, "What do you make here?"

"This is a food processing plant. Not the most glamorous job, but an important one. You'll make sure everyone has food on their tables, which is especially important after everything that has happened." Sara cheerfully said, "Follow me, please!" then stepped down onto the sidewalk where she waited for everyone to disembark.

Sara led them down the wide sidewalk to the gleaming glass doors at the front of the building. She opened one of the doors, motioning for them to enter.

The lobby was more than large enough to accommodate everyone, but only a dozen of the lucky ones got to sit on the chairs. The receptionist sitting behind the counter glanced up at them, then returned to her duties. Behind her was a sign with the company's motto: "Quality People, Quality Food".

The HR representative weaved through the crowd, making her way to the door on the other side, swiping her ID badge over the security pad. A buzzer rang out, releasing the lock. Sara opened the door, saying to the group, "Ten at a time, please." She counted the men and women as they walked single-file past her. John made the first cut.

Sara escorted the group down the hallway. There were five metal doors on each side. She instructed them to choose one. "Once inside, you'll need to disrobe and put on a paper gown. A doctor will come in to evaluate you."

John opened one of the doors. The room smelled of body

193

odor, but he reasoned the previous occupants had come straight from a detainment camp so it was to be expected. He took off his jeans and t-shirt, laying them neatly on the chair, then sat in his underwear on the paper-lined exam table, awkwardly wrapping the paper gown around himself. He waited for the doctor to arrive.

Instead, it was a stout nurse who entered the room carrying a small plastic basket filled with syringes and glass tubes. She briskly told him, "We're going to need a blood sample. You faint easily?" John shook his head. The nurse expertly strapped rubber tubing below his bicep. After finding a suitable vein, she jabbed it with a needle, filling a vial with his blood. She placed the sample in the plastic basket, then, before leaving, informed him, "The doctor will be in here shortly."

194

Thirty minutes later, a doctor entered the room carrying a tablet, which he set on the counter. "All right, let's take a look at you." He pulled out a handheld device from his lab coat pocket, using it to peer into John's ears, eyes and nose. "Stick out your tongue, please." The doctor took a peek, then turned around and entered a few notes into his tablet. He stared at the screen a moment. "Okay, now I just need to confirm that you are you." He picked up the tablet, holding it in front of John's face. A beep rang out. Seeming satisfied, the doctor said, "Go ahead and get dressed. And when you're ready, open the door. Someone will come for you." He left the room.

Fifteen minutes passed before Sara strolled down the hallway, calling out, "Everyone! Follow me, please!"

The future employees exited the rooms, following Sara to the end of the hallway where she shepherded them up the stairwell. When she opened the door at the top of the steps, the sounds of machinery working at full speed on the production floor bombarded the group, making it difficult to hear her instructions as they proceeded along a steel-grid catwalk. They came to an office suspended over the storage area below. Everyone shuffled inside.

Sara shut the door and the factory noises subsided. "Okay, here's what's happening. You'll sit here until I call your name, then you'll head into the next room to get your picture taken for your employee ID. And after that, you'll receive your first work assignment. Okay, ladies first." She glanced at her clipboard, reading from the list, "Connie Pérez."

The woman opened the door, which automatically closed behind her as she entered the next room.

After a few minutes, a buzzer rang out, cueing the coordinator to announce the next name, "Mary Romano."

The woman got out of her chair and nervously headed to the door.

This happened three more times before it was the men's turn.

Sara called John's name.

He stepped into the other room, surprised that it was so dark inside. His eyes didn't have time to adjust before two men crept out of the shadows from behind him. One pressed a device against the back of John's neck, injecting him with a serum that rendered him senseless. The men grabbed his arms as he fell, then hauled his body out the door at the opposite end of the room.

The factory noises drowned out the sound of John's body hitting the wire-grid platform. One of the workers, wearing blue coveralls with his name embroidered on it, grabbed a pair of industrial scissors, cutting through the unconscious man's t-shirt, jeans and underwear, peeling off his clothes, throwing them over the railing. The items sailed into the dumpster below. The other worker reached above his head, grabbing a large metal rack shaped like an inverted "U". Its cables lengthened as he pulled it down. He used his body weight to press the rack flat onto the floor. Together, the workers placed the victim on the rack, quickly spreading his arms and legs wide, securing his wrists and ankles with electronic metal cuffs.

One of the workers took a few steps over to a control panel, moving the joystick in the center. The rack's cables tightened, and the top end rose into the air until the entire contraption was fully vertical. John's head slumped forward. He resembled a crucified man as he was hoisted higher, sailing over the railing. The rack was guided by an overhead track that descended as it crossed the three-story room, leveling out before curving around a wall.

On the other side, John joined a horrifying lineup. The women who had preceded him also hung naked on their racks, which had temporarily stalled. But, unlike him, they had regained consciousness and were screaming and fighting against their restraints. A double-glass wall insulated the rest of the factory from their cries for help.

Ahead of them was an enormous saw blade, shrieking an ear-piercing battle cry, waiting to slice the victims in half as soon as they arrived above the stainless-steel trough designed to catch the spilled blood. Beyond the blade, a mechanical mouth was open and eager to consume their bodies. Their flesh would be cooked off the bones, then shredded into a tidy end-product chocked full of protein, hormones and adrenaline. At the far end, vacuum-sealed cans labeled "Minced Meat, Grade A" traveled along the conveyor belt to where blue-eyed workers packed them into boxes, which were stacked onto pallets. Forklift operators moved the pallets to the loading docks.

John opened his eyes, groggily lifting his head. He saw the lineup of screaming women in front of him, twisting and struggling, trying to free themselves. Fear threw his adrenaline into overdrive. He wildly yanked on his shackles, tearing at his flesh.

The group panicked when a buzzer rang out. The assembly line inched forward, taking them closer to the spinning blade.

At the forefront of this ghastly procession, jets of water bombarded the first woman in line, blasting off all of the grime she had accumulated at the detainment camp. As the drenched woman emerged out of the power wash, electricity surged from the cuffs, searing her wrists and ankles. She screamed in pain and terror as the current tore through her body. Her back arched. Strands of energy sizzled over the rack, scorching her wet skin. The woman pitched herself back and forth, jerking on her metal bonds. Her fear level escalated so high, she went into shock. Her screams abruptly stopped and her eyes stared blankly, but the rack continued chugging ahead, escorting her limp "Grade A" flesh toward the deadly blade.

The torture began again. Electricity tore through the next woman in line as she exited the power wash. She screamed and struggled, reacting like a caged animal willing to chew off her own appendages to escape.

At that moment, Tom Running Deer emerged inside this genocidal chamber, remaining invisible as he tried to figure out why screams filled the air. Despite the confusion, he spotted John,

197

then went to his side where he let himself become semi-physical.

Stunned by the sight of Tom's strange appearance, John stopped struggling. Confused, he wondered if both of them had died and now existed as spirits.

Tom shouted in John's ear to be heard over the screams and buzzing saw, "I'll explain later! Let's get you out of here!"

Based on Tom's words, the young man assumed they were still alive, so he yelled, "Okay, but save everyone!"

Tom wasn't sure what he could do within such a short time frame. The racks continued advancing forward. Another shackled and unconscious man slid around the bend, taking his place at the back of the lineup. Tom studied this assembly line of unending victims. Even if he saved these people, there would be a fresh batch within the hour.

The saw blade spun only inches from the comatose woman at the forefront.

With only a second to think, Tom noticed the rack holding John was fastened to an overhead track that carried all of the racks throughout the factory. The entire system was connected. With no time to spare, he touched John's arm.

The factory's exterior shell, and its attached overhead conveyor system and inner structures, landed on top of a green wheat field. The inverted "U"-shaped racks squeaked as they slowly stopped swinging. Each one was empty, except for the one holding John.

Tom released his grip on the young man, giving him a moment to adjust. A flock of sparrows flew through the open dock bays, continuing on their way.

John hung there in disbelief. "How did you do this?"

"It was the virus. I'm mutating. Cecile's mutating."

John shook his head. "I don't understand."

"I'll explain later."

The young man looked at the barren racks. "Why didn't the others come?"

"I think it was a permission thing."

Both men were solemn, knowing the others remained captive at the slaughterhouse.

After a respectful amount of time passed, Tom said, "Well, let's get you off that thing and go home. Well...not home, but...you ready?"

The young man nodded.

Back at the food processing factory, now void of its facilities, the hybrids, who had been working in the second-floor offices and on the catwalks, plunged to their deaths after the inner structures were whisked away from beneath their feet. They hit the concrete slab. The sun beat down on their twisted and broken bodies.

The naked victims, who had been strapped to the racks that were no longer there, dropped a few feet to the floor—a bruising, but nonlethal, fall. A few of them sat up, wondering what had happened. The spinning saw blade eased to a stop. The conveyor belt was motionless. One man jumped to his feet, streaking through where the wall of the building had been a moment earlier, bypassing the idling big rigs and eighteen-wheelers. He was not going to miss his one shot at freedom. Several of the potential "employees", still waiting in the wall-less lobby, watched the streaker run through the parking lot.

A bus pulled up to the curb with a fresh load of people who would not be processed today.

199

CHAPTER 21
Saving Billy

THE TRANSLUCENT HARUTO arrived inside an empty prison cell. She stared at the spot on the floor where Billy sat the time before. She hadn't expected him to be gone. Her mind called to him, *Where are you?* But no vision or answer came to her. Panic set in. Afraid he might be dead, she had an overpowering desire to search for him, but didn't know how to find him without being able to connect with his consciousness.

Without any specific destination, Haruto moved her ethereal body through the block wall, entering the murky hallway lit by dim and infrequent overhead lights. She aimlessly drifted down the prisoners' row where moans seeped out from under the reinforced metal doors.

In an attempt to locate her lost lover, as well as distance herself from the surrounding misery, Haruto imagined herself at the laboratory where she had once been shackled. When she arrived, she saw the familiar gurneys lined in a row, empty, waiting for their next victims. The sight resurrected painful memories as she remembered the inhumane experiments the aliens had performed on her. Because of this, she was glad Billy wasn't strapped to a gurney, but she was also disappointed. *It would have been so easy to take him out of here.* She wondered where else he might be.

Just then, three small-statured aliens, wearing black hooded cloaks, walked past the glass doors as they moved down the hallway. One of the aliens glanced inside the laboratory, his face hidden in the shadow of his hood. Forgetting she was invisible, Haruto held her breath, standing perfectly still, expecting to be discovered. Instead, the alien moved out of sight with the others. She breathed a sigh of relief, but then wondered where they were headed. *Maybe they will lead me to Billy.* She knew it was a long shot, but it was the only one she had right now.

Haruto floated down the long desolate corridor behind the aliens, who walked without talking, intent on reaching their destination. They eventually came to a "T" intersection, turning right, walking down yet another passageway.

The monotony wore on Haruto, who felt she wasn't making any progress. Just when she was about to give up on this endeavor, the aliens passed by a set of steel doors. Haruto decided to see what was behind them.

She glided into a dark industrial-sized space. A phosphorescent green mist rose out of the metal vats lining the wall on the right-hand side. On the left, eight-foot-tall glass capsules stood in the gloomy room. The nearest one contained a male body floating in embryonic fluid.

Haruto hoped it wasn't Billy as she hesitantly moved closer, dreading the answer.

The specimen bobbed in the capsule's artificial current, slowly rotating.

Its face bumped against the glass.

It was part alien and part man.

Haruto screamed, but no sound came out of her invisible mouth.

Down the corridor, the aliens stopped walking, sensing something was amiss. They turned around, the hems of their hooded cloaks following their motion. Their shrouded eyes searched for anything out of the ordinary, but the long corridor stood empty and quiet. They resumed moving forward.

Standing before the capsule, Haruto shook with fear. *What are these aliens doing with these...creatures? Only God knows what they're doing to Billy.* She needed to find him before it was too late—if it wasn't already.

She vanished from the room, reemerging behind the aliens. It took her a moment to calm down enough to realize they were waiting for an elevator to arrive.

The steel doors slid open. Haruto followed the aliens inside. The elevator began its descent. She felt strange being so close to these hooded creatures, especially in such tight quarters. None of them felt her presence.

They arrived at their floor. The aliens exited, walking past two hybrid guards who did not acknowledge them. After a short distance, they stopped in front of a mercury-like door, its form constantly swirling. One of them stepped up to the security pad, extending his gray four-digit hand from beneath his long draping sleeve, placing an exceptionally long finger on the touchpad. A blue light flashed over the silvery door, causing it to dematerialize.

The aliens crossed the threshold. Haruto trailed behind them, entering the circular-shaped room furnished with curved metal benches. At the far end, a tall reptilian commander studied a grid of holographic screens displaying different areas within the underground complex: a lobby, a laboratory, corridors, and prison cells holding anguished people crumpled in misery. He stood with his clawed hands clasped behind his back, wearing a black double-breasted military uniform with gold trim and buttons. A black metallic sash was draped over one shoulder. His reptilian face did not betray his anger.

The short aliens stood in the center of the room and bowed. One of them said, "We are at your service, Commander Guado."

The commander continued staring at the images as he asked, "Have you recaptured her?"

"No, sir."

He turned around to face them. "Explain yourselves."

"Yes, sir. After the woman disappeared from the laboratory, her DNA was detected back in Japan."

Haruto realized they were talking about her.

"She was discovered during a routine search, but once again escaped. Hours later, the woman showed herself, seemingly on purpose, setting off a DNA detector. What's most interesting about her is she seems to be able to transform her body at will. Changing from physical to what can only be described as a visible ghost—instantly. Unfortunately, it's only her physical form that sets off our DNA detectors."

"Why didn't you know this would happen?"

"We conducted extensive testing for decades on hundreds of thousands of people, and none had this mutation. But the Omega Project infected billions—a much larger pool."

Commander Guado breathed deeply as if cooling his rage. "This could ruin milleniums of planning. She and any others like her *need* to be eliminated."

"Yes, sir! We are working on it day and night, sir."

"Our Supreme Leader will want an answer soon. Understood?"

"Yes, sir."

"Dismissed."

The cloaked ones bowed, then left.

The commander returned to staring at the surveillance images. Haruto approached him. She could see his skin was almost as thick as armor. When he breathed, a hissing sound, along with his forked tongue, came out of his mouth.

Repulsed, she turned away to view the holographic screens. One showed the aliens that had just left the room and were now entering the elevator. Another screen showed a six-foot-tall praying mantis, which wore a tunic that was open on both sides, exposing its spindly barbed arms and legs. The praying mantis leered over a man, strapped in a chair, whose head was covered by a black hood that expanded and collapsed with each gasping breath he took. Wires coming out of a nearby machine were attached to the man's neck, arms and chest. Hybrid soldiers stood guard. Two alien scientists observed the proceedings.

The silent monitor offered no clues to what the praying mantis said to the man, but the oversized insect was seen flipping a switch on the machine. The man slumped, seemingly unconscious.

Haruto didn't know exactly what the man had just endured, but it was obvious he was being tortured. Without thinking about the consequences or the Galactic Council's instructions, she left Commander Guado's post and entered the torture chamber just as the praying mantis fiddled with a knob on the machine, sending a jolt of electricity throughout the man's body, surging him awake. He cried out in pain.

The praying mantis sneered in a raspy voice, "Are you ready to summon her yet?"

The man breathed heavily beneath the hood, but didn't answer.

The arthropod creature taunted him, "Until you tell us where she is, this will continue."

The man remained silent.

Taking advantage of the lull, as well as the victim's conscious state, the undetected Haruto floated beside the man, sending her thoughts into his mind. *I can save you. Do you want to come with me?*

The forlorn man lifted his head slightly, silently asking, *Haruto?*

Billy? Haruto's heart jumped with joy! Billy was alive! For a moment, guilt overtook her. She realized she should have tried again and again to connect with his mind, because eventually she would have caught him at a moment when his consciousness wasn't overcome by the torturer's machine. But then she concluded this self-admonishment was a foolish waste of time. The only thing that mattered was she had found him alive.

Billy's thoughts called to her, *Thank, God, it's you! Get me out of here! No, wait!* He shared his concern with her, *I'm chipped. You can't risk leading them—*

It won't matter. Trust me. All right?

All right.

She put her unseen hand on his shoulder, making him invisible. Next, she imagined the black hood and microchip becoming physical. The black hood dropped onto the chair; and the microchip, which had been implanted under Billy's skin, fell to the floor. The room was silent as the microchip rolled across the floor, coming to a stop at the praying mantis's spiny foot. A small tap rang out, inadvertently mocking the torturer.

When Billy arrived at his new home in Alteria, the beauty of the lake and surrounding forest astounded him. This place was a splendid dream compared to the nightmare he had just endured within the aliens' grasp.

He gazed at Haruto, her dark brown eyes meeting his. They hugged each other tightly. After a long moment, Billy held her at arm's length, asking, "Where are we?"

"Inner earth."

He shielded his eyes to glance at the red ball in the odd-colored sky.

"It never moves," she told him. "Day or night, it stays right there at the top."

Billy was confounded, trying to soak it all in.

Zachary was relaxing under the shade of a tree, watching Eva play with her furry friends, when he noticed Billy's arrival. A smile swept across the young man's face. He jumped up, briskly strolling across the grass. He reached the newcomer, cheerfully saying, "Hello, Billy!"

They firmly shook hands.

Although normally a reserved man, Billy had tears in his eyes. His emotions were on overdrive because of all the torture and trauma he had endured. "Man, I've never been so glad to see you. Those aliens are fucked up!"

Zachary laughed. "Glad to see they didn't break your spirit, even if you do look like shit. And smell like it, too." He held his fingers under his nose to emphasize his point.

A look of concern crossed Billy's face. He stretched out his t-shirt, bringing it to his nose, taking a whiff. He winced, becoming self-conscious. Without saying a word, he jaunted down the lush knoll toward the lake.

Haruto and Zachary watched him wade into the water until it was waist deep, then dive beneath the surface.

Inspired by Billy's spontaneity, the two chased after him, rushing into the lake, laughing.

Billy came up for air. He undid his tangled braid, running his hands through his hair while dipping his head back into the water to wash it.

Zachary called out, "Hey! Stinky! Washed that smell off yet!?"

"What'd you say?" Billy swam toward his friend.

"Stinky!"

Billy splashed him.

"Hey!" Zachary splashed him back.

A full-fledged water fight ensued between them.

Haruto laughed until she cried. The water sprays cascaded around her.

Zachary dove into the water to escape the barrage.

Billy swam over to Haruto, his long black hair flowing behind him as he slid beside her. His handsome face glistened in the sun. With a low voice, choked by emotion, he said to her, "Thank you for saving me."

Her rosebud mouth widened into a smile as she wrapped her arms around him.

CHAPTER 22
Finding Shelter and Food

CECILE AND TOM appeared on a lonely strip of highway. Here, a Western trading post had been built out of logs, complete with a residential unit above the store. An oversized statue of a grinning cowboy, kicking up his heels, was affixed to the rooftop, its neon no longer glowing. A lone car was parked in the side parking lot. Behind the lot, a man stood at the base of a rusty windmill pumping water into a bucket.

At the opposite end of the trading post were numerous full-size teepees that had been set up as models on top of the dusty ground. Display signs stated the teepees were capable of sleeping ten or more people. The canvas walls were hand-painted with Native American warriors riding bareback, soaring eagles and mountain scenes. The interiors were furnished with Southwestern-styled blankets and pillows. Dreamcatchers dangled from the ceilings.

"How do you want to do this?" Tom asked his wife. "Take 'em or trade 'em?"

Cecile answered, "Trade 'em."

Thirty minutes later, the teepees were gone, and in exchange, loaded on the store's front porch next to the sun-bleached rocking chairs, were shrink-wrapped pallets of beer, beans and rice.

A fair trade.

The well-crafted, almost luxurious, teepees were relocated to the Bear Claw's new campsite in Alteria. The nomadic dwellings were positioned at one end of the lake—their nostalgic and noble presence beautifully complemented the natural surroundings, making the tribe members feel wealthy in spirit.

While Tom and Cecile assigned the living quarters, Zachary decided to make himself useful by getting food supplies. He transported himself to an unmanned distribution warehouse still untouched by looters. Sunlight streamed through the sidelights near the multi-story ceiling, highlighting the particles of dust. Rows of metal shelving held cardboard boxes, resting on palettes filled with food items, clothing, kitchen accessories and bath products.

The desolate building was spooky. Zachary could hear the ghosts of the former workers—echoes of their footsteps, conversations and forklift engines. But the sounds faded when he got to work, walking down the aisles to assess his choices. *Toothpaste. Toilet paper. Shampoo. Chips. Beer. Cereal.*

He found a palette of canned pinto beans. These were a necessity, so he decided they would be his first delivery.

Zachary brought the load back to the teepee that had been designated as both the pantry and kitchen. He placed the palette beside the slanting wall. The teepee was roomy, but this delivery took up a big portion of it. He decided to limit the next trip to boxes.

Adeelah peered through the flaps. "Wow! That's a lot of beans!"

Zachary chuckled. "It sure is, but I'm going back for more. Well, not beans. Other stuff. You want anything?"

"Yeah. I'd like to come."

209

"Um...sure. I could use some help, I guess."

He held out his hand. She shyly took it. Together, they went to the warehouse.

Adeelah looked around, mesmerized by the bounty of food and wares. She walked down an aisle, skimming the labels, mentioning each item, "Beets...spinach...green beans. You know, we barely had these essentials on the rez before the viro hit? Now look. We have all we need." She stopped talking, remembering the tragic events that had brought them to this place. She became ashamed. "All they needed" had come at too steep of a price. She solemnly said, "Things are never going to be the same. Are they?"

Not wanting to discuss the morose subject, Zachary changed it. "Did you know I used to live in the jungle?"

His out-of-the-blue comment snapped Adeelah out of her gloomy mood. She asked, "How'd you end up there?"

"Oh, the usual. I fell in love. Conchita was the shaman's daughter—beautiful, kind and courageous. We met in the spirit realm as Earth Sentinels. After our attempts to save the world failed miserably, I left my home in Pennsylvania, and traveled through the Amazon to find her. We had two children together, but the virus took our baby and her father, and...I don't know...she lost her mind with grief, I guess. She left me and Eva, and then the tribe threw us out."

"That's really sad."

"Yes, it is. And I got bit by an anaconda, and almost died from an infection."

"What!?"

"I know! Crazy, right? Well...the truth is, I didn't almost die. I did die."

Her eyes became wide with amazement. "Wow!"

"Yep, I saw the light at the end of the tunnel and everything."

Adeelah inquired, although she tried to seem casual about it, "So...you still married?"

Zachary hesitated to answer, realizing it would be the first time he said it out loud. "In the tribe, a woman divorces her husband by moving out. Pretty simple, really. She left. And that was that."

"I'm sorry. Both of my parents died. And my aunts and uncles, younger cousins and my grandmother. God, I miss them all so much." Tears welled up in her eyes.

He understood. Everyone had his or her own sad tale of woe and sorrow.

She lowered her head, letting her long black hair fall in front of her face to hide her tears. Zachary walked up to Adeelah, holding her. She sobbed into his chest. They stood in the middle of the gigantic warehouse, overshadowed by the tall racks, sheltering themselves from the pain of the past.

After she had a good cry, he released her, asking, "Ready to get to work?"

Adeelah gave him a slight smile as she wiped away her tears. "Sure."

The pair made numerous trips back and forth. After the last one, Adeelah left to tell her friends about the snacks that had arrived. Meanwhile, Zachary examined their handiwork. The inner earth's sun softly glowed through the canvas walls, illuminating the stockpiles of canned fruit and vegetables, tuna, flour, sugar, salsa, chips, juices, and bags of rice. He felt good about the food situation.

Eva peeked through the teepee flaps. Jabbar was perched on her shoulder with his tail curled around her neck. The spotted jaguar stood behind them making deep purring sounds, which caused Zachary's heart to skip a beat. He fought against his instinct to run from the predator, instead smiling at his daughter, who asked him, "Did you get something for me?"

"As a matter of fact, I did." He rummaged through the boxes, looking for a particular one. While his back was turned, the teenagers, led by Adeelah, appeared behind the little girl, jostling with each other, anxious to see what goodies would be handed out. When Zachary spun around with a lollipop between his fingers, he was surprised to see the older kids eyeing the treat meant for Eva, but he knew the situation could be easily remedied. He jokingly said to them, "But wait! There's more!" as he motioned like a game-show host. He dug through the box again, grabbing a handful of lollipops, which he held out to the teenagers who eagerly snatched his or her favorite flavor.

Eva took one, although she wasn't sure what to do with it until she watched Manuel unwrap a ball of flavored sugar and stick it in his mouth. She followed his example. As soon as the sucker touched her tongue, her eyes lit up. "Yum!"

The monkey pouted. His mouth turned down at the corners, the tips of his long white mustache coming together. He wanted a treat as well.

Eva pulled her sucker out of her mouth. "Daddy?"

"Yes?"

"Can Jabbar have one, too?"

The monkey stared earnestly at the keeper of the food, who responded, "Of course." Zachary rummaged through the box again, thinking, *He'd probably like a fruity one. Ah, here's pineapple.* He removed the wrapper, handing it to the tiny monkey, who licked the lollipop, bobbing with excitement.

"Daddy?"

"Yes?"

"Ferta's hungry, too."

This comment caught Zachary's full attention. Nobody wanted a hungry jaguar roaming the village. Ferta stared at the young man while licking her chops. This made him even more nervous. "Okay, pumpkin, I'll go get cat food for her." Before leaving, he emphasized, "Don't go anywhere. Okay? I'll be right back," then he disappeared.

The big cat narrowed her eyes and flicked her tail, believing she had been left out. Eva consoled her friend. "Don't worry," she said, mimicking her father, "He'll be right back."

CHAPTER 23
Revisiting Japan

THE MIKOS HAD gathered at a table in the vast dining hall meant for a hundred monks. They were quietly eating rice drizzled with honey, vegetable soup, and hard-boiled eggs laid by their own chickens. Steam wafted out of their mugs brimming with green tea.

Konomi gazed out the expansive set of windows, viewing the foothills in the distance. The young woman was experiencing pangs of guilt over the last argument she had with Haruto. She replayed the scene in her mind, remembering her demands that Haruto leave before the soldiers returned and detected her mutant DNA. Haruto's sad face haunted her.

The young Miko was startled out of her thoughts when the semi-transparent Haruto appeared in the dining hall. A smile came over Konomi's face as she rushed to her friend whose arrival somehow implied forgiveness. She wanted to hug Haruto, but was unsure of how to touch her spectral body, so she simply stood beside her, gushing, "It's so good to see you!"

The other women got up to greet Haruto as well, crowding around their fugitive cohort.

The oldest, Hoshino, took the lead, inquiring, "Tell us, how have you been?"

Haruto replied, "I've been fine. And you?"

"We're fine, thank you. Can you tell us what's going on out there? We heard on the radio that martial law is still in effect, and they're working to restore order."

"The truth and what you're told are two different things."

"What do you mean?"

"It's a long story. Please sit down, and I'll tell you all about it."

The women apprehensively returned to their seats, wondering what bad news awaited them.

Haruto took her usual place at the head of the table, opposite of Hoshino. Her ghostly body perched on her chair. "What I'm about to say is most unusual, so please keep an open mind."

"Of course, we will," said Hoshino.

"There is a much bigger problem in this world than just recovering from an epidemic and things returning to normal, which isn't going to happen by the way, because the virus was purposely spread."

215

Hoshino was skeptical. "Who would do such a thing?"

"Aliens. Aliens spread the virus."

The women remained quiet, wondering if the virus had damaged Haruto's brain or if the trauma of being taken by the soldiers had led to this bizarre claim of aliens.

Haruto continued, "The virus was meant to kill the humans least useful to their agenda—the youngest and the oldest. These aliens have been manipulating our bodies since the beginning of time. Their agenda has always been to create hybrids that connect to their hive mind—"

"Wait," Hoshino interrupted. "Aliens? A hive mind?"

"I'm not explaining this very well. Perhaps I should start over."

"No, please keep going." Hoshino did not want to extend this conversation any longer than necessary.

"Very well. These hybrids look just like us, except they are connected to the aliens' hive mind and hold positions of power. For instance, the UN leaders overseeing our soldiers are hybrids."

The Mikos had seen the fair-haired UN leader with their own eyes, and there was no doubt in their minds he was human.

Haruto sensed their reluctance to believe her, but she persevered, "Those who don't connect to the hive mind are put into detainment camps or prisons, or made part of horrific experiments, and then eaten. Do you remember the Earth Sentinels?"

"Of course, we do," replied Hoshino.

"Well, Tom and Cecile rescued their tribe from a detainment camp, and brought them to a safe place, and I would like to do the same for you. You could live with the others and me. I think you would like it there. It's beautiful, much like here."

Hoshino resisted the idea. She thought of her vegetable garden, and the way the sun shone in her room each morning. And how she felt like a queen when she descended the stone staircase. She didn't want to leave this temple and go with Haruto to some unknown destination. "It seems silly to leave our home when we're safe here."

"I don't think you are safe—not in the long run. The world is being run by aliens, who think of humans as a food source. And those UN leaders are aliens in human form. With them controlling the armies, nothing can stop them from doing whatever they want."

"Haruto..." Hoshino sighed. "It's hard to argue with something so ridiculous. This is crazy talk! The soldiers already came here after you left, and, as you can see, we're fine. I think it's far more dangerous to be wherever you are. Aren't you the one the soldiers are looking for?"

The other women averted their eyes, embarrassed, because they agreed with Hoshino's rhetorical question.

"I felt it was safe enough to take Billy there," Haruto said, defending her offer to relocate her fellow Mikos.

"Oh, I'm so glad Billy's all right," Konomi politely mentioned.

Haruto gave the young woman a half-smile, knowing her fellow Miko never really cared for him. "Yes, he's fine now, but I saved him from being tortured by those aliens, and I'm afraid of what they might do to you. I strongly urge you to come with me. There's a good chance the soldiers will come here again, if only because of me rescuing Billy."

"If you're not here, I think we'll be all right." Hoshino's words were tinged with aggression as she boldly stepped into her role as the permanent leader now that it was obvious Haruto would no longer be living among them. "Thank you for your kind offer, but we will stay here for now."

"You know me. Have I ever led you astray?"

"You've been under a lot of pressure lately. Let's drop the subject. Okay?"

Haruto was disappointed. These women were like family to her, but she respected their right to decide for themselves. "I wish you well. If you should change your mind, call to me in your dreams." She bowed, then disappeared from their sight.

In the parsonage living room, among the mahogany bookcases and leather furniture, Father Chong sat praying in his favorite high-back chair. He was so engrossed that he didn't notice when the semi-transparent Haruto appeared, standing nearby. She had come to visit her friend, mostly because he had crossed her mind while she was visiting the Mikos. She patiently waited for him to finish, watching his lips fervently move, but after a minute had passed and he showed no signs of wrapping it up, she began to feel like an interloper so she cleared her throat to announce her presence.

The priest's eyes snapped open as he yelped in surprise, startled by what he believed to be an intruder. When he saw it was only Haruto, he released a deep sigh of relief, putting his hand over his pounding heart. "Oh, my goodness, you scared me."

"I'm so sorry, Father. I didn't mean to—"

"No, no, it's fine. I understand. Where are my manners?" He stood up, motioning with his hand. "Please have a seat. It's good to see you again. Tell me how you've been." He lowered himself back into his chair, ready to listen.

Haruto sat on the edge of the leather sofa, clasping her ethereal hands on her lap. "Father, so much has happened that I don't know where to begin. How about you? Any news on when the church will reopen its doors?"

"Funny, you should ask. That's just what I was praying about." He reached over, picking up a Bible from the coffee table, displaying its cover to her, which, for some reason, seemed to trouble him deeply, yet it looked like an ordinary cover to Haruto so she didn't understand his concern.

The priest used his finger to underline the title, *New World Version, Holy Scriptures.* "They've changed it," he explained. "They changed the Bible! Can you believe that? Sure they've

218

removed or added books over the centuries. For example, when they translated it from Hebrew to English, but now they've given me a version where the New Testament has been completely removed!" He repeated, "Removed!" to emphasize his point. "This is sacrilege! They told me the new Pope mandated this change, but I don't believe them. He would never do such a thing."

Haruto wasn't sure how to respond, or even if she fully understood, so she suggested, "Perhaps you should start at the beginning."

"Yes, yes, of course." He took a deep breath, then began, "A UN leader and bishop visited me this morning. Sat right where you're sitting. They brought along several armed soldiers who stayed near the door, which I found odd. Then the bishop announced this new version." Father Chong tapped the book that was lying on the coffee table for clarification. "He told me how the United Nations wants only one religion to unite the people during this time of crisis. They took the Old Testament and combined it with the Torah and Quran to create a single holy book. All the major religions mishmashed together. Like it was a stew or something.

"The most disturbing part is the bishop told me the changes were mandatory. That the priests from this point forward needed to act as intermediaries between the people and God, removing Jesus totally from the equation. This goes against the whole foundation of Catholicism."

He rubbed his forehead with frustration. "Maybe I should just hang up my frock and teach at the university when it reopens. I can't profess something I don't believe in." He shook his head. "This is what happens when religion gets mixed up with politics. Truth doesn't matter."

219

Haruto felt she should warn the priest that his decision to step down would, in her opinion, endanger his life, so she said to him, "This may be related. You remember me telling you about being taken to the alien laboratory in the underground subway? It was the day I became invisible—"

"That day will be etched in my brain forever."

"Yes, well, after I left here, I met up with my old friends, who also mutated—"

"Wait a minute. There's more like you? Who just happen to be your friends? That's a pretty wild coincidence."

"Normally, it would be, but you see, I met these people when I joined the Earth Sentinels...the Storm Creators." She let the information sink in.

A new awareness dawned in the priest's mind. He, like most of the world, had heard of the Earth Sentinels when they created the supernatural storms to grab the governments' attention. He was visibly impressed. "You're an Earth Sentinel? Why didn't you say so before?"

She shrugged. "Not everyone was overly fond of us. And, in my opinion, the mission didn't go so well."

"But still, it was an amazing effort," Father Chong complimented her. "I feel like having you autograph my recycling can or something," he joked to lighten the mood.

His comment amused Haruto.

The priest became serious again, asking, "So you think aliens have something to do with the new Bible?"

"Yes."

He was doubtful, but decided to keep an open mind. "In order to hear the rest of this, I think I need a smoke. Do you mind? It calms my nerves."

"Feel free."

The priest selected a pipe from the stand on the coffee table, packing it with tobacco while Haruto explained, "Bechard was the leader of the Earth Sentinels—"

"Wait, I remember him. He's a fallen angel, isn't he?"

Haruto nodded.

A shiver went down the priest's spine. He couldn't shake his preconceived notion of fallen angels being demons. "What's he like? This Bechard character."

"Hmmm. Well...let's just say he's trying. But I have so much more to tell you."

He lit his pipe with a match, took a puff, then exhaled, saying, "Then start at the beginning."

So Haruto did. "Hundreds of thousands of years ago, the Anunnaki flew to earth from their planet Nibiru—"

"Hundreds of thousands of years? How long is this going to take?"

She smiled. "Trust me, it won't take that long."

"All right, then. Proceed."

"Their planet crosses our solar system every 3,600 years—"

"So you're saying we have an additional planet?"

"Yes. With a very long elliptical orbit. The Anunnaki traveled here to mine for gold, but the digging took too long. Something about gravity making the work difficult and the workers revolting. But the Anunnaki needed the gold to replenish their dissipating atmosphere, so they genetically altered the next available species— our ancestors, the Neanderthals—splicing their genes with their own to create slave laborers. These were the predecessors to

Modern Man."

The priest choked on his pipe smoke. After his coughing calmed down, he took a sip of tea to clear his throat, then, speaking in a hoarse voice, he said, "You're trying to tell me that we were created by aliens. And not God?"

"Yes and no."

"Make up your mind!"

"Well, what I'm trying to say is, the Anunnaki came to earth, genetically modified the cavemen, and then declared themselves to be gods over their newly created slaves. It was easy for them to do. The Anunnaki aged so slowly they seemed immortal. They were nearly nine-feet tall, and brought amazing technology with them. And on top of all that, their first creations had no history to draw from. No point of reference. No longer Neanderthals, they had lost their connection to the earth. They were like ducklings hatching out of eggs—imprinted by the first creatures they saw— believing everything they were told."

"Well, I think you're wrong about this one."

Because of her disastrous conversation with the Mikos, Haruto felt she needed to push her point a little harder. She did not want anything bad to happen to Father Chong should he decide to step down from the church. "I wish I were wrong. I really do. I know this is difficult for you, but from what I've seen, I don't think I am. Please, let me explain."

"If you must." The priest bit tightly on his pipe stem as he braced himself to listen to her words.

She asked, "Can I borrow this?" pointing to the old unrevised Bible setting on the coffee table.

"Sure." He picked it up, handing it to her.

Haruto opened the Bible to the first book of Genesis. Her semi-physical hands flipped through the pages. She quickly found the verse she wanted to share with him. "What I'm about to say makes more sense if you replace all the references of 'God' with the word 'Anunnaki'."

"What?"

"Stay with me. For instance, here where it says, 'And the Lord God took the man, and put him into the garden of Eden to *till it* and to *keep it*.'" She looked up at the priest, saying, "Even the Bible states man was made to work for his *god*."

"I prefer the word 'serve', but that hardly proves anything."

"Yes, not in and of itself, but I also learned from Bechard that the first humans weren't able to have children. They were sterile like mules. The Anunnaki preferred it this way because it helped them to keep the slave population in check, especially since they were living to be nearly a thousand years old. You have references in the Bible of men living this long.

"So anyway, everything was going great for the Anunnaki until another race interfered. This race, the reptilian Dracos, the serpent, snuck into the garden to tempt Eve, who was hard at *work, serving* her god."

The priest noticed Haruto's little dig.

"Of course, there was more than one Eve, but, to keep this simple, I'll refer to the collective as one." Haruto continued reading from the Bible, "'And the serpent said unto the woman, ye shall not surely die; For God doth know that in the day ye eat thereof, then your eyes shall be opened, and ye shall be as God...'" She expanded on this passage, "'Ye shall be as God,' signifies the ability to procreate like their Anunnaki masters, who had proclaimed themselves to be God. If you read further, to where the Bible says, 'Adam and Eve became aware of their nakedness.' It means they became aware of their ability to have sex and reproduce."

"I know what the Bible says," commented Father Chong with a hint of irritation. "But your interpretation is a bit of a stretch since the Bible also says that God commanded them to be fruitful and multiply. They couldn't do that if they were sterile."

Haruto argued, "Yes, but there's no mention of children until *after* 'the fall', and even then, God curses the woman—telling her that childbirth will cause her sorrow, and throws her and Adam out of the Garden of Eden."

"But that's only because she listened to the serpent—"

"Exactly. Eve ate the fruit from the Tree of Life. The tree represents our DNA. She agreed to the Dracos' genetic modification that allowed her to have children, and then she got the man to go along with it. Nowhere before 'the fall' does the Bible mention Adam and Eve having children. It's only afterwards."

"But Adam and Eve in the Bible existed only 10,000 years ago. Yet your timeline involves hundreds of thousands of years."

"The Bible references a specific lineage. Obviously, there were other people already in existence. Adam and Eve's children had to marry someone, right? The text is a strange combination of the original events and later descendants, which makes it confusing. The story leaps from the beginning and bypasses 200,000 years—"

"I don't care what you say. I've heard God's voice. I *know* he exists. And I know he's not an alien."

"Father, I believe in a divine Creator as well, but not the

one from your Old Testament, which I believe was a cruel hoax inflicted on the unsuspecting genetically altered humans to make them submissive and obedient. Even the Anunnaki geneticists must have believed in something bigger than themselves. Surely, they had a god or gods they worshipped."

He shrugged.

Haruto said, "Back to my original concern. I believe quitting the church could be very dangerous for you. The reason I say that is the Dracos, the serpent of the Bible, will kill anyone who threatens their agenda. They have been busy altering our genetics since the beginning. Busy creating hybrid humans that will align to their hive mind. They're not going to risk—"

"What is all this? Hybrids? Hive mind?"

"Another name for the hive mind would be 'collective consciousness'. The hive mind is what the Dracos consider to be their legacy because earth's conditions have been slowly taking its toll on their reptilian bodies. To continue as a species, they've decided to reside within the human form, which they consider inferior, but necessary for perpetuating their hive mind. Those who connect with the hive mind are rewarded with positions of power, and those who don't either get eaten or work in the mines, and then get eaten."

"Eating hybrid humans? I'm confused. Are they eating their own kind or humans?"

"It is confusing, because we're all hybrids to some degree. To make this conversation less confusing, I'll refer to those who are fully connected to the hive mind as hybrids, and everyone else as humans."

Haruto took a breather, then said, "Let me sum it up for

225

you. First, the Anunnaki genetically modified the Neanderthals to create sterile human slaves, which the Dracos later modified. Their modification allowed us to procreate, but it also altered part of our brain, referred to as the Reptilian Brain. The Dracos continued refining mankind during our evolution until some of us fully connected to their hive mind. For example, the UN leaders are hybrids who are carrying out the Dracos' agenda, which includes religion, it seems.

"Keep in mind the Bible, Quran and Torah all speak of the same alien god, so combining them wouldn't be that difficult." She paused. "But if you think about it, it would have taken more than a month to compile, translate and print the New World Version they just gave you. They must have planned all of this long ago."

Overwrought, the priest slumped in his chair. Haruto had painted a picture he didn't find very attractive. He rubbed his forehead, mentioning, "Today has been awful. I'm getting a headache." He sighed.

Haruto was worried about him. "I can stop if you—"

"No, no, it's like a Band-Aid, just rip it off."

"All right. My point is, the Dracos will use you, me or anyone to reach their goal of total domination of this planet. Do you really think you have a choice about which version of the Bible you can use? Most likely the bishop is a hybrid. And worst of all—"

"There's more?"

"Unfortunately. And this is the worst one of them all. The Dracos have technology that allows them to extract a person's soul, or consciousness, or whatever you want to call it, and insert it into a hybrid fetus."

Father Chong weakly said, "That's not possible. Only God

controls our souls."

"But I've seen it—" Haruto stopped talking when she noticed how pale his face had become. "Do you need some water?"

The distraught priest wasn't listening anymore. "I need to lie down." He placed his cold pipe in the ashtray, then stood up without saying another word, walking to the stairs, slowly climbing them.

CHAPTER 24
Faulty Alliances

THE CRYSTAL SANCTUARY walls glistened around the Earth Sentinels, who faced the twelve Galactic Council members standing on the crescent-shaped platform. It was time to begin the discussion that would impact mankind's fate for better or worse.

The leader, Synege, clasped her palms together. "Greetings. It is good to see you again. We understand the rescue was successful."

Cecile answered, "There were a few serious problems, but everyone is safe."

"We are glad to hear this."

"Thank you."

"And are you settling into your new home?"

"Yes, it's beautiful."

"Wonderful."

Bechard materialized in the room, standing tall beside Zachary. "Greetings, everyone. Sorry, I'm late."

"Hello, Bechard." Zachary held out his hand.

The fallen angel reached down and shook it firmly. "As always, a pleasure."

Tom and Billy acknowledged Bechard with a nod of their heads.

Synege said, "It is good to have all of you here, although we, like you, wish it were under better circumstances. As you are aware, the Dracos' UN leaders are controlling the human armies, and it's only a matter of time before the armies are unleashed to destroy the fallen angels' domain, and then our Alteria. We believe the most effective way to stop the Dracos would be to dismantle their hive mind. This would unlink them from the UN leaders and all the other hybrids on this planet. But, in order to dismantle the hive mind, we need something the fallen angels possess. Something they stole eons ago. Let me show you what I am talking about." She gracefully waved her arms, and beams of light streamed down from the ceiling, banding together, forming into a holographic movie, playing in the center of the room. She said, "This is a scene from long ago."

The Giza pyramids appeared in the three-dimensional projection, but, instead of desolate sand, lush gardens surrounded the giant structures. The Great Pyramid had a gold-clad capstone with a beam of light shooting out of its peak, streaming toward the heavens. Standing at its foundation were two young fallen angels wearing black robes. One of them pressed his hand against the slanted wall. An enormous block of granite swiveled open, revealing a hidden doorway.

The fallen angels stepped through the gap. They stormed down the narrow sloped passageway dimly lit by a golden glow coming from deep within the center, growing brighter as they moved along. Their black-tipped wings brushed against the walls.

Meanwhile, within the guts of the pyramid was a room with a high gabled ceiling. Here, two priests prayed over a milky stone highlighted with swirling flecks that radiated the colors of the rainbow. The stone was kept inside a large chest made of gilded acacia-wood, which was stored in a granite crypt the size of a man's

229

coffin. Without the chest's lid in place, the stone's intense golden light illuminated the priests' faces and their garments, which were finely woven out of pure strands of gold intertwined with blue, purple and scarlet linen threads to create beautiful patterns. Each of their waists was cinched with an embroidered belt. The bells sewn on the hems jingled when they moved. To counteract the stone's overpowering and potentially deadly energy, the priests wore long gold chains that draped over their shoulders and down their bodies, touching the granite floor to ground them. Their heads were crowned with elaborate turbans worn for the glory of their god. Incense burned, and multiple layers of goat-hair curtains lined the walls.

A booming voice, riddled with static, transmitted through the milky stone. "By the sweat of your brow, secure the stone and conceal it before the fallen ones taketh it."

A priest answered, "As you command, O Lord of the gods."

The transmission ended. Only the hum of the stone's energy remained.

After making the sign of the cross with their hands, the priests reverently walked across the room to retrieve the chest's weighty gold-clad lid, adorned with statues of angels in prayer, which rested on two wooden poles lying on the floor.

The priests transferred the ornate lid over to the chest, lowering it in place. Entombed, the stone's humming sound was muffled, and only a few rays of light filtered through the seams.

The fallen angels stormed out of the darkened passageway, stopping at the threshold, sensing the danger of entering the dimly lit sanctuary.

A priest called out to the intruders, "This is the Lord's house.

You have no right to be here."

The fallen angels examined the room, their eyes settling on the chest.

"You'll die if you come closer," the priest warned them, but his eyes unintentionally glanced at the lid, knowing his cautionary words were no longer true. The lid imprisoned the stone's powers. The fallen angels knew it as well.

Without saying a word, one of the fallen angels drew his sword from his sheath, expertly throwing it. The blade circled through the air like a rotary knife, slicing through the priest's neck above his gold chains.

It was a clean cut.

The priest's head toppled, dropping along with his body to the floor, the bells on his robe clanking. The sword continued flying through the air, cutting through several layers of goat-hair curtains before falling to the floor, clanking as it hit.

231

The other priest sought cover, running toward the chest, attempting to pull the lid off single-handedly, but, before he could, the second fallen angel expertly threw his spinning sword, lopping off his head.

Boldly entering the room, the fallen angels stepped over the decapitated bodies, severed heads and pools of blood to retrieve their swords, then picked up the two wooden poles from off the floor, which they thrust through the rings on each corner of the chest. With their great strength, they hoisted the heavy chest out of the crypt, carrying the mouthpiece to the gods out of the room.

The holographic scene abruptly came to a standstill, blurring into rays of light, fading from view.

Synege expanded on what they had just seen, "The chest stolen by the fallen angels contained the Destiny Stone. This unique mineral entity was brought to earth from the planet Nibiru. It was used to facilitate the communications between the Anunnaki's home planet and their kingdom here on earth, but what interests us the most is the stone's ability to amplify the earth's vibrations. It did back then, and will do so again when it is returned to its rightful place in the pyramid. Unfortunately, it's not the only piece to the puzzle. There are crystals that also need to be placed back into the sacred vortexes around the planet. But the Destiny Stone is the keystone. Once the stone and crystals are in place, we expect earth's vibrations to rise and dissolve the Dracos' hive mind, and thereby relinquishing their control over the UN leaders and other hybrids."

232

Zachary asked, "But you're not sure?"

"We are sure. When the Destiny Stone resided within the pyramid, so very long ago, the hive mind was rendered inoperable because the earth's vibrations were too high for it to function."

"But why did the fallen angels steal it? Didn't they consider it might awaken the hive mind?"

"We do not know for certain why the fallen angels stole it. They may have thought they could harness the stone's powers to restore their aging bodies, but, judging from their current appearance, they were unsuccessful. Another possibility is they used the stone to communicate with others on their home planet. Regarding the hive mind, we can only assume the fallen angels didn't want it to work again, but perhaps, they felt the trade off was worth it, because, at that time, the Dracos were not much of a threat."

"They were wrong about that," Telphane uttered, the ethereal being's voice trickling through everyone's minds.

"Yes, they underestimated the Dracos."

Geet, the elephant man, wrapped his thick arms around his large belly, his stubby fingers clasped as he spoke solemnly, "We need to keep in mind, the Dracos know where all the sacred vortexes are. Now that they control the human armies, they could easily steal, maybe even destroy, the stone and crystals."

"I don't understand how a stone and crystals could raise the earth's vibrations," Zachary confessed. "I mean the earth is huge! How could such small stones have that kind of power?"

Synege said to Geet, "Please explain it so he and the others can better understand."

Geet flapped his large ears and nodded. "I would be glad to." He began, "There are many pyramids around the world besides those in Egypt." The shimmering lights of the holographic movie danced, causing the image to change. A small island off the southern coast of Yonaguni, Japan, appeared. The scene dipped beneath the Pacific Ocean, heading to the seafloor where the submerged ruins and canals, created out of mammoth blocks of granite, lay in waste and covered with algae. Fish darted in and out of the ancient rubble that once had stood proudly as pyramids.

Geet continued, "These pyramids are just a few of those that have been lost to time. Some still stand, like those in Egypt, while others have been restored, such as the Mayan pyramids in Chichen Itza. Pyramids were very popular for marking the sacred spots because stone is durable and a great vibrational conductor, but not all the markers were pyramids, such as this one at Easter Island."

A remote uninhabited island off the coast of Chile appeared in the holographic projection. Huge stone bodies with oversized

233

heads, partially buried in the ground, stood along the shoreline as if waiting for their gods to return. Geet explained, "These figures were carved out of volcanic rock. The people understood the sacredness of this locale and honored it. And while these carvings are a beautiful testament, they are not capable of raising earth's vibrations. That was done by a crystal, the size of a man's body, which was buried inland between the volcanoes and the sea. The crystal was taken and stored by us after the Destiny Stone was stolen. We hoped to replace it one day."

Synege said, "Hopefully that day is now."

"Yes, indeed." Geet continued, "All of the vortexes are marked in some way. Some of the markers are ancient, and some are more recent. For example, cathedrals and castles, the Vatican, and even the U.S. Capitol are built on top of sacred vortexes. In addition, some of the markers are natural, such as Mount Shasta.

"All of the sacred vortexes are connected by ley lines, also known as the earth's energy grid. Once the crystals and Destiny Stone are returned to their rightful places, they will connect with the earth's vibrations, working in harmony to raise it. And because the quartz crystals are piezoelectric, they can convert one form of energy into another. Quartz is also an excellent transmitter and amplifier. The ancient crystals are especially powerful, which is why we have carefully hidden them."

"Thank you, Geet," said Synege, then she addressed the Earth Sentinels, "The council is wondering if one of you would be willing to try to locate the Destiny Stone and steal it back?"

Tom responded, "Sure, I'll give it a try."

"Thank you, but before you do, a word of caution. Make sure the stone remains in the chest. Do not touch the stone. Its power has killed many."

The man raised his eyebrows, thinking the warning should have been given first, but he still accepted the task, closing his eyes, hoping a vision would present itself. The others waited with bated anticipation. Cecile studied her husband, concerned for his safety. A minute passed, but Tom had not gone anywhere. When he opened his eyes, he didn't seem pleased. "The stone sits in a chest inside a cavern. The walls are covered with what looks like ice, but I'm not sure. The vision was hazy. I couldn't tell where it was, and I couldn't connect with the stone well enough to go there."

Phosulent commented, a thousand points of light moving his lips, "A force field must be in place."

Synege asked, "Could you try again? Perhaps look outside the cavern and describe the scenery. We might recognize the location from your description."

Tom nodded, closing his eyes once more. But a short while later, he gave up, shaking his head with frustration. He told the others, "The farther I pulled away, the fuzzier it got until the connection just quit."

"Well, that is disappointing. This was our best option." Synege sighed, seeming unsure of which direction to move from this point. "Would someone else like to see if they have better luck?"

"I'll give it a try," Haruto said. She closed her eyes, silently calling to the stone. She saw a fuzzy scene of the chest in a dark cave. She heard the stone call to her, saying, *Help me!* But the woman was unable to do more than that. Haruto gave up trying, and said to the group, "I can't connect either. I'm sorry."

"Thank you for trying, Haruto," Synege replied.

"The stone could be anywhere," stated Geet. "We're not even sure if it's hidden on this planet."

Synege nodded her bald head. "True, but our mission will be very difficult, maybe even impossible, without that stone. We will have to offer the fallen angels something of value in exchange for it, because without it, we will never dismantle the Dracos' hive mind. And if we don't do it now, I'm afraid it will never be possible, which puts Alteria in grave danger."

"Trade something of value?" Zachary was confused. "Like what?"

"What do we have the fallen angels would want?" Tom asked.

The other council members lowered their heads, knowing the seriousness of what Synege was about to suggest. "We can offer them our protection."

"Protection!?" Zachary cried out in disbelief. "But they're the enemy!"

Synege was troubled by her own suggestion as well.

"Protection from who?" Billy asked.

"From the human armies. The Dracos will surely order them to attack the fallen angels. The reptilians are extremely territorial, and will eliminate their competitors now that they can. But they won't stop there. They will attack us next. However, we have a plan. One that should take the least amount of life possible. If it goes well, less than a thousand hybrids will die, plus the Dracos."

"How many Dracos are there?" Cecile asked.

"Approximately a hundred ancient bodies. It is a small number, but the Dracos control millions of soldiers and hybrids. That is our main problem."

"I don't understand how the Dracos gained such power with

so few numbers."

Faylinn fluttered her fairy wings, in her high-pitched voice she asked the council leader, "Would you like me to explain it to them?"

Synege nodded.

Faylinn began, "The Dracos, after genetically manipulating the Anunnaki's Adams and Eves, bided their time, living unnoticed on the fringes. They knew the Anunnaki and other alien races were capable of being mortally wounded, which happened quite often in their endless petty battles. It was only a matter of time before the gods dwindled in numbers or returned home. So the Dracos waited. Once the gods were gone, the lofty lizards claimed their spot at the top of the food chain—"

Zachary interrupted, "But didn't the outcast fallen angels also remain?"

"Yes, thank you for pointing that out. The rebels who were left behind by the Anunnaki wisely remained hidden from sight. The Dracos, on the other hand, didn't handle their power well and ran amuck, devouring people in broad daylight. Needless to say, this did not bode well with the humans, who ganged together, sometimes whole clans or villages, killing them on sight. The great legends of 'slaying the dragon' are based on this time period. The hunts were relentless. The Dracos were driven underground. They couldn't live here in Alteria—we refused their presence. And the fallen angels, who live in the northern region of inner earth, refused them as well. Out of options, the Dracos created a subterranean tunnel system around the world, which still exists today."

Synege stepped into the conversation. "The Dracos have never benefited mankind in any way. Their genetic mutations of humans were solely for the purpose of creating living vessels, hybrids, that one day would perpetuate their hive mind. Earth's environment had taken its toll on their alien reptilian bodies, and they knew it was only a matter of time before their species died out completely. If that happened, they would live out their days trapped within the hive mind with no physical bodies—an endless purgatory. They absolutely needed the hybrid program to work if they were to enjoy life in a body."

Telphane said, "Not everyone worries about having a physical body." The being's beige essence flickered.

"The Dracos have a primitive mind set, Telphane," Synege commented. "You know that." She spoke to the Earth Sentinels again, "Granted, the Anunnaki weren't much better—creating you to be their workforce, but on the other side of that coin, even as they let you repopulate after the flood, they knew that one day you would free yourselves. The earth's short orbit around the sun speeds up your evolution—physically, mentally and spiritually. The Anunnaki felt your upgrade and eventual freedom was their gift to you as repayment for your enslavement. Keep in mind, the 250,000 years since your inception is just seventy years on their planet."

Billy spouted angrily, "You can't just mess with people's DNA and make them slaves, then tell them it's a favor!" He stopped talking, shaking his head, realizing it was pointless to be mad at the ancient astronauts whose planet had been destroyed. They were all dead. He lifted his black hat, smoothing his hair back, his face still flush with anger.

"Of course not. I'm not justifying their actions," Synege stated.

"The Anunnaki went against the universal Law of Oneness, and their actions had devastating effects on this planet as well as their own. In addition, the Anunnaki rebels, the fallen angels, who were exiled here on earth are much less palatable than your original creators. Without a doubt, the fallen angels are untrustworthy and sinister," she paused before adding, "but they possess the Destiny Stone."

"'Which way to turn?' wondered the windmill." Guru was speaking in riddles. "We seek to manipulate the manipulators. Round and round we go."

Synege looked at him with her large green eyes, contemplating his cryptic message. "It's a vicious cycle we hope to break free of once we raise earth's vibrations. Unfortunately, with the Dracos' UN leaders controlling the human armies, we cannot install the crystals, or the Destiny Stone once we have it, because all of these precious catalysts would be in danger of being stolen or destroyed by the Dracos before the process was completed. The easiest and least bloody way to ensure we can install the stones is to kill the Dracos and the UN leaders first. However, because we are unable to steal the Destiny Stone from the fallen angels, we do not have any choice other than to offer them our protection in exchange for the stone. But this mission would require a great service from you, Earth Sentinels."

Tom, Cecile, Zachary, Haruto and Billy became apprehensive, wondering what Synege was about to ask of them.

"Are you willing to escort our Alterian warriors directly into the lairs of the Draco leaders so they can assassinate them? And the same with the UN leaders? And then install the UN impostors? Only then will we control the armies."

239

Haruto said, "I knew it! Every time we get together, we always end up fighting someone. Well, I'm not doing it. Last time, we almost cost people their lives, and gained very little for our efforts."

Synege responded to Haruto's outburst, "This plan is not ideal, but the Dracos' actions are causing all of mankind to suffer as we speak. If they attack us, the casualties will be in the millions. Compare all those lives to a mere hundred Dracos and a thousand UN leaders. A fair exchange if you ask me. Yes, there will be blood on our hands, but much less than the number of humans slaughtered for food every single day, not to mention the billions killed by the virus. How many more have to suffer and die?"

She turned her head, speaking to all of the Earth Sentinels before her, "Without you, we won't succeed. You are needed to transport our warriors. Otherwise, we will never find the Dracos hidden within the tunnels—not in time to implement our plan."

Tom asked her, "Who would replace the UN leaders?"

"The council recommends recruiting your Earth Sentinel members. These are people who have fought bravely with you and proven their loyalty."

Tom continued his line of questioning, "But would we need to install the stone if the Dracos and UN leaders are killed? Perhaps we could do this on our own without offering the fallen angels our protection."

"I wish it were possible, but after the Dracos are killed, their spirits will still have access to the hive mind. They would simply instruct the next hybrids in line to take the dead UN leaders' places. The Destiny Stone is needed to shut down the hive mind. By killing and replacing the UN leaders, we will hopefully interrupt their communications long enough for the earth's vibrations to rise. We will only have a small window of time before they realize what we have done. We must work quickly."

Geet added, "Kill those at the top and hope the rest scatter."

Cecile offered her opinion, "Killing the Dracos and UN leaders sounds like a fine plan until it's actually time to plunge the sword."

"To attack anyone is to attack one's self," Guru said to no one in particular.

"To me, it's unacceptable," Haruto uttered.

Tom shook his head, displeased, saying to the council, "So the only plan you have is to trade with the flying bastards, and have us transport your warriors to kill the Dracos and their UN hybrids, and then replace them?"

Gladise added, "And install the stones."

Synege pointed out, "War makes for strange bedfellows. And don't forget, you are now Alterian citizens. These are your warriors as well." She then directed a question at the fallen angel in their midst, "Bechard, would you be willing to handle the negotiations?"

"I would be honored," he replied, "but you know it is unlikely Abaddon will agree to this proposal, even with Hagsmar's safety at stake."

She replied, "You are a master negotiator, Bechard. If anyone can get him to agree to this, it is you."

"Bechard?" Zachary called to him.

"Yes?"

"This is even worse than the first time we got together."

Bechard remained silent, knowing that despite their best

efforts, everything was, once again, going straight to hell.

Cecile complained, "And when we're done, what will change? Will mankind continue to fight wars that don't benefit them—all for forces they don't even know exist?"

"When this is finished," Synege said, "we will petition the senate to hand the reins over to us instead of the fallen angels. We will teach the humans how to live peacefully. Some things have to be learned. Then hopefully, one day, they can rule themselves. Without the Dracos' hive mind instigating wars and conflict, it might work. It should have never been otherwise."

Zachary asked, "But what if the senate decides to let the fallen angels rule?"

"We will deal with that when the time comes." Feeling all the questions had been answered, Synege asked the Earth Sentinels, "Will you help us save mankind and inner earth?"

None of them were pleased with the plan, but Tom, Cecile, Zachary and Billy agreed to help.

CHAPTER 25
Lord God Abaddon

FLAMES FLICKERED FROM the urns on each side of the stone throne where an imposing figure sat wearing a black robe. His ebony-iridescent wings were pressed against the high back. He gripped a scepter whose tip was adorned with a silver crescent cradling an obsidian disc. His dull gold crown was encrusted with precious jewels that no longer sparkled. From out of his ashen face, his gray eyes warily studied the uninvited visitor, who stood in the center of the great hall. The ruler's discolored teeth showed through his cracked lips as he asked, "What brings you here, Bechard?"

Bechard was shocked by his cousin's appearance, but he politely concealed his repulsion. "Abaddon, I've come—"

The ruler slammed his fist on the throne arm, shouting, "In my house, call me, Lord God!" Spittle seeped from the corners of his mouth.

Bechard raised his eyebrows at the egoistical outburst.

The ruler regained his composure, fiercely glaring at the defector.

Bechard knew Abaddon had no love for him, but the Galactic Council had given him this assignment and he planned to finish it. "I've come because of the situation with the Dracos, which I'm sure you're well aware of..."

Thunder rumbled from deep within the ruler's chest, precipitating a black mist filled with demons, which heaved out of his cadaverous mouth. Hisses, screams and shrieks echoed throughout the sanctuary. Abaddon's ashen skin grew ghastlier. Fine lines etched across his face and hands. Dust fell from his body as if he was crumbling. His inhalation sucked the ominous cloud back into his bowels, then he venomously spewed, "Of course, I know! Why have you come here!?"

Bechard recited, "I've come to propose an alliance on behalf of the Galactic Council. We would..."

Abaddon turned away from Bechard, focusing his attention toward the back of the room where one of the massive gilded doors, dusty from neglect, swung open. A human slave entered. The emaciated man wore only a loincloth. With both hands, he held a silver tray bearing a pitcher and goblet. He nervously walked the length of the sanctuary, bypassing Bechard to approach the throne where he knelt, bowing his head.

The ruler ordered, "Give it to me."

The slave rose, standing to the side so he would not block his master's view, holding out the tray with his trembling hands. Abaddon snatched the goblet, drinking all its contents in one greedy gulp, holding it out to be filled again. The slave picked up the pitcher, concentrating so he would not spill a precious drop of the blood being poured into the cup.

Bechard looked away, disgusted.

Abaddon drank once more, and as the blood flowed down his throat, a major transformation took place. His stone-like body became flesh again. His gray eyes turned blue. The lines on his face and hands became smooth. The color of his wings flashed from black to indigo, for just a moment before losing their brilliance. With his thirst quenched, he wiped his mouth with the back of his hand, leaving a crimson smear. He set the goblet on the tray, motioning for the slave to leave.

The bodily fluids infiltrated Abaddon's system. The rush of human hormones caused his eyes to dilate. His hands clenched. He suppressed a moan, experiencing intense, almost orgasmic, pleasure, breathing heavily.

Bechard averted his eyes, saying to his cousin, "Blood is a pale substitute."

Abaddon didn't hear the comment, remaining a willful prisoner in his cage of euphoria.

"Do you remember when you were a thing of beauty?" Bechard inquired. "With a light so bright, you mesmerized everyone."

The words cut through Abaddon's ecstasy. He became enraged by the interruption, bellowing with a legion of voices, "Don't speak to me of light! What has the light brought you? You small useless creature. No armies of your own. No empires. You are weak. The only reason you are alive today is because of our kinship. But the next time I see you, I will kill you, then cast your soul into hell for all of eternity! You have been warned. Now leave."

A multitude of fallen angels with raven-black wings marched into the sanctuary carrying swords—a procession of black hooded robes. They split into two groups, forming a line on each side of the great hall. They stood erect, menacingly facing Bechard.

"I don't believe I need to introduce our friends," Abaddon stated dryly.

Indeed, the ruler was right. Bechard knew all the fallen angels by name, but he persevered with the conversation despite

245

the threat, talking in a diplomatic manner, "You might be aware that some of the Earth Sentinels have mutated, and now possess a power that could be of service to you."

Abaddon smoldered, but he listened to what Bechard had to say.

"The Earth Sentinels are able to transport the Alterian soldiers directly into the Dracos' dens and UN leaders headquarters. Instantly. No barriers to fight through. No fort that can't be entered. And after the soldiers kill them, the Dracos' will be gone forever. And Hagsmar will be safe."

Abaddon stroked his broad chin, asking, "What are your demands?"

"The council wants the Destiny Stone."

Abaddon didn't answer.

Bechard wasn't surprised by his cousin's hesitation and tried to persuade him. "The Dracos have millions of human soldiers at their disposal. Their assaults will be relentless. The stone's powers won't be enough to protect you against those armies." Bechard pressured him. "Give it to us. You know we won't use it for ill intent."

Without committing, Abaddon inquired, "Is there anything else?"

"After the Dracos and UN hybrids are killed, we will fill their vacancies—"

"You forget yourself, Bechard. The humans are my domain, as is earth's surface. I will fill the UN positions."

"The positions must be filled immediately upon the UN hybrids' deaths, otherwise, the vacancies will be noticed—"

"I have millions to choose from!"

The two of them stared at each other. Bechard was not pleased with Abaddon's demand to fill the UN positions himself, but it was not entirely unexpected.

Without warning, the self-proclaimed god unfurled his large black wings, leaning forward, staring directly at Bechard. His alarming posture prompted his soldiers to straighten their backs. Abaddon tersely stated, "It will be me and my soldiers who kill the lizards and their minions. Not one, single Alterian soldier is to step foot on earth's surface. Is that understood? The only useful thing you have offered me is the Earth Sentinels' powers."

Bechard said, "The Earth Sentinels can take you wherever you want to go." Knowing the fallen angels' dwindling numbers made every casualty a severe blow, he added, "And they have other powers—powers that can protect you during battle." He waited for Abaddon to answer.

"Summon your friends. I will need proof of their powers before I relinquish the stone."

"Of course."

247

CHAPTER 26
Display of Powers

TOM, CECILE, ZACHARY and Bechard arrived inside the fallen angels' castle, standing on the mosaic pentagram in the center of the floor, their airy bodies barely perceivable. The nearby throne sat vacant. The nightly mist, which had not yet lifted, created a foggy veil between the land and sky—gray and dark like a rainy afternoon, making the sanctuary especially gloomy.

There was a creaking sound as two human servants pushed open the sanctuary doors, holding them wide. A small army of black-robed fallen angels, wearing protective armor and holding double-edged swords, marched into the room, their footsteps echoing throughout the great hall, their faces hidden beneath their hoods, stomping as they advanced in unison. They lined the walls, snapping to attention, facing the Earth Sentinels.

Zachary couldn't dispel the ominous feeling in the pit of his stomach. He wished he had found a different way to be of service—like Haruto who had volunteered to retrieve the Destiny Stone. She, like him, disapproved of the Earth Sentinels' participation in this aggressive foray. Truthfully, he wasn't sure any of them approved.

A slave appeared on the rounded balcony that jutted out near the throne. The man wore a blue velvet cape lined with white ermine fur dotted with the black tail tips of unfortunate weasels over his loincloth. The slave put a trumpet to his mouth. His cheeks puffed as the sound bellowed throughout the great room. He lowered the instrument, shouting, "All bow to our Lord God!"

The soldiers knelt on one knee, bowing their heads. The trumpeter and slaves prostrated themselves.

Wearing a chest plate over his robe, Abaddon arrogantly strode out of a hidden chamber and crossed the raised platform to stand beside his throne, glaring at the Earth Sentinels who refused to submit. He wanted to smite them, but, alas, he could not. Not today. So he acted as if nothing was wrong, resting his arm on the chair's high back. His other hand lingered over his sword. The ruler looked strong and refreshed, despite the tinges of gray in the creases of his face. Abaddon commanded his soldiers, "Rise, my faithful ones!"

The fallen angels rose from their knees, standing erect once more.

The slaves took their cue and scuttled out of the room, shutting the doors behind them.

Abaddon turned toward the Earth Sentinels. "It is time to demonstrate your powers."

The ruler motioned for one of the soldiers to step away from the lineup to act as the test subject. The black-hooded figure's wings remained folded as he dutifully marched across the floor, stopping a body's length away from Zachary, Tom and Cecile. Bechard stepped away to give his friends room to work.

"Please show us what you can do, Earth Sentinels." Abaddon's cordial request was overshadowed by his dark heart.

Tom took a deep breath, stepping beside the soldier, repulsed and somewhat scared at being so close to this ancient creature,

249

who he forewarned, "I will need to touch you to demonstrate. Do you agree to this?"

The soldier nodded, his hood lifting up and down.

As soon as Tom made contact with him, they both became semi-transparent. The man instructed the soldier to hold up his spectral sword, then he focused on the shadowy weapon, transforming it into gleaming metal. Abaddon was amazed his soldier's phantom arm was capable of holding up such a heavy blade.

"While in this state," Tom explained, "nothing I know of can hurt us."

The ruler stroked his chin examining the ethereal soldier and deadly sword, pleased by what he saw. He asked, "And how do you know where to find these reptilian filth and their weak-minded fools?"

"You will tell us who it is you seek, then we will take you there. How it works? I'm not sure. It just does."

"What else can you do?"

Tom accepted the challenge, causing himself and the soldier to become invisible—even the sword disappeared. Zachary and Cecile could see the two souls suspended in their translucent bodies, but the others in attendance could not.

"Very nice..." Abaddon smiled sinisterly as he considered the possibilities.

Tom let go of the soldier, who became physical again, but he neglected to transform himself and remained hidden from the fallen angels' sight.

Abaddon grew apprehensive, paranoid the supernatural being might sneak up on him, so he demanded, "Show yourself,

Earth Sentinel!"

Tom appeared as a gossamer body, standing in the same spot.

With Abaddon's immediate fear averted, he focused on the mission at hand, saying to his soldiers, "It is time for me to choose who will fight beside the Earth Sentinels." He scanned the lineup. "Luxus. Bebue. Please step forward. You will go this day and give honor to our people."

The ruler turned his chiseled face toward Zachary, stating, "You and I will fight together. Come to me."

The demand caused an immediate resistance in the young man. Of all those before him, Abaddon was the least palatable. Zachary's feet refused to budge and his spirit refused to comply with this evil creature's order. He looked the ruler in the eyes, and said, "I will meet you halfway," even though he wanted to say, "Go to hell!" failing to remember the fallen angels were master mind readers.

251

No one had ever refused Abaddon during his entire reign. The ruler's anger welled up like an alpha wolf being confronted by an omega male. Blood rushed to his face even as his skin grew ashen, creating a fine layer of dust. The soldiers averted their eyes, expecting the worst.

Instead of expressing his rage, the ruler clapped his hands twice. The doors at the end of the sanctuary were pushed open. Slaves appeared. They bowed, then waited for instructions. Abaddon's booming voice rang out, "Bring us our nourishment!"

The humans scampered away to retrieve the requested sustenance, which sat ready in the outside hall.

Meanwhile, Abaddon issued instructions to his soldiers, "Those who have been chosen, drink up. You have an arduous task before you—"

"Pardon me," Bechard said, "but, before we begin, we will need the Destiny Stone."

Abaddon glared at his dissident cousin, hating him and hating giving up the stone, but the matter at hand was urgent, so he looked up and down the rows of soldiers, calling out, "Oxair. Monatec." The two soldiers stepped forward. "Take Bechard to the stone."

The pair simultaneously replied, "Yes, my Lord—"

Bechard clarified, "It will be Haruto and I. She will carry the stone."

Abaddon waved his hand to indicate he didn't care about the details.

With the approval given, Bechard said to the chosen escorts, "I will return with the Earth Sentinel. Meet me in the grand foyer," then he disappeared.

CHAPTER 27
The Destiny Stone

INSIDE THE CASTLE'S grand foyer, tarnished suits of armor—remnants of enemies killed in past battles—were displayed for morbid curiosity. Spider webs were knitted among the metal plates and strewn across the moldy walls.

Bechard appeared here. The semi-transparent Haruto arrived right after him. Bechard had warned her to never become physical in the presence of the fallen angels—despite everyone's belief that she, Tom, Cecile and Zachary had become immortal, but it was a belief that had yet to be proven.

"Wonder where they are?" Haruto asked, uneasy at being inside the enemy's fortress.

"Be patient," replied Bechard.

Just then, the two fallen angels strode into the chambers.

Bechard greeted them, "Oxair. Monatec."

The soldiers ignored him as they strode toward the entrance. They would have preferred to kill Bechard, but instead obeyed their orders.

Monatec opened one of the massive doors, which had been built for strength, not aesthetics, then, with disdain, he said to the visitors, "Follow us."

The soldiers went outside, stepping down the stairs, walking toward a silver disc-shaped hovercraft, which emitted a humming sound as it hovered over the rocky ground. Haruto and Bechard trailed behind them. Outside, the air was crisp and cool from the rising mist, a refreshing contrast to the musty castle. The hatch door on the saucer lifted and a set of stairs extended out. The two soldiers climbed aboard, one after the other. Haruto's spectral body glided through the shell, moving inside, while Bechard lost a few feathers squeezing through the hatch.

The circular flight deck contained two captain's chairs near the instrument panel and four passenger seats at the rear. Small round windows were evenly spaced around the circumference of the cockpit, offering a panoramic view of dismal Hagsmar.

"Sit down," Monatec instructed, taking his position at the controls, pressing several buttons. The humming sound increased. Haruto floated above the floor, not needing to sit. Bechard had barely taken his seat before the hovercraft zoomed straight up, shooting over the valley toward a black mountain with jagged peaks.

A few minutes later, the hovercraft touched down.

Oxair got out of his seat, motioning for everyone to follow him outside. He led them on a short jaunt to the base of the mountain. Here, a buzzing sound was heard, although neither Haruto or Bechard could determine where it was coming from. The fallen angel stepped closer to the cragged wall, placing his hand inside a stone crevice, touching a hidden sensor pad. The buzzing sound ceased, and a secret door began moving inside the mountain, churning up dust as it crept along. When the door came to a stop, Oxair walked through the opening, followed by the others.

At the far end of the cavern, the Destiny Stone's light shone through the seams of the ancient chest, causing the crystal-covered walls and low-hanging stalactites to sparkle like fresh-fallen snow in the moonlight. Golden statues of angels prayed over the gilded lid.

Oxair stopped halfway. "From here, we take no responsibility for your well-being."

Bechard and Haruto nodded, indicating they understood the dangers of the stone's powers.

Both of Abaddon's soldiers crossed their arms, waiting for the deed to be done.

"I'll do it alone," Haruto told Bechard. "It's safer for me."

He agreed by lifting his chin, but felt concern for her safety.

Oxair and Monatec curiously observed the proceedings, hoping for the worst.

Haruto floated in front of the chest. She hesitated a moment because she was afraid of the stone's powers, but she gathered her courage and touched the lid with her vaporous hand. Nothing unusual was felt. Either her ethereal state protected her or the chest did, or both. Now all Haruto had to do was transport the precious cargo to the Mammoth Cave in Alteria. "Bechard?"

"Yes?"

"I'll meet you there." Haruto and the chest disappeared.

Bechard was right behind her.

CHAPTER 28
Killing the Dracos

THE SUPREME LEADER'S bedroom resembled a large cave. And perhaps it was. Here, Zycar lay on a king-sized bed with twisting and snarling snakes, dragons and gargoyles carved into the wooden headboard—all devouring humans. The bed cover, a heavy tapestry, was pulled snug over his slumbering body. His long white plumage of hair hung over his pillow. Curved ram-like horns extended out of both sides of his head. His scaly face hung loose from age. Some of his pointed teeth protruded over his bony lips that were open in the midst of a snore. He was blissfully unaware Zachary had escorted Abaddon into his private chambers.

Invisible, Abaddon examined the sparse room, paying special attention to the shadows where a guard might lurk. After deeming it safe, he nodded to Zachary, giving him the signal to transform themselves from the unseen into a semi-transparent state. Now both ghostly, Zachary let the ruler's sword become physical.

Abaddon raised his weapon, ready to strike at Zycar's neck, seeming to savor the moment.

The Draco's red eyes flashed open, his slitted pupils wide at the sight of the sword hovering above his head, held by the spectral fallen angel. But the Supreme Leader didn't scream, in fact, he showed no fear as he accused his assassin in a raspy voice, "Coward!"

Abaddon would have loved to duel his nemesis, if only to quell the reptilian's pride, but too much was at stake, so instead he sneered, "Zycar, die!"

The sword cut through the air.

Zycar raised his thick-skinned arms to protect his throat while rolling out of the way. The sword cut off one of his hands and slashed the side of his throat. For humans, this would have led to a quick death, but not for the Draco whose jugular vein ran down the center of his neck.

The Supreme Leader escaped from the bed, his feet hitting the floor. Blue blood ran down his chest and spurted out of his wounded arm. His red eyes glared with anger. He didn't expect to win a fight against an ethereal being, but he did intend to stall his death long enough to issue a warning via the hive mind. His intention worked. The highest-ranking Draco leaders heard Zycar's thoughts clearly while the lowest ones sensed something was wrong, even if they couldn't quite put their fears into words.

The bedroom door burst open. Two reptilian guards rushed in with their lasers drawn. They spotted the intruders and opened fire, but the laser beams zipped through the ethereal bodies with no impact.

"Move with me," Abaddon instructed Zachary as he stepped closer to Zycar. The young man followed, careful not to lose touch of the fallen angel, who shouted with vengeance, "Die!" plunging his sword into the Draco's heart. The reptilian leader fell to his knees. A moment later, his body collapsed onto the floor.

The guards threw down their laser guns, pulling out handheld devices from their gun belts. The weapons sent powerful beams of energy that struck Abaddon and Zachary, but only impacted the

257

young man whose mind went blank. He couldn't see, or hear, or think.

Even though Abaddon's mind was too strong to be overpowered, the fallen angel became physical when Zachary was unable to concentrate. To protect himself, the ruler rushed toward the guards, swinging his sword at their necks, cutting off both of their heads with one blow. Their bodies crumpled, and the mind-control devices dropped from their lifeless hands.

The beams of energy ceased.

Zachary's mind cleared. Unfortunately, the first thing he saw was the two decapitated guards lying on the floor in pools of blue blood and their severed heads nearby. A pair of dead red eyes stared directly at him. He gagged.

"Take me to the next in command!" Abaddon demanded, disgusted by the young man's softness.

Trying his best not to vomit, Zachary reached for him. They both disappeared.

The military control center was filled with holographic surveillance monitors manned by hybrid soldiers.

The three Draco leaders, who sat in the high-backed chairs in the center, heard Zycar's warning echoing throughout the hive mind. They stood up, walking in unison across the floor to a curved glass door, which spun open. They stepped inside a circular safe room. The glass door reeled shut, and a force field became active, but not before the invisible Zachary and Abaddon emerged in the midst of the control center.

Abaddon silently said to his escort, *Make me a ghost. I want them to see me.*

Zachary transformed him from an invisible state into a semi-transparent one, continuing to hold onto the ruler who smiled with anticipation as he glided toward the safe room. On the other side of the glass door, one of the Draco leaders was seen pushing a button. A toxic mist streamed out of the ceiling in the main room. The intent was to kill the invaders, but it was only the soldiers who gasped for air.

As a last measure, the Draco leaders pulled out their laser guns, aiming at the fallen angel through the glass, but the beams shot through Abaddon's shadowy figure without any effect. A look of resignation crept across the reptilians' faces.

Abaddon drifted through the glass door, hovering before the leaders who were trapped inside like goldfish in a bowl. He nodded at Zachary, who caused the ruler's airy sword to become physical. The refined steel was thrust through the chest of one of the Dracos, who made no sound as blue blood gushed out of his wound. The reptilian simply stared at Abaddon with fierce hate until he succumbed to his mortal injury, dropping to the floor. Then the fallen angel thrust his sword through the next leader, and then the next.

Abaddon gloated over his kills a moment before saying to Zachary, "Make my sword a ghost so I can remove it."

The young man did as he was asked.

The ghostly ruler floated out of the safe room. It was then he noticed an image on one of the holographic monitors on the other side of the control center. He sailed over the dying soldiers to take a closer look. Zachary moved beside him. Hovering in front of the holographic monitor, Abaddon saw a satellite transmission of warships carrying fighter jets, heading north. A terrible realization struck him. Frustrated that he could not see Zachary, he shouted in all directions, "Take me back to Hagsmar! Now!"

But what about the mission? Zachary asked, unsure of how to proceed.

"You fool! I must prepare for war! Depart! Now!"

But if we just finish this, the humans will be free, and—

"I don't give a damn about the humans! Leave! Now!"

CHAPTER 29

Hagsmar Prepares for War

ON THE TARMAC, fallen angels, wearing armor over their black robes, scurried in and around the fleet of silver hovercraft as they prepared for war.

Abaddon boldly strode across the way. In his arms, he held scrolls that were tightly rolled and bound with leather straps. Two trusted soldiers kept pace beside him. When the ruler reached a well-used hovercraft, he looked back at his castle on the hill as if it might be the last time he saw his kingdom. He said to his soldiers, "I will unleash hell, and you will protect our domain. Understood?"

"Yes, my lord," both of the soldiers answered.

Abaddon expertly made his way through the hatch, tucking his wings. He went to the cockpit, settling into the pilot seat.

The humming hovercraft shot straight up into the air, speeding over the land, quickly moving out of sight.

CHAPTER 30
Plan B

SYNEGE, WHO STOOD in the center of the council members, stated, "It's deeply disappointing the fallen angels did not finish killing the Dracos and UN leaders. But, like them, we have to deal with the human armies advancing toward Hagsmar, because if the humans win that battle, they will invade here next, destroying all of inner earth. But we are prepared to stop them. We have stationed troops near the Great Magma Divide to prevent the Dracos' forces from crossing over. Unfortunately, the fallen angels will not allow our armies to enter their territory—that would lessen the threat considerably."

"What about the opening at the South Pole?" Zachary asked. "Can't the human armies enter there as well?"

"Normally, yes, but, fortunately, it's wintertime in the southern hemisphere. The Antarctica's subzero temperatures not only freezes fuel, it also causes metal to become brittle. There are logistical problems as well, such as the brutal winds, which cause plane engines to burn more fuel and fly unsteadily as their wings threaten to snap off—few, if any, would make it to the Great Opening. Driving is even more hazardous than flying, and not really an option since it is impossible to drive down the nearly vertical tunnel. However, to be on the safe side, we have stationed a squadron near the opening. Armed with electromagnetic pulse devices, they will be able to disable any planes that try to enter there."

Haruto solemnly commented, "We're about to kill the same people we're trying to save."

The sanctuary became quiet.

"A sad irony," Synege affirmed. "I wish we had better answers, but with the EMPs, we should be able to stop the army planes without too much bloodshed."

A bright glow appeared outside the crystal walls. A rainbow of colors refracted through the thick quartz as a ball of light entered the sanctuary. Once inside, it split into the familiar five orbs, which spoke in unison, "Forgive our intrusion, dear council, but we have an urgent message."

Synege steeled herself. "Proceed."

"The human armies have bombed the pyramids of Giza, and are headed toward the other sacred vortexes as we speak."

The small Arcturian's shoulders slumped as she lamented, "Mankind has no sense of self-preservation."

The talking head, Phosulent, concurred, "True. Humans have always been slaves and know nothing of freedom. They blindly follow whoever claims to be their master, remaining unaware that by destroying their history, they are destroying the last remaining clues to their origins."

Synege raised her shoulders. "You're right. They just don't know any better."

Tom shook his head, tired of the never-ending complications. "Now we have two problems."

"True, but..." Bechard pointed out enthusiastically as the idea took form, "both could be fixed by using the EMPs!" He spoke directly to the Earth Sentinels, "With your ability to instantly transport yourselves anywhere, you could use the EMPs to disable all of the military weaponry on earth. This would be efficient and humane."

Zachary, Haruto, Tom and Cecile didn't answer immediately. Zachary felt the situation was spiraling out of control, again. Tom was calculating the logistics and time frame. Haruto felt her heart skip a beat as it warned her this situation would escalate—there would always be one more battle to fight.

Geet cautioned, "That's fine, but we need to be strategic about it. We can't disable everything in sight. It would set the humans back a hundred years. Their computers would be fried. TVs, radios, cars and trucks, and phones—all useless. How would we communicate with them? Provide food? Eventually the electricity will be turned on. It would be nice if their communication devices worked." The mouse on his shoulder tilted his head, waiting for an answer.

Bechard suggested, "If we tighten the EMPs' range, we will avoid hitting the surrounding infrastructure needed by the humans to get back on their feet."

"Focus solely on the bases?" Synege reiterated, shaking her head. "That will take considerably longer than a broader strike."

"Yes, but it is doable." Bechard continued with his thought process, "And after we hit the bases, the armies won't be much of a threat if we replace the UN leaders before the weaponry is repaired."

"More killing?" Haruto uttered forlornly.

Bechard responded, "A thousand lives to avoid killing millions. It's a fair exchange."

Billy offered his opinion, "Those UN leaders aren't guiltless. They're Dracos in human form, and they wouldn't think twice about killing us."

Haruto countered, "But I don't want to be like them."

He adjusted his black hat. "Sometimes you gotta do, what you gotta do."

CHAPTER 31
EMP Attacks

THE AIRCRAFT CARRIERS from China, Russia and the United
States were anchored in the Arctic Ocean. On top of each deck
was a short runway with jets ready to lift off. A fleet of Chinese
military jets, identified by red stars outlined with yellow on the
gray tails, took to flight. Right behind them was the Russian team
flying Su-27s and T-50s. The sleek bodies were covered with
geometrical-shaped camouflage. Coming up from the rear were
the United States' F-22A Raptors, F-18 Hornets, A-10s and F-35s
gleaned from the Air Force, Marines, and Navy divisions.

The multi-national squadron flew over the Arctic's mass of ice,
topped by mountains of snow. Their great numbers blocked out the
pale sun as they headed toward the North Pole. Here, even though
it was summer, the temperature remained just below freezing—
an unending season of cold. The jets approached the northern
entrance of inner earth, which was nearly sixty-miles wide at the
outer circumference before its snowy terrain sloped downward,
narrowing into a tunnel. The fighter planes flew to the midpoint
of the massive-sized hole, then dipped their noses, speeding past
the enormous icicles dripping over the tunnel's edges, some bigger
than the planes themselves. The aircraft began free falling inside
the passageway. To avoid stalling, they crisscrossed like downhill
skiers. The pilots fiercely concentrated to avoid colliding with

their fellow pilots, their hands tightly gripping the control wheels. As the jets zigzagged through the tunnel, the sun's light became faint, and soon the vestibule was pitch black. The planes' landing lights lit the way—buzzing fireflies weaving toward their targets.

They flew.

And flew.

Hundreds of miles later, midway through the earth's crust, zero gravity took effect. The planes became weightless, wobbling uncertainly, but the engines propelled them forward through the darkness while the glowing needles on their compasses spun round and round.

When the jets finally left behind the no man's land between upper and inner earth, the gravitational pull switched.

Down became up.

They ascended toward the fallen angel's domain. The tunnel thundered as the jet engines strained. Soon, a light appeared at the top of the tunnel, providing a beacon for the pilots. Unbeknownst to them, the light was a temptress, luring them to the surface where Abaddon's fleet waited for them.

At the first sound of the jets, the fallen angels fired lasers down the hole.

The humans' jets, and the bombs they carried, exploded, causing massive shockwaves and fireballs. The fighter planes crashed on top of each other—toppling like rows of fiery dominoes.

Some of the incoming jets managed to avoid being hit, whizzing up and out of the tunnel. The fallen angels' hovercraft zoomed in every direction, picking off the strays with bursts of laser beams.

By sheer luck, a Chinese jet flew through the bombardment

267

and escaped unscathed. It raced toward its number one target: Abaddon's castle and surrounding territory.

A fallen angel noticed the rogue fighter plane and spun his silver saucer around, chasing the invader, quickly gaining airspace. He lined up the target.

A flashing light on the dashboard alerted the Chinese pilot. He responded by releasing a series of flares that spiraled behind his aircraft like fireworks, creating a thick veil of smoke, heat and trails of sparks, which flared out like the Angel of Death's wings.

Because of the tactical veil, the fallen angel could not accurately pinpoint the Chinese jet, so he simply aimed in the general direction and pushed a button on his control wheel. A series of laser beams shot out.

Untouched, the Chinese jet rose out of the haze, flying close to the speed of sound toward its target.

Fast behind it, the fallen angel lined up his second shot.

But, from behind him, an American jet intervened by shooting missiles that utilized infra-red and search-and-track capabilities.

A warning blared in the fallen angel's cockpit. He took a defensive maneuver, but an incoming missile hit its mark, blowing up his hovercraft.

The unhindered Chinese jet plowed through the gray skies, speeding up and over the cliffs at the edge of the sea. Abaddon's castle, sitting high on the peak of a black cragged mountain, was in sight. The warplane shot several missiles.

Toroidal fireballs consumed the castle and adjacent air force base.

Tom appeared just in time to watch the explosions unfold in the sky. The moment was bitter sweet. He was glad Abaddon's empire had fallen, but he was also concerned the human army was making too much progress, so he aimed his EMP gun at the planes escaping from the tunnel. The device resembled a short-barreled bazooka with a clear, half-round quartz sight at its end. He flipped a switch near the handle. The gun hummed. He pulled the trigger, causing gamma rays to charge the electrons in the air. The heat generated from the displaced electrons sent a surge of energy that burned up all the electrical circuitry within range.

The modern jets lost their computer-controlled stability and dropped like a flock of mallard ducks during hunting season. Explosions battered the landscape as each jet struck the ground. Only the fallen angels' hovercraft remained afloat.

Some of the human pilots managed to eject and unfurl their parachutes, but the fallen angels used them for target practice.

Tom surveyed the smoldering castle in the distance and the plane wreckages all around him. There was nothing left for him to do here, so he set the intention to go to earth's surface where Zachary and Cecile were already using the EMP devices to disable the military's weaponry.

Zachary arrived, floating above the Fort Bragg military base, just in time to see a jet lift off, quickly gaining altitude.

Ignoring the one that got away, Zachary raised the EMP device in his hand, holding it tight against his shoulder, sweeping it from one end of the base to the other. Unseen and unheard, these incredibly powerful energy waves incinerated the electronics on all the aircraft and ground-support vehicles as well as the base's phone and electrical systems, heating and air conditioning units, generators, computers, and more.

There were no explosions, fires or even a sound. It was very anticlimactic. A ground vehicle rolled to a stop.

Next, Zachary pointed the EMP device at the jet that had taken off. Flying at supersonic speed, it was already a speck on the horizon. Because of the recent attacks on the Dracos, the young man was less resistant to taking a life (not something he was proud of), yet he hesitated to pull the trigger.

Suddenly, a lightning bolt burst out of the clear blue sky, striking the aircraft, which exploded. A great round of thunder rolled over the land.

The startled young man studied the orange ball of flames, then uttered the name of the perpetrator, "Bechard."

CHAPTER 32
Plan C

AFTER THE EMP strikes were completed, the Earth Sentinels returned to the Galactic Council's chambers. The beauty of the sparkling crystal walls belied the somber tone of the room. Tom, Cecile and Zachary looked tired, only Haruto and Billy were clear eyed.

Synege said, "We need to kill the UN leaders and replace them as quickly as possible." She spoke directly to Bechard, "Have you been able to contact Abaddon?"

Bechard answered, "No. He was either killed in battle or is in hiding, and no one has stepped up to take his place."

"The council and I discussed this possibility, and have the following suggestion: Let's finish the mission without the fallen angels. You, Earth Sentinels, can use our Alterian soldiers to assassinate the UN hybrids, and then install your own members into the vacancies."

Tom asked, "What about the remaining Draco leaders? Should they be killed as well?"

The council members telepathically conferred with one another.

Finally, Synege answered Tom, "The highest-ranking Dracos have been taken care of. For now, let's focus on eliminating and replacing the UN leaders." She then directed her words to all of the Earth Sentinels, "Are you willing to finish this mission? I know it won't be easy, and you are tired, but it must be done."

They all agreed, except for Haruto.

CHAPTER 33
New Recruits

BECHARD TOOK IT upon himself to find recruits he could trust to take over the UN leadership positions, which would soon be forcibly vacated, so he issued a request that spiraled around the world, beckoning the former Earth Sentinels to return to the spirit realm.

The fallen angel's voice entered the mind of an African shaman wearing colorful clothing, which belied his hopeless situation as he sat in a tent alongside a dozen other members of his tribe—all held captive in a detainment camp. The man heard Bechard's voice, carried by the wind, calling, "Come, come, Earth Sentinels!" The man smiled, then closed his eyes, letting his spirit follow the familiar sound.

At another campsite, a Siberian shamaness with braided gray hair, wrapped with a colorful scarf, heard Bechard's voice summoning her. She clasped her hands, her silver bracelets clinking, then closed her eyes, freeing her spirit.

Soon thousands of spirits stepped through the ethereal blue doors that led into the spirit realm. They moved toward the cobblestone courtyard where Bechard waited for the shamans, mudangs, Ngakpas, Jhakri, Noros, klong folk, Alignalghi, Sangomas, Hatałii, curanderos, Geiki and Machi to arrive. The old friends were noisy and jovial as they greeted each other.

The fallen angel raised his hands to quiet the crowd, loudly calling out, "Welcome back, Earth Sentinels!" The crowd hushed. "It's an honor and pleasure to see you again. Thank you for coming, because, once again, we have important work to do."

He briefed them on the virus outbreak and its impact on a few of the Earth Sentinels who were mutating; and on the war between the fallen angels and Dracos whose hive mind commanded the UN hybrid leaders who, in turn, controlled the human armies and all aspects of civilization.

After answering their questions, Bechard told them why he had invited them here, "At any moment, the Alterian soldiers will begin assassinating the UN hybrids. These positions need to be filled by people of high moral character, who will act fairly and follow the guidance of the Galactic Council. Make no doubt about it, these are dangerous positions subject to assassination attempts, so I will understand if you don't want to volunteer. But if you don't, please leave now. No judgment. Because it would be better if you left now, rather than later."

A few dozen people slunk away, exiting through the blue doors.

"I appreciate their honesty. Anyone else?"

No one moved.

As a final confirmation, Bechard addressed those who stayed, "If you think you have the qualities to help mankind during this difficult transition, please step forward."

Everyone took a step over the cobblestones.

Bechard smiled like a teacher well pleased with his students.

CHAPTER 34
UN Replacements

IN A CLEARING of a great forest, troll warriors waited for Zachary's arrival. They were dressed for battle, wearing rugged furs over their woven garments. On top of their nubby heads were helmets with ram horns protruding from the sides, pulled low over their bulging foreheads, resting just above their bushy eyebrows. Some wielded swords or knives, but all held clubs. The trolls' large mouths and thick lips were pulled back in sneers as they mentally prepared themselves for the carnage about to ensue. The women and children stood nearby to wish the warriors well before they left, expecting them to come back as heroes known throughout Alteria, and honored in the legends sure to follow.

Zachary appeared out of thin air.

The leader, Junya, approached him, his thick tree-trunk legs stomping across the dusty ground, his musky smell preceding him. The troll looked down on the puny human, speaking in a gruff voice, "Welcome to Miramar, land of the trolls. From here to the sea, we are many. And we accept the call to..." he shouted back at his clansmen, "smash some heads!"

The warriors roared, shaking their clubs.

Zachary felt out of his league—not understanding how anyone could look forward to killing. After the shouting subsided, he informed them, "I need one of you to go with me—"

All of the warriors rushed forward, nearly trampling Zachary who jumped out of the way to avoid being crushed.

Junya spoke, "I go!"

"Me, too!"

"And, me!"

One of them shouted, "Kantra, you not take my place!"

The trolls at the forefront wrestled with each other. One grabbed another by the neck.

Zachary cupped his hands around his mouth, shouting, "Stop! Stop it!" He put his hands down, conceding, "Okay, the four of you can come."

They let go of each other. The other warriors groaned wishing they had joined the scuffle.

"Don't worry. You'll each have a turn," Zachary assured them.

The selected trolls straightened their animal skins and helmets, preparing themselves for the attack.

Meanwhile, at the Fort Bragg military base, the UN leader, Commander Lewis, sat in his office having a terse conversation with his officers. "So what did you find out?"

With a southern drawl, an officer answered, "The driver who went to Seymour said the other base is in the same boat as us, but, interestingly, the towns in-between were unaffected by the EMP strikes, sir."

"That is interesting." Commander Lewis sat thinking, unsure of how to proceed until he heard an order transmitting through the Dracos' hive mind. *All the planes must be repaired. Our survival depends on it. Do whatever it takes.* A different voice followed. *Find salvage parts.* The silent messages prompted the

UN leader to say to his men, "Let's search the areas away from the bases for salvage parts."

"Yes, sir."

"I'll decide which sites to search first, but before I do..." He adjusted his belt. "I need to take a piss." Two empty Diet Coke cans sat on his desk. He got up. The officers stood at attention as he left.

Commander Lewis made his way down the unlit hallway. The latrine door had been propped open with a wooden wedge, allowing the sunlight from an office window across the hall to filter in. He walked to the porcelain urinal, hidden in the shadows, unzipping his fly.

That's when Zachary and his band of trolls stepped in behind the UN leader, remaining invisible. The young man checked to make sure they were alone, then transformed himself and the assassination team into a semi-transparent state. Next, he made the trolls' clubs become physical, which caused the well-used weapons to emit a pungent odor.

Commander Lewis sniffed in disgust as he urinated, assuming someone either forgot to flush the toilet or the sewer line was backed up. He zipped up his pants, then turned around, coming face to face with the shadowy ogres. He didn't have time to comprehend the bizarre sight before one of the trolls swung a club at his head. The blunt force killed the hybrid instantly.

One of the trolls picked up the body, holding it up like a rag doll, gruffly saying, "Go now."

There was no time to delay. Blood trickled out of the UN leader's cracked skull, and the uniform needed to be kept spotless. The trolls put their hairy hands on top of each other's, and Zachary put his hand on top of theirs, transporting all of them back to their village.

The women, children and warriors-in-waiting cheered upon their arrival. But there was still work to be done. The uniform needed to be delivered to the UN impostor, and it needed to be done quickly before the dead commander's absence raised questions. Zachary made the uniform invisible, which caused the flesh-and-blood body to tumble out of it, collapsing onto the ground.

A female troll grabbed the corpse, dragging it over to a cauldron that hung over a fire. She picked up an ax and chopped off the man's arm, throwing it into the simmering stew.

Zachary grimaced and turned away from the grisly scene, saying to the warriors, "The next part I will do alone." The trolls grunted angrily at the prospect of being left behind. They were only slightly pacified when he assured them, "Don't worry. I'll be back."

The young man went to another part of Alteria—to where the Bear Claw tribe resided. Billy was waiting for him near the lake, standing in the shade of a tree.

"Ready?" Zachary asked him.

Billy nodded. "So the deed is done?"

"Yes, and we need to hurry." Zachary held out the uniform that Billy needed to put on.

Billy removed his black hat, revealing a military-styled crew cut. His long hair had been sacrificed for the mission. Zachary tried to hide his shock at the difference the haircut made in the man's appearance. Somewhat embarrassed, Billy ran his hand over his short hair, saying to his friend, "Not a word," then he stripped down to his skivvies and got dressed, pulling on the jacket sleeves to lengthen them. It wasn't a perfect fit, but it was close enough. He said, "Let's go."

Invisible, the two of them emerged inside the dark unoccupied latrine. The coast was clear, so Zachary changed Billy's body into a physical form, advising him, "Last office on your left."

Billy strode down the hallway.

The officers, who had been impatiently waiting for their commander to return, stood to salute when Billy entered the room. The unknown UN leader didn't fit the usual profile, but he wore the right uniform. He nodded at the men as he walked past them, sitting behind the desk.

Without missing a beat, Billy swiveled in his chair, facing the officers. "At ease. Have a seat."

The officers glanced at each other as they sat down, wondering what was going on.

Billy introduced himself, "Name's Commander White..." He caught himself before saying the last part of his name. "I'll be in charge from here on out."

This change of commanders was so sudden and strange, it left the officers confused. After all, who leaves in the middle of an important meeting?

One inquired, "Sir, Commander Lewis didn't mention anything about being replaced."

"Yes...it was unexpected. Now can you fill me in on what's going on here? And can someone get me a coffee?"

"Yes, sir," another officer answered, "but it's brewed on a propane stove so you'll have to excuse the taste. Bitter as hell, sir."

"That'll be just fine." Billy was pleased no one suspected he was an impostor, because he planned to hinder all their efforts of repairing the damage caused by the EMP strike.

The rock folk had lived in this lush valley for as long as they could remember. There were no males, mostly because they weren't needed. To reproduce, each female simply broke off the tip of a finger, planted it in a mound she had built, and then waited for it to grow. After decades of gestation, eventually a rock baby crawled out from the dirt to be welcomed by its extended family. All of the rock folk had been spawned from the same stone, making their kinship fiercely loyal.

Their faces were lifted toward the red sun that warmed their hard bodies, infusing them with its energy. They were praying for their safety during the impending attacks.

280

When Cecile arrived, the rock folk sensed her presence and turned to look at her with their vague eyes, which were nothing more than slight indentations in their faces. The stone warriors got to their feet, moving their heavy legs toward the visitor.

The first to reach Cecile said, "Welcome, I am Feldmar." When she spoke, her hands moved with graceful gestures despite her bulky frame. "We've been waiting for your arrival."

"It's a pleasure to meet you. I'm Cecile Two Feathers."

"The pleasure is ours."

Cecile told them, "What we're about to do isn't remotely pleasant."

"We are aware of this."

"Then we should go." Cecile held out her hand. Feldmar gently placed her cool palm on top of hers.

Inside the headquarters of the Xiangshui Hsu Air Base, a worried UN leader sat in his office. His cold-blue eyes stared at the Asian officers standing stiffly in front of his desk. He said to them, "I sense something's wrong. Double the guards around the perimeters."

"Yes, sir!" the officers responded in unison, saluting, and then marching out the door.

Cecile and Feldmar arrived behind the UN leader, who could not see the invisible pair. Since no one else was in the room, the Earth Sentinel made the stone warrior become physical. The UN leader caught a glimpse of Feldmar out of the corner of his eye, but, before he could turn his head, she pounded down on his skull with her rugged fist. The dead commander fell over his desk, bumping his face on the metal surface before sliding out of his chair and onto the floor.

Cecile moved quickly to grasp Feldspar's hand while reaching down to touch the hybrid's shoulder, taking all three of them out of there.

The blue-skinned king lounged on an oversized cushion resembling a giant lotus flower, propping himself up with one of his four arms. He wore a gold crown with a sculpted cobra in its center and an elaborately embroidered red *sherwani* that draped regally over his muscular body. There were a dozen four-armed warriors stationed nearby, who wore free-flowing black pants and stood with two arms crossed over their bare chests while their other arms hung by their sides ready to grasp, at a moment's notice, the curved swords tucked inside their waistbands.

The king was pleased by Tom's arrival and stood to formally

greet him, speaking in a deep smooth voice, "Welcome to Ventura. I am King Shavore. My men are most honored to be of service."

Tom replied, "Your help is greatly appreciated."

"As is yours. I've handpicked my best fighters. May the gods bless our cause."

"Thank you. Are they ready now?"

"They are."

"Good, but I only need one at a time."

"Very well." King Shavore motioned for one of the warriors to step forward. "This is Hanperto."

Hanperto bowed to his ruler, and then to Tom. "Thank you for this honor. I stand ready."

Tom touched the man's shoulder, making the both of them invisible.

The two of them arrived in an office located on the French Châteaudun Air Base. The UN leader stood by the window, which was the only source of light. He was trying to decide how to deal with the recent EMP strikes as he studied the grounded planes.

Tom glanced out the doorway. The hallway was empty, so he transformed Hanperto into a tangible body. The blue-skinned assassin reached out with his four hands, grabbing the UN leader's head while firmly holding onto his shoulders, cleanly snapping his neck.

After the UN leaders on the military bases were assassinated and replaced with the Earth Sentinel impostors, Cecile and Zachary lay down to get some much-needed rest. Tom was exhausted as well, but there was one more UN leader he needed to take care of. This particular hybrid didn't reside on a military base and wasn't on the official list, but Tom was going to deal with him personally.

CHAPTER 35
Replacing the Crystals

MAMMOTH CAVE. HARUTO stood with Synege in front of the gold-covered chest that contained the Destiny Stone. Light escaped from under the lid, highlighting the treasure trove of gold coins and trinkets scattered across the rugged floor. Partially buried in the dirt beside the cave walls, twelve ancient crystals gleamed. Their quartz bodies were nearly the length of a man.

Synege addressed Haruto, "Thank you for agreeing to do this."

"You're welcomed. I am glad to do it."

"Before you commence, I want to remind you to place the crystals and Destiny Stone in the stone cradles or crypts from whence they came. Stone is an excellent conductor and will help their vibrations to rise faster—and the sooner we raise earth's vibrations, the sooner the hive mind will shut down."

"But the Great Pyramid has been destroyed," Haruto lamented. "It will be impossible to return the Destiny Stone to its original location."

"Perhaps if you place it directly beneath the rubble, it will have the same effect." Synege paused. "This was their intention... to prevent us from reactivating the vortexes—ever."

Haruto nodded. "I will ask the stone and crystals for their advice on where they would like to be placed."

"Will that work?"

"I believe so, but I won't know until I try."

"It must work. Would you like me or someone else to stay here to see if we can be of help?"

"No, thanks. I think I'll concentrate better if I'm alone."

"Very well. Please let the council know immediately if you have any problems. We're in this together." She touched Haruto's arm. "Godspeed to you."

Haruto bowed.

The small Arcturian turned to leave, lifting her white robe above her ankles. The sound of clinking gold coins followed her footsteps to the cave entrance.

Haruto waited for the air to quiet, then she walked to the pink crystal. "Hello, my friend, you will be the first. Please tell me where to take you." She rested her hand on its cool smooth surface, letting her mind connect with it.

285

An image appeared. It was of Easter Island in the Pacific Ocean—easily identified by the monolithic figures, which had been carved out of lava, protruding out of the ground near the shoreline. The vision focused on a grassy area between the inactive volcanoes and the sea. The image dipped beneath the black topsoil, moving past a layer of brownish-red dirt, finally arriving at the bedrock below, which had a hand-chiseled depression—most likely created at the same time the monoliths were carved. Unfortunately, it was covered by the dirt that had collapsed after the crystal was removed millenniums ago. The scene lingered here, making it obvious this was where the crystal wanted to be placed, but the dirt needed to be excavated first.

To deal with the situation, Haruto transformed herself into a semi-transparent state, and then went to the underground location alone. Her golden glow lit the small dark cavity. With her ghostly hand, she touched the fallen dirt, making it semi-transparent, then she floated with it through the top soil, taking the mound to the surface, resting it on the grassy field. With that done, it was time to retrieve the crystal.

Haruto returned to Mammoth Cave. She touched the crystal, making it ethereal like herself. "Ready?" she said to it.

The crystal rang out a high-pitched tone.

She transported the crystal to the underground vortex, and tenderly placed it on the stone cradle. It was a perfect fit, so she transformed the crystal back into its natural state. Immediately, the quartz vibrated and glowed. The ground quivered as its vibrations raised.

286

Mount Shasta is a dormant volcano that is considered to be the first chakra of the planet. Strange cloud formations, in the shape of giant saucers, are common over its high-reaching snow-covered summit.

Haruto held the ethereal red crystal as she floated above the landscape. She waited for the crystal to guide her to its desired location within the sleeping volcano. The crystal's inner light grew brighter as it awakened, prompting Haruto to glide through the side of the mountain, moving through the great expanse of petrified lava until they reached the hollow core. She and the crystal floated down to the hardened-ash floor. She thought they would stop here, but the crystal urged her to continue farther below.

They moved deeper into the base of the mountain, coming to a giant channel that once flowed with fiery slag, but now held cool water. "Here?" Haruto asked. The crystal vibrated. Its desire to be home was so strong that it threatened to leap out of her hands. Haruto kneeled close to the waterline, letting the crystal slide into the water, becoming physical after it left her hands. As the red crystal sank into the ashen crypt, it vibrated and emitted an intense light, causing the water to glow like hot lava.

After Haruto had installed all of the sacred crystals within the earth's vortexes, it was time to replace the Destiny Stone. She stood in front of the ancient acacia-wood chest decorated with golden angels—a tribute to the Anunnaki who had brought the stone from their planet.

She spoke to the stone concealed within the chest, "Your former home, the Great Pyramid of Giza, has been bombed. Where would you like me to place you instead?"

The rays of light streaming from under the chest lid became brighter. An angelic voice entered Haruto's mind, saying, *I long for a place far, far away. A place where my power is neither special nor feared.*

"I understand you are alien to this planet, but would you be willing to help mankind one last time? We need your energy to raise the earth's vibrations to defeat the Draco's—"

Ah, the serpents. I understand. Yes, I am willing. Regarding the placement, rest me under the foundation of the pyramid, above the river that flows beneath. There is an underground chamber betwixt the two. There, I will magnify the energies of the earth.

The connection between them ceased.

It was time to act.

287

Haruto made herself ethereal, then touched the chest, making it and the Destiny Stone ethereal as well. This transformation allowed her to see the stone's essence within the container.

She escorted both of them to Egypt where they floated above what was left of the pyramids—three mounds of rubble. Haruto shook her head at the travesty. *Stupid humans.* The nearby Sphinx's head had been blown off its cat-like lounging figure and lay in the sand, its blind eyes staring up at the desert sun. The sight broke Haruto's heart, but she had a mission to fulfill, so she envisioned the chamber the Destiny Stone had spoken of. She saw a subterranean room, beneath the Great Pyramid, carved out of the limestone bedrock. In the center was a pit that dropped eleven-feet before sloping toward the Nile River. "Here?"

"Yes," the stone answered.

Haruto transported the ghostly chest and stone to the underground chamber, placing them on the slab floor, a safe distance from the pit.

The stone confirmed, *This is a good place to call my home. Please take me out of my prison. Here, I shall share my energy with the earth.*

Haruto lifted the still-ethereal stone out of the chest, and carefully placed it into a slight hollow in the bedrock. With a final respectful glance at the Destiny Stone, she disappeared, letting the stone become physical in her absence. Its great powers were unleashed. Energy exploded throughout the chamber.

To ensure everything went as planned, Haruto floated above the demolished pyramids. She saw rays of light escaping from the cracks in the bombed landscape, and felt the intensity of the Destiny Stone's vibrations. The air distorted like a heat wave.

She smiled, embracing the Destiny Stone's energy. The ley line circuitry was now complete. The free-flowing energy amplified the earth's vibrations, which began to slowly rise.

CHAPTER 36
Mari Saves Herself

ALTERIA. THE RISING vibrations seemed to improve everyone's mood. A handful of teenage girls and boys sat on a park bench listening to Rowtag play his guitar. The other tribe members talked among themselves while Haruto and Cecile cooked deer meat on an outdoor grill fueled by a 500-pound propane tank. Refried beans simmered in several saucepans. Traditional Fry Bread dough danced in a skillet, snapping and sizzling in the hot oil. The delectable aroma tempted those nearby.

Cecile called out, "Come and get it!"

The people heeded her call and formed a line, letting the women serve them before finding a place to eat.

After everyone was served, Cecile walked over to where Mari sat. The young woman was resting her back against a tree trunk. The food on her plate remained mostly untouched. "May I sit here?" Cecile asked her.

Mari nodded. She had not spoken a word since she had been raped. The once vibrant woman was now despondent.

Cecile sat beside her. "I was thinking that, later, just us women could take a swim. Care to join us?"

Although Mari had refused many such invitations before, for some reason, this time she agreed by nodding her head.

An hour later, Cecile strolled with Mari toward the lake while the teenage girls followed closely behind them, giggling. They all wore bathing suits and carried bright-colored towels. Eva tagged along. Jabbar was perched on her shoulder while Ferta padded beside her.

As the group crossed the grass, Adeelah shrieked, "I do not!"

Cecile asked over her shoulder, "What's going on?"

One of the girls piped up, "Adeelah has a crush on Rowtag."

"I do not!"

"You do!"

Cecile smiled and shook her head, deciding not to get involved.

At the water's edge, the towels were dropped onto the grass. The women and girls stepped into the cool lake, which was fed by the streams flowing down the mountainside whose tall peaks attracted rainclouds like a beautiful woman attracted lovers.

The girls waded into the water, trying to avoid stepping on the smooth stones scattered across the sandy bottom. They didn't venture far, choosing to stay in the warmer shallows where they could sit and talk while the sun's energy nourished their souls.

Things didn't go as well for Eva. The monkey shrieked when she stepped into the amethyst lake. Jabbar's fear of the water forced the little girl to return to the grassy embankment where she sat wishing she could join the other girls. But even more than that, she wished her mother was here.

Unlike the monkey, the jaguar liked the water, and scouted for minnows, nipping at them with her sharp teeth.

Mari and Cecile waded into the depths of the lake.

Cecile stopped when the water reached her chest, running her hands through it as she watched the teenagers giggle and talk.

291

A group of fairies flew into view, hovering above the girls, their sparkling lights dancing around them.

Mari swam farther out, paddling over the murky bottom where the pond weeds waved in the slow current. She trod water for a moment, then decided to float on her back. The sun warmed her exposed body. A breeze caressed her face. A flock of birds flew from one side of the shore to the other. Feeling safe, Mari let down her guard. And in that moment, her freed mind allowed a repressed memory to squeeze into her awareness—a flash of the horrible incident she had so carefully hidden away. His cold blue eyes stared at her, delighting in her pain and moaning with pleasure while she screamed. Her mind slammed shut, but it was too late. The trauma from the rape overtook her. Tears trickled out of the corners of her eyes. Her nerves became raw wires with too high of a voltage coursing through them. Overwrought, numb and helpless, Mari stopped fighting.

292

Limp, she let her feet sink below the water, taking the rest of her with them. The sound of the giggling girls fell away as her head slipped beneath the surface. Slowly sinking, she gazed up at the sunlight streaming through the water above her, growing fainter and fainter, her black hair billowing around her face as she slipped deeper, bubbles trickling out of her nose. Her feet hit the cold muck that swirled around her legs.

Cecile took a break from watching the girls and noticed Mari was nowhere in sight. Fear welled up in her as she spun around scanning the water. *Where could she be!?* In her panic, Cecile had forgotten she could transport herself with a simple intention, but then she remembered. Instantly, she appeared next to Mari at the bottom of the lake, looking at her through the cloudy water. Mari returned Cecile's gaze—dismayed by the fear expressed on her friend's face. That's when it occurred to Mari that she was tired of being saved. Tired of being the victim. She pushed off the bottom, racing toward the surface, clawing her way to the top, bursting out of the water, gasping for air, filling her lungs with oxygen. Mari had decided to save herself.

Cecile and Mari lay on the colorful towels watching the teenagers who were still in the water. The red sun in the lavender sky dried the women's long black hair and warmed their bodies.

"I was so afraid of losing you," Cecile confided. "I know it's going to take time, but if you ever feel like you can't go on, please let me know."

Tears welled in Mari's eyes, and, for the first time since that fateful day, she spoke, her words quietly uttered, "At the bottom, with no breath left in me, it felt like I had died, but I wanted to live." She sniffed. "I was a butterfly breaking free of my cocoon." She seemed embarrassed. "I know it doesn't make sense. Does it?"

"It does," Cecile comforted her.

"I wish I was like you, powerful, so I could have left that place before—"

"I know."

The teenagers got out of the lake, shivering. They grabbed their towels, then headed toward where Cecile and Mari lay. With Jabbar on her shoulder, Eva followed them.

Standing in front of the two women, Adeelah asked Cecile, "Can we have a snack?" Then she noticed Mari's tear-stained eyes. "Is everything okay?"

The teenagers were pleasantly shocked when Mari responded,

"I'm hungry, too." She stood up, wrapping the towel around her waist. "Ready?"

CHAPTER 37
Conchita

ZACHARY TOSSED AND turned in his sleep. He was worried the rising vibrations might not dismantle the Dracos' hive mind. He wanted to provide a safe world for Eva to live in. He dreamed of a ticking clock. *Tick, tock. Too late. Tick, tock. Won't work.* The illusionary clock alarm rang out. He woke up, sweating.

The young man looked over at Eva and her furry friends, who lay beside her blissfully enjoying their slumber. The Alterian sun, which was dimmed by the nightly mist, glowed faintly through the canvas teepee, highlighting Eva's features. Zachary ran his hand over his daughter's head, thinking of Conchita. He fretfully pondered, *What if Takwa had lied? What if Conchita never abandoned us? Is it possible she still loves us?* Although the answers might break his heart again, he had to know.

The invisible Zachary arrived in Pahtia's old hut. Conchita stood near a slatted wall holding a bundle of fresh herbs, looking for an empty spot among the multitude of other bundles. The familiar sounds of the jungle filtered inside. Parrots screeched. Monkeys hooted. How Zachary missed this place and his wife. His heart ached at the sight of Conchita's beautiful face. The amulet that Pahtia had given her hung from her neck. Sadness overtook Zachary when he realized Conchita's presence here did not bode well for him because it meant she really had gone to live in her father's dwelling, just as Takwa had claimed.

Zachary's attention was jolted by the sight of his dead infant's rattle lying in the center of the worktable, nestled between the medicinal herbs. The presence of the baby's toy made his heart ache. Grief and anguish hammered his mind. He faltered, lacking the courage to confront Conchita.

The shaman's daughter finished tacking the herb bundle to the wall, then unknowingly walked through Zachary's essence as she headed toward the doorway, grabbing a pouch off a peg before stepping outside. She followed the path toward the river.

As Zachary watched her step away, he wondered how she could justify deserting him and Eva. *Did life go on for her?* Needing answers, he willed himself to become physical, feeling his heart pounding. His throat tightened. Despite his fears, he hoarsely shouted, "Conchita!"

The young woman stopped, slowly turning around. She stared at him a moment as if not believing it was really him, then she smiled joyfully. Her expression confused Zachary. Did he dare to believe she still loved him? But why had she forsaken her family? He searched her face for clues.

Conchita took a hesitant step toward Zachary, asking, "Does Eva live, too?"

In a guarded voice, he answered, "Eva's fine."

She let out a quivering sigh of relief. "Day and night I have mourned for the two of you, hoping you had survived the journey. I asked the spirit guides for answers, but they said it was not for me to know."

Zachary couldn't understand how she could speak of her own pain when she had caused him and Eva so much of it. "Why did you leave us, and let the tribe send us away? It was a death sentence."

"No! Let me explain!"

He shook his head. "There's no excuse."

"I'm sorry, I was not there."

"How could you let them do that to us!?"

"I did not! Please listen to me!" she insisted.

The fire in her eyes convinced Zachary to hear what she had to say.

In a solemn voice, Conchita conveyed the details of that fateful day. She had run out of their family's hut, going to her father's place to be alone. After a good cry, she decided enough was enough. She needed to find peace for herself and her family. She lit a fire in the pit, then sprinkled an herb over the flames, breathing in the smoke, letting it bring a vision to her, hoping the spirit guides would offer their guidance. But it was her dead father's face that appeared in the ever-shifting smoke. He said to her, "Conchita, remember there is no death. You are a shaman. You never have to worry about being strong enough by yourself. I will help you. The spirits will help you. Let the loving energy restore your spirit. Breathe deeply."

She did as he suggested, and a moment later, Conchita heard the familiar laughter of her dead son. She couldn't see him, but she could feel his presence.

Pahtia said, "Your son is loved by many here. You need to tend to the living. You are a shaman. Be strong."

"I will," she promised.

"Go now. Your family needs you. Go before it's too late!"

Conchita jumped to her feet, rushing out of the hut. She

297

briskly moved down the path under the low-hanging vines. The overgrown foliage brushed against her arms.

At the edge of the village, two hunters stood on the path blocking her way. When she approached them, they remained in place. This confused Conchita, who said to them, "Let me pass," but they refused to budge.

Not wanting to waste time, she stepped off the path to go around them, but one of the hunters issued her an order, "You need to return to your father's hut."

"Who are you to talk to me this way?"

Their confrontation was interrupted by Eva's voice screeching from the other side of the thick underbrush, "Mommy! Mommy!" Conchita's eyes became wide with fear. She tried to answer her daughter, but one of the hunters tightly pressed his hand over her mouth. The other one grabbed her arms. Together, they dragged her back to her father's hut.

"They made me a prisoner," Conchita explained to Zachary. "I suspected what had happened to you and Eva, so I devised a plan to escape and find you. I put a wet rag over my nose and mouth, then burned an herb that makes people sleepy. I fanned the smoke with a palm leaf so it would drift over the men standing guard outside. It took many hours, but finally they fell asleep. Then I ran to the river. I could see your tracks along the bank. I knew which direction you were headed, but I also knew Takwa would come looking for me. It was a risk because if I caught up to you, it would not be long before they caught up with all of us. But I thought without my help, you would not make it."

Conchita became solemn as she described what happened next. She had journeyed through the afternoon storm, continually slipping on the wet sloped ground. Her legs and arms were covered with cuts and bruises. Finally, the rain ceased, and the sun blazed through the clearing along the river. She had lost their trail for a small stretch, but picked it up again in the soggy soil, closing in on the outcast pair, coming to where their fresh footprints led from a raised bank down to the sandy shore. But here, a disturbing sight presented itself. There were caiman tracks where the human impressions ended. Her heart pounded. She was afraid she was looking at the scene where her husband and daughter had been attacked, but oddly, there were no signs of a struggle.

"You had vanished. I searched along the river until Takwa and his men found me, and forced me to return to the village. They said they would kill you if I did not go with them. I believed them.

"I could not forgive Takwa or the others for what they did to you, and me, so I moved into my father's hut, away from them—" Her explanation was cut short.

Bushes rustled. Hunters, whose bodies were painted with red-and-black lines, stormed down the path toward Conchita and Zachary. The tribesmen stopped a short distance away from the pair, glaring menacingly at the pale-skinned intruder. Takwa stood at the forefront. His eyes were vengeful as he stepped forward, gripping a spear. He sneered, "Your *bruja* can't save you now."

Zachary suddenly understood how men could kill each other in battle. He despised this arrogant hunter, who, because of his lust and possessiveness for Conchita, had risked his family's lives. He charged at his adversary, wanting to break his neck, and was mid-stride to doing so when Takwa thrust a spear into his heart. Zachary clutched the weapon near his wound, sinking to his knees.

299

Conchita screamed, rushing to his side.

Everything seemed lost until Zachary transformed himself into a semi-physical state, which healed the wound. The spear fell through his intangible body, clanking on the ground.

Conchita was confused, but, at the same time, in awe of her husband's supernatural abilities.

Terrified of Zachary's powers, all the hunters ran away, except for Takwa, who smiled eerily at him, proclaiming, "I knew Eva was a *bruja*, and now I know you are, too." He spoke directly to Conchita, "Is this what you want? An evil spirit as a husband?"

Takwa's taunting fueled Zachary's anger. The Earth Sentinel cast his hands, emitting an energy surge that sent the hunter spiraling through the air, smashing his back against a palm tree. Takwa was momentarily stunned, but then he sprung to his feet, charging at Zachary who, in return, wrapped his apparitional hands around his rival's neck, strangling the life out of him. The hunter was no match for the strength that Zachary possessed while in this supernatural state. Takwa punched at the young man's shadowy form without any impact, except to use up his own precious oxygen and strength, his face turning purple.

The sight of her compassionate husband killing someone was more than Conchita could bear. "No, Zachary! Do not be like him!"

He continued squeezing Takwa's neck.

"Zachary!"

He looked at her.

Her eyes pleaded with him.

He threw Takwa to the ground. The hunter lay there gasping for air.

Zachary returned to Conchita, holding out his hand. "Let's get out of here."

She reached for him, spanning the gap between them.

Phump.

With their fingers only inches apart, Conchita felt a sting in her neck and faltered. Takwa had shot her with a poisonous dart from where he lay. The young woman's muscles became paralyzed. Knowing she only had a brief moment to live, Conchita looked at her husband, wanting his face to be the last thing she saw from this life, then she collapsed, but Zachary caught her in his arms, converting her body into a semi-physical state—the same as his. The poisonous dart dropped from her vaporous neck, landing in the dirt, its effects no longer a concern, her body renewed from the metamorphosis.

Zachary encouraged Conchita to stand. "You're okay."

She tested her step, amazed she could move. She turned to face Zachary, gazing into his eyes. Conchita didn't understand her transformation, or his for that matter, but she knew this wasn't the time to discuss it. For now, it was enough to know they were alive.

After nearly losing her, Zachary could no longer hide his feelings. He loved her. He would always love her. He leaned in to kiss Conchita. She returned his embrace, but their gossamer bodies dulled the sensation. Wanting to fully feel her, Zachary made both of them become flesh and blood. After a lingering kiss, he wrapped his arms around her, holding her close, nuzzling his face in her silken black hair.

The sight of the two lovers entwined was more than Takwa could bear. He jumped to his feet, screeching a battle call, intending to murder one or both of them. Startled, the pair turned their heads. Zachary saw his enemy lunged for them, but as Takwa soared, Zachary and Conchita disappeared. The tribesman fell through the empty space, tumbling across the ground. Body and ego bruised, Takwa sat up, seething and breathing heavily. But not for long.

A black jaguar leaped down from an overhead branch, pouncing on the hunter. The snarling predator struck quickly, biting the back of his neck, paralyzing Takwa who remained conscious as the big cat sunk its canine teeth into his skull, dragging him into the secluded underbrush.

CHAPTER 38
CERN

IN THE FOOTHILLS of the Swiss Alps, near Geneva, a silver hovercraft slipped out of the clouds, descending into a valley shrouded with mist, lowering onto a landing pad. The hatch door lifted and a set of stairs lowered. Abaddon climbed out, his face determined as he stomped past the two soldiers who waited for him with their heads bowed and fists held over their hearts.

The soldiers followed their ruler across the landing. The high winds fluttered their black robes and ruffled their wings. Abaddon led them to a barely discernible metal door in the mountainside. He stepped inside, his heavy footsteps clanging on the steel catwalk that spanned the deep pit below.

Abaddon reached the door at the other end, flinging it open, ducking his head under the doorframe as he entered a modern headquarters. Carpet ran the length of the hallway. Affixed to the wall was a sign crafted out of black glass and embellished with the gold-metal letters "C.E.R.N.". The acronym stood for the French *Conseil Européen pour la Recherche Nucléaire* or in English: the European Council for Nuclear Research. This was the birthplace of the World Wide Web as well as the home of the Hadron Collider— the world's largest particle smasher.

The main hallway led past numerous offices with glass fronts where administrators were busy working on their computers. A few of them glanced up, but the sight of the fallen angels stomping past their windows prompted them to quickly resume their work, pretending they had seen nothing unusual.

Abaddon stormed to the elevators where he jabbed the "down" button. He pushed his way inside before the doors had a chance to fully open, pressing the button marked "C". The car sped down, passing the data-processing facilities and laboratories. The fallen angels were riding in one of the fastest elevators in the world, yet it took nearly a minute to complete the descent.

The doors opened to reveal a half-dozen men and women wearing white lab coats and hard helmets, all standing with their heads bowed. Abaddon and his soldiers stepped into the wide corridor.

The lead physicist nervously said, "We are pleased to receive you, my Lord God."

Ignoring the pleasantries, Abaddon tersely replied, "Take me there, now."

The man's throat tightened even more. "Yes, my lord." He and the other physicists escorted Abaddon and his soldiers to the two electric vehicles parked alongside the wall. A trailer was hitched to one of them and held an oversized high-back chair upholstered in black velvet.

Abaddon stepped over the side rail and sat in the chair. "Let's go!"

The physicists quickly took their seats.

The vehicles hummed down the half-mile-long corridor while the soldiers walked behind them, their long legs easily keeping pace. Despite the efficiency, Abaddon impatiently seethed. He just wanted to be there, now.

When they reached the office at the end of the corridor, the lead physicist jumped out of the driver's seat, rushing to open the door for Abaddon.

Inside was a large observation room, which offered a view of a thirty-foot-high darkened tunnel. Abaddon sat on the throne-like chair in the center of the room. The physicists took their seats at the control panel under the observation window. The foot soldiers stationed themselves near the door.

Abaddon tersely asked, "Is the black cube in place?"

The lead physicist answered, "Yes, my lord."

"Then let us begin."

"Just a word of caution, my lord. The earth's vibrations have been steadily rising. We're not sure why. This could be—"

"Start it!" Abaddon was tired of these fools.

"Yes, sir. I mean, Lord."

The physicists pushed buttons and double-checked gauges on the control panel. One by one, the indicator lights switched from red to green.

The lead physicist confirmed with his colleagues, "Ready?" They all nodded. "Engage."

The events were set in motion.

The enormous twelve-sided tunnel came to life. Lights flickered on to reveal the metal plates, wires, tubing and superconducting magnets contained within the ultrahigh vacuum, cooled by liquid helium to -271.3° Celsius.

The lead physicist pushed another button. His action released a high-energy particle beam from a containment compartment, which passed through a transparent black cube before shooting into the first of three tunnels. There, the particles built up speed before rushing into the second larger tunnel, continuing to gain velocity until they were ready for the third and final step. The accelerated particles, hurtling at close to the speed of light, were unleashed into a 27-kilometers circular tunnel that straddled the borders of Switzerland and France. Inside this tunnel were two tubes. The particles whizzed through each in opposite directions, and, at intersecting points, a portion of the particles collided. But these particle collisions were more powerful than they had ever been in the past. Earth's rising vibrations were affecting the process.

The observation room shook. Dust fell from the ceiling tiles.

The lead physicist turned to Abaddon, stating, "My lord, the explosions are too much for the tunnel to handle. We need to shut it down."

Abaddon glared wordlessly at him, his gray eyes penetrating the man's soul. Afraid, the lead physicist turned away, but his words of caution held true. The escalating particle blasts activated the Rhône-Simplon fault line, causing the earth's tectonic plates to thunder as they shifted.

One of the physicist shouted, "It's an earthquake!"

The CERN tunnel developed cracks, but kept working. Sub-zero air hissed through the crevices. The exploding particles began creating dark matter upon impact—the single-most powerful and dangerous substance known to man. The amount of dark matter grew exponentially.

Time distorted.

The mountain seemed to disappear, and, in its wake, a newly formed black hole emerged. Every speck of light was sucked out from the far end of the tunnel.

The window in the observation room threatened to buckle. The physicists stared at the black hole, not knowing what to do or expect.

Pandora's Box had been opened.

The black hole's presence provided a passageway from another dimension. From out of its great void, an ominous cloud rushed toward the observation room, glowing red with demons.

The physicists screamed, tipping over their chairs, falling over each other, as they tried to flee.

Abaddon sat in his chair with an eerie smile pasted on his face.

The ominous cloud swarmed closer, shrieking and tearing at the fabric of reality. The legion of demons rushed into the room, gnashing their teeth, their howls vibrating the walls. In unison, the demons sinisterly asked the ruler, "May we?"

Abaddon nodded.

The demons entered the physicists' bodies, possessing the men and women whose screams of terror suddenly ceased, their eyes becoming catatonic.

Demented and crazed, a woman threw herself against the wall.

Another physicist convulsed on the floor, braying maniacally.

One man examined his lab coat sleeve, then pushed it up to reveal his bare arm. He bit into his own flesh, taking out a chunk. He chewed. Blood dribbled down his chin as he creepily commented, "Delicious."

Abaddon ignored the chaos around him, his eyes fixated on the black hole. Waiting.

CHAPTER 39
Rising Vibrations

THE GALACTIC COUNCIL and the Earth Sentinels anxiously stared at the holographic number 251 slowly spinning in the center of the sanctuary, indicating the current Hertz reading of the earth's vibrations.

The number rose to 252.

The rising vibrations were affecting inner earth as well, causing the surrounding crystal walls to emit high-pitched ringing sounds.

Synege clasped her hands in front of herself. Her large green eyes watched the number change to 253.

Zachary wrapped his arm around Conchita as they waited nervously.

254.

Cecile was jittery with anticipation. Tom stood beside her, hoping this time their efforts would go as planned.

255.

Billy held his black hat reverently at his side while Haruto prayed, "Sweet Devas, please let this benefit mankind."

256.

CHAPTER 40
Draco's Emergency Meeting

THE SUPREME LEADER, Zycar, and the other top Draco commanders who had been assassinated by the fallen angels with the Earth Sentinels' help had called an emergency meeting through the hive mind. The officers who were lucky enough to have avoided the assassinations were physically present in the room. Commander Guado stoically sat at the long stone table wearing a black double-breasted military uniform. His distinctive black metallic sash was draped over one shoulder. The other officers nervously waited in their seats. The assassinated leaders' chairs remained vacant out of respect.

309

Zycar's fuming spirit started the meeting, his thoughts boomed to everyone in the room. *Millenniums of planning—gone! All because of those EMP strikes! All of our weaponry is down, and we don't know who did it. Alterians? Fallen angels? Invaders? And why haven't we been able to talk with any of our UN leaders to get some answers? Commander Guado?*

Commander Guado answered his leader through the hive mind, *The UN leaders were working on repairing the machinery and weaponry, and seemed to be making progress, but we lost contact with them. One by one. We do not know why. Our scientists detected the earth's vibrations are rising, but it hasn't reached the point where it would impact our intercommunication—*

Why has no one checked on the UN leaders!?

Sir, we visited some of the bases, but the UN leaders were either off finding salvage parts or in the field.

Get out there and find them! Do not take 'no' for an answer! Understood!?

Yes, sir!

What have the scientists said about the rising vibrations?

They suspect the crystals have been returned to the vortexes, but no one can say for certain. Our planes and tanks are not functional yet, so we deployed older jeeps not affected by the EMPs, but strong winds and lightning storms have made it impossible to get within miles of the sites.

Storms? Sounds like Bechard. If that's true, Alteria is involved. We need to know! The Supreme Leader growled. *Get the soldiers out there and find those UN leaders! Make sure those armies stay under our control!*

Yes, sir!

For the vortexes, destroy them with the satellite lasers.

Commander Guado cleared his throat. *Not possible, sir.*

Why!?

The armed satellites are gone.

Gone?

Disappeared.

Zycar's reptilian eyes nearly bugged out of his scaly head. He seethed, *We have to destroy those vortexes! Find a—* His words cut off mid-sentence.

Commander Guado attempted to communicate with the Supreme Leader, *Sorry, sir...lost...moment.*

What!?

Commander Guado tried again, but his message was garbled within the hive mind.

Zycar shouted, *I can't...answer...someone better...*

Still unable to understand what his leader was trying to say, Commander Guado tried one more time, *Can...hear...?*

There was no response.

The hive mind had fallen silent.

BOOK DISCUSSION QUESTIONS

Below are questions to help get the conversation started at your book club or group. General questions are provided at the end.

CHAPTER 1 — Amazon Jungle

- The author asks the reader to believe that a virus can be spread through the use of planes. Do you think it's possible to spread a virus around the globe in one day?

- How does the fishing episode convey the relationships between Zachary and Takwa (the rival hunter), his father-in-law, Pahtia, and the tribe?

CHAPTER 2 — Curator's House

- What does Haruto's reluctance to marry Billy tell you about her, and their relationship?

- How does Haruto and Father Chong's interaction at the temple set the tone for their interactions later?

- The owl means different things to Haruto and Billy. Is the owl a sign from the universe? (One strange example of the owl's meaning is found within the secretive, real-life Bohemian Society. Its members include the top 1% of the 1% richest people as well as leaders, influencers and past US presidents, such as Richard Nixon, Gerald Ford, Ronald Reagan, and both George H. W. Bush and George W. Bush. The Bohemian Society members put on priest costumes and worship a forty-foot-tall Great Owl of Bohemia statue, which looms over a bonfire and burning coffin as they perform a mock sacrifice. Their motto is "Weaving Spiders Come Not Here" [notice this theme in Tom's storytelling in Chapter 3]. This men-only event takes place every July in Northern California.)

CHAPTER 3 — Spider Webs

- Tom tells a story about a spider that spins webs to keep the stars in place, but she loses a star and goes after it. In her absence, a sneaky spider takes control. What does each spider represent? Is the missing star symbolic of someone or something else?

CHAPTER 4 — The Amazon Bruja

- Does Conchita overreact to the death of her son and father?
- When the Blue Morpho butterflies rest on Eva, does it make you wonder if she has special powers?

CHAPTER 5 — The Soldiers Arrive

- When Haruto rings the bell to warn the Mikos of the soldiers approaching the temple, does her action inflame the situation? Or would it have played out the same?
- Bechard the fallen angel appears for the first time. Judging by Billy and Haruto's reactions, what kind of relationship does this couple have with him?
- The soldiers inject Haruto and Billy with electrical currents and a sedative, and then drag them away from the temple. If the soldiers understood the underlying factors would they have acted differently or still followed orders?

CHAPTER 6 — Outcasts

- Zachary and Eva are outcast from the tribe. Is this symbolic of being cast out of the Garden of Eden, especially after being bitten by a snake?

- Eva convinces the jaguar to save Takwa. Should she have?

- The caiman's presence is interpreted by Zachary as threatening, yet the creature only wants to rescue them. What does this say about perceptions and preconceived fears?

- Does Pahtia's earlier prediction that he would reincarnate as a caiman lead you to believe he is the caiman that helps Zachary and Eva?

CHAPTER 7 — To Hell and Back

- Why do you think the alien scientists are performing experiments and taking bodily samples from Haruto and the other women?

- When Haruto magically returns to her home at the temple, her fellow Mikos seem more concerned about how her reappearance affects them (soldiers coming to look for Haruto), than how they can help her. Are their concerns justified? Would you have reacted the same way?

- Bechard makes his second appearance and offers advice to Haruto. Should he help her more?

CHAPTER 8 — Leaving the Temple

- A strange windstorm prevents Haruto's presence from being detected by the soldiers who are patrolling the city. Do you think the windstorm was a natural occurrence?

- When Haruto visits Father Chong at the parsonage, he opens up his home to her. Should she have been honest with him about trying to escape from the soldiers?

CHAPTER 9 — Darkest Before the Dawn

- When Zachary is discovered by the missionaries on the shore of the Amazon River, he is near death, yet with their help (and Bechard's), he recovers. Why does the author keep putting people who follow different belief systems together?

CHAPTER 10 — The Desolate Reservation

- The Bear Claw First Nation tribe members being taken as prisoners by the soldiers is eerily reminiscent of when the Native Americans were imprisoned on the reservations in the late 1700s through the early 1900s. Is the author making a connection?

- Why do you think the tribe members are taken?

CHAPTER 11 — Haruto's Transformation

- Father Chong and Haruto seem to have a good relationship after spending time in each other's company. What is the author saying about tolerance?

- When Haruto asks Father Chong whether a fallen angel could be forgiven by God, is she really talking about Bechard?

- Haruto transforms into an invisible state when she hears the soldiers storming through the priest's house towards her. Does every great transformation take a traumatic event for it to occur?

- When Haruto learns she can transform herself, she believes herself to be invincible. Does this mean she has become immortal?

- Was it foolish for Haruto to expose herself to the soldiers just so she could test whether or not they could detect her presence?

CHAPTER 12 — Zachary's Transformation

• When Zachary transforms, his body crumbles like brittle clay. Clay is mentioned in the text of an ancient Sumerian tablet. It reads:

> In the clay, god and man
>
> Shall be bound,
>
> To a unity brought together;
>
> So that to the end of days
>
> The flesh and the soul
>
> Which in a god have ripened –
>
> That soul in a blood-kinship be bound.

In addition, clay is mentioned in the Bible: "And then the Lord God formed man from the clay of the earth, and he breathed into his face the breath of life, and man became a living soul." Genesis 2:7. (Some Bible versions use the word "dust" instead of "clay".) Clay is also in the title of this book. What does clay represent?

CHAPTER 13 — Together Again

• The main characters seem to have little in common with each other—all come from different backgrounds and cultures. What do they have in common?

• Is the Bear Claw reservation a good place to hide out?

CHAPTER 14 — Our Origins

• Bechard explains mankind's origins to the Earth Sentinels. What parts of his explanation do you believe to be true: Ancient astronauts, genetic engineering, chemtrails, aliens/hybrids living among us, soul extraction, Illuminati, government cover up?

CHAPTER 15 — Practicing

- The Earth Sentinels have acquired amazing powers, yet know very little about them. If you discovered you had these powers, what would be the first thing you did?

CHAPTER 16 — Scouting

- Haruto and Zachary discover inner earth. Is this place physically possible?
- Why Didn't Bechard tell his fellow Earth Sentinels about inner earth?

CHAPTER 17 — The Galactic Council

- The Galactic Council speaks about the Law of Oneness: "Many people have pre-planned their destinies so however we proceed must honor that, even if it seems cruel, even to them. We don't want to Interfere." Does this mean that the Galactic Council can't directly help people? Is that why they need the help of the Earth Sentinels (humans)?

CHAPTER 18 — The Tribe's Rescue

- When John is scanned by the UN leader, the label "Level 4" comes up on the tablet screen. What do you think is the criteria for "Level 4"?
- What do you think the purpose of the detainment camps is? Do you think they are a temporary or long-term solution for the Dracos' agenda?

CHAPTER 19 — Rescue on the Reservation

- Do you think the military jets were sent in response to the tribe members being taken from the detainment camp? Or were they bombing all the settlements?
- Would human soldiers be willing to bomb their own countryside?

CHAPTER 20 — Saving John

- John is taken to a food processing plant where he is told he will be employed. Why do the hybrids guide the unsuspecting victims through the "employment" process?
- Do you think it would be hard to recruit employees who would be willing to kill humans for food?

CHAPTER 21 — Saving Billy

- Haruto's "tour" through the aliens' headquarters gives her insights into their prison system, genetic experiments and military structure. Is this valuable information for understanding what is going on behind the scenes? Does it help you to better understand the Dracos?
- Zachary and Billy reunite after being apart for five years. What kind of relationship do you think they had in the past?

CHAPTER 22 — Finding Shelter and Food

- Of all their options, Tom and Cecile choose teepees instead of houses or mansions to bring to inner earth for their tribe members to live in. What does this say about them?

CHAPTER 23 — Revisiting Japan

- Why are the Mikos resistant to Haruto's invitation to live in a new, safer location?

- Was Haruto too blunt when informing Father Chong about the aliens and their control over religion and society?

- What do you think about the biblical references Haruto used to support her claims? Is it possible the Bible, Torah, Quran and other scriptures were written about the same ancient astronauts instead of a divine creator? Do you think there could be another interpretation?

CHAPTER 24 — Faulty Alliances

- Are the chest and Destiny Stone symbolic of anything else? Is the chest what is referred to in the Bible as the Arc of the Covenant? ("Ark" is the Greek word for chest.)

- Do you think it is wise to form an alliance with the fallen angels in order to obtain the Destiny Stone?

CHAPTER 25 — Lord God Abaddon

- What insights to Bechard's personality do you gain from his interaction with the fallen angels' ruler, Abaddon, who happens to be his cousin? What do you learn about Abaddon?

CHAPTER 26 — Display of Powers

- Tom showcases the Earth Sentinels' powers to Abaddon, who agrees to give them the Destiny Stone in exchange for their magical abilities to transport him and his soldiers. Zachary obviously has reservations. Should he follow his heart instead?

CHAPTER 27 — The Destiny Stone

- The Destiny Stone's strong powers has killed many in the past.

Why doesn't it harm Haruto?

CHAPTER 28 — Killing the Dracos

- The Earth Sentinels use the fallen angels as assassins to avoid doing the dirty work themselves, but are they just as guilty?

CHAPTER 29 — Hagsmar Prepares for War

- Abaddon gets into his hovercraft and leaves before the human armies attack. Why do you think he leaves before the battle?
- Abaddon tells his soldiers he will "unleash hell". Do you feel his words are figurative or literal?

CHAPTER 30 — Plan B

- Although Bechard doesn't claim to be the leader, he plans the EMP attacks. Why does everyone listen to his counsel?

CHAPTER 31 — EMP Attacks

- Would you use the EMPs more broadly (other than just focusing on the military bases) to speed up the process?

CHAPTER 32 — Plan C

- Should the council have ordered the death of the Draco leaders first, and then the UN leaders?

CHAPTER 33 — New Recruits

- Earth Sentinels members are recruited to help mankind. Would you be willing to do the same despite the dangers?

CHAPTER 34 — UN Replacements

- Is killing the UN hybrid leaders necessary? Is there a better way?
- Who does Tom want to kill personally?
- The author introduces the trolls in Miramar, the rock folk who live in the Rockfolk Valley, and the blue-skinned four-armed warriors of Ventura. Did these glimpses offer a better understanding of what it's like to live in inner earth?

CHAPTER 35 — Replacing the Crystals

- Do you think the Seven Wonders of the World are located on sacred vortexes (Colossus of Rhodes, Great Pyramid of Giza, Hanging Gardens of Babylon, Lighthouse of Alexandra, Mausoleum at Halicarnassus, Statue of Zeus at Olympia, Temple of Artemis at Ephesus)?

CHAPTER 36 — Mari Saves Herself

- Mari decides to save herself, but only after nearly drowning. Do you think earth's rising vibrations, caused by the placement of the crystals, help Mari to choose life instead of suicide?

CHAPTER 37 — Conchita

- Is Conchita's excuse for not being with her family when they were thrown out of the tribe good enough?
- Does Takwa get what he deserves?

CHAPTER 38 — CERN

- Abaddon is waiting for something to come through the tunnel. Any idea who or what it might be?

CHAPTER 39 — Rising Vibrations

- Do you think the rising vibrations will fulfill the Earth Sentinels will cause new problems?

CHAPTER 40 — Draco's Emergency Meeting

- If you were a Draco leader, what would be your next step for regaining control of earth's population?

GENERAL QUESTIONS

- What was your initial reaction to the book? Did it hook you immediately or take some time to get into?

- How did you feel about the characters? Which ones do you like or not like, and why?

- Which character did you relate to the most, and what is it about them that you connect with?

- Did the characters seem real and believable? Can you relate to their predicaments? To what extent do they remind you of yourself or someone you know?

- How did the characters change or evolve throughout the course of the story? What events trigger these changes?

- Did the events in the book reveal the author's world view?

- Do certain parts of the book make you uncomfortable? If so, why do you feel this way? Did this lead to a new understanding or awareness of some aspect of your life you might not have thought about before?

- Do you like the book? If you read any of the author's other books, how does this one compare?

- What moral/ethical choices did the characters make? What do you think of those choices? How would you have chosen differently?
- How authentic are the cultures represented in the book?
- Why do you think the author wrote this? What is her most important message?
- How do you think the characters' points of view are similar or different from the author's point of view or background?
- Are the characters' actions the result of freedom of choice, destiny or adherence to traditional beliefs?
- Is there any moral responsibility that was abdicated?
- Are there any symbols that may have cultural, political or religious reference? e.g. owl, crucifix, Destiny Stone and its chest, crystals, inner earth, colors, etc.
- What tone did the author set with her choice of words? Is it optimistic, pessimistic, prophetic, cautionary, darkly humorous, depressing, cathartic, other?
- How do you feel about the ending? Would you have stopped there?

ABOUT THE AUTHOR

 ELIZABETH M. HERRERA is a shamanic healer and teacher, and author of *Shaman Stone Soup* (memoir), *Dreams of Heaven,* and *Earth Sentinels: The Storm Creators.*

She was raised in a Christian home, but lost her faith in her early twenties. For over a decade, she searched for something to fill the void, eventually discovering Native American spirituality (shamanism). Through this spiritual practice, she unexpectedly became a catalyst for healing and miracles. These experiences led her back to a belief in a higher power.

Always drawn to the spiritual side of life, Elizabeth began her shamanic path in Michigan where she learned to shamanic journey. Elizabeth continued her studies through the Foundation for Shamanic Studies for shamanic journeying, soul retrieval, and death and dying (psychopomp), but her major source of learning has been from her spirit guides, who offer limitless guidance and lessons on living a more spiritual life. She is also a student of *A Course In Miracles*, which she discovered is the perfect companion for shamanism.

Elizabeth inherited her rebellious spirit from her father and grandfather. Her grandfather was a full-blooded Apache who smuggled sugar and flour from Mexico into Texas, exchanged gunfire with Texas Rangers and crossed paths with Pancho Villa.